D1335043

The Secret Sky

ATIA ABAWI

The Secret Sky

*A Novel of Forbidden Love
in Afghanistan*

Philomel Books • An Imprint of Penguin Group (USA)

PHILOMEL BOOKS

Published by the Penguin Group
Penguin Group (USA) LLC
375 Hudson Street, New York, NY 10014

USA | Canada | UK | Ireland | Australia | New Zealand | India | South Africa | China
penguin.com
A Penguin Random House Company

Copyright © 2014 by Atia Abawi.
Penguin supports copyright. Copyright fuels creativity, encourages diverse voices,
promotes free speech, and creates a vibrant culture. Thank you for buying an autho-
rized edition of this book and for complying with copyright laws by not reproducing,
scanning, or distributing any part of it in any form without permission. You are supporting writers and allowing Penguin to continue to publish books for every reader.

Library of Congress Cataloging-in-Publication Data
Abawi, Atia.
The secret sky : a novel of forbidden love in Afghanistan / Atia Abawi. pages cm
Summary: Two teens from different ethnic groups in present-day Afghanistan must
fight their culture, tradition, families, and the Taliban to stay together as they and
another village boy relate the story of their forbidden love. 1. Hazaras—
Afghanistan—Fiction. [1. Love—Fiction. 2. Ethnic relations—Fiction. 3. Family life—
Afghanistan—Fiction. 4. Pushtuns—Afghanistan—Fiction. 5. Taliban—Fiction.
6. Afghanistan—Fiction.] I. Title. PZ7.A136Sec 2014 [Fic]—dc23 2013026895

Printed in the United States of America.
ISBN 978-0-399-16992-2
1 3 5 7 9 10 8 6 4 2
Edited by Jill Santopolo.   Design by Semadar Megged.
Text set in 11.5-point Adobe Devanagari.
Dari alphabet provided by Abdul Wahid Abawi.
The publisher does not have any control over and does not assume any responsibility
for third-party websites or their content.

To the people who taught me love in all its forms—
my parents, Wahid and Mahnaz; my brother, Tawab;
and the true love I was destined to find, Conor.

THIS IS LOVE: TO FLY TOWARD A SECRET SKY, TO CAUSE A HUNDRED VEILS TO FALL EACH MOMENT. FIRST TO LET GO OF LIFE. FINALLY, TO TAKE A STEP WITHOUT FEET.

—*Jalal ad-Din Rumi*

INTRODUCTION

I was in my mother's womb when my parents and two-year-old brother fled Afghanistan with only the money in their pockets and two suitcases. They left on a sweltering Kabul summer day during the Soviet War in a chilling and stressful escape that involved their plane being stopped on the tarmac and the communist police walking up and down the aisle for four hours before they could take off. The flight first took them to Moscow on their way to their destination, West Germany. I was born a month later, and we moved to the United States a year after that. I will always be grateful and in awe of my parents for having had the courage to leave everything they had ever known to try and give their children a better life.

As I grew up, my parents shared their memories of a land they so desperately wanted to see again. "When we return . . ." was the start of so many sentences throughout the 1980s. They even enrolled my brother and me in an Afghan school on Saturdays, believing we should know how to read and write at least one of the Afghan languages, as it would be useful upon our eventual return. They immersed our lives in the Afghan culture inside the home while allowing us to embrace our new culture outside of the home. My mother's glowing descriptions of Afghanistan and its various ethnic groups made me envision the country as a virtual Candyland—different tribes of people dispersed through various parts of the country, making it a land of diverse beauty and kindness. It was not until I was older that I read about the ethnic divisions and bloody rivalries. I almost felt betrayed by the truth.

As the years went on and one war in Afghanistan turned into another, my brother and I no longer heard the words "when we return . . ." I could see the devastation in my parents' eyes as they watched the news and saw the country they loved shatter into pieces night after night. It's hard to witness your parents' dreams fade away before your eyes. I would listen as their friends talked politics over endless cups of green tea with a sprinkle of cardamom about a situation they knew they were too far away from to have any effect on. This was a scene played in the homes of most in the Afghan Diaspora all over the world.

It was after the United States led an invasion in 2001 that the country became a topic of conversation again throughout the world, not just in Afghan homes. I went to Afghanistan for the first time in 2005 to shoot a documentary and hoped to see a country rebuilding. It was a museum of war relics, with Soviet tanks still lining the runway of Kabul Airport, disabled Afghan men and women maimed from the fighting and tales of horror from those who had survived the years of barbarism from one war to the next. I heard story after story of devastation and triumph. Although the people were exhausted, there was still hope that things would get better—"How could it get worse?" they said. During that five-week trip, I had the incredible opportunity to spend time in a small remote village in central Afghanistan, cut off from the rest of the country and governmental rule of law. It was a village that had survived through the efforts of its people, a mix of ethnic Pashtuns and ethnic Hazaras—a village similar to the one described in this book.

In 2008, I moved to Afghanistan full-time as an American television correspondent, first for CNN and then for NBC News, and immersed myself in the country and its people. I may be of Afghan origin, and I may speak the language, but in the end, I knew I was an outsider and my mission was to share the voices of those who didn't have a way to connect with a world now involved in their story. In the more than four years I lived in Afghanistan, I experienced life in the most spectacular ways—and death in the most horrific. I learned quickly that Afghanistan is a land of contradictions. It holds unimaginable beauty and inconceivable ugliness. I've known good people who were needlessly killed and bad people who got away with the slaughter of so many. There were times my safety was put in jeopardy by people I did not know, and times when the threat came from those I knew all too well. I saw the best and worst in life on a daily basis.

But even through the despair and hardships Afghanistan

has experienced during the years, I do believe it holds a magic that is hard to define. My heart broke a little during the nearly five years I lived there, listening to and witnessing all the suffering. But I strongly believe that God works in mysterious ways, and God granted me the greatest gift of all in Afghanistan—love. First, the love of a family who knew to flee in order to give me a better life and then the love of a husband I met while covering a heartbreaking war. And it is that love that has helped piece together the broken bits and make my heart whole again.

This novel was inspired by my time in Afghanistan. The cities and villages I've seen, the people I've met, and the hope many have for a brighter tomorrow. I've illustrated real-life experiences in Afghanistan to the best of my ability, hoping the reader will get a small glimpse into a beautiful and tragic world unseen by so many. Afghanistan is a large country with millions of people who have different thoughts and different beliefs, and many of their lives differ greatly from the ones depicted in this novel. But though this story is fiction, it's influenced by real events and real people. I hope it touches your heart the way the people who inspired it touched mine.

Atia Abawi

Part One

One

I know this worn path better than I know myself. As I walk through the nut-colored haze, I can taste the salty bitterness of the parched ground meeting the air and then meeting my mouth. Since I was a child, I've always tried to walk in front of everyone, so the dirt wouldn't hit my clothes. There's nothing worse than the smell of earth on your clothing when you are lying on your mat and trying to sleep at night. It lingers, making its way into your dreams.

But still, the path brings me comfort. It's something I am familiar with. I don't know the new curves on my body the way I know the bends on the footpath.

I look down and am glad that I can hide myself under an oversized *payron*. I'm jealous of my three-year-old sister, Afifa. She doesn't have to worry about becoming a woman. At least, not yet. I turn and see her behind me, jumping onto the footprints I've made, carefree like I used to be.

"What are you doing, crazy girl?" my best friend, Zohra, asks my little Afifa.

"I'm jumping so I don't drown!" she says with determination, sticking her tongue out to the side as she lands on another print.

"Drown in what? We're walking on dirt." Zohra shakes her head.

"No, it's a river!" Afifa responds. "And Fato's footprints are the rocks I need to jump on so I don't drown!"

"Okay, you *dewanagak*," Zohra says, laughing. "Fatima, your sister has a lot of imagination. I don't think we were that colorful when we were her age."

"I think we were," I say. "At least I was. You were always so scared of everything, including your own shadow." I can't help but laugh.

"What do you know?" Zohra pouts, just as I thought she would. The best part about teasing her is that she is horrible at pestering back. She's my best friend for many reasons, and that is definitely one of them.

I keep chuckling, and eventually Zohra starts to giggle too. She's never been able to stay mad at me, even when I deserve it.

We're nearly at the well when we both see the tree log. It's a log we pass almost daily, and every time, it brings back memories of what life used to be like, when all the kids from the village spent the days playing together. My mother says that it's no longer proper for a girl of my shape to go out and play, that it will be seen as indecent. But even if she did let me play outside, I don't have anyone left to run in the fields with. Most of the girls around my age aren't allowed to leave their homes, and the boys have begun helping their fathers in the fields and shops.

Zohra and I are still allowed to see each other, but even time with her isn't the same as it used to be. She doesn't want to run around anymore; she would rather sit and gossip about the village, sharing all the information she hears from her parents while braiding my hair.

For the first time in my life, I feel alone. Lonely. Even though my little brothers and sister are always around, it seems like I no longer belong in my family—at least not the new me—the bizarre, curvy, grown-up me. This feeling of no-whereness makes me empty inside in a way that I can't explain to anyone, not even Zohra. She seems to be embracing all the changes that I can't.

I wish I could be like that log. It's always been the same— able to fit the tiny backsides of a dozen or so children, squeezed tightly together. We'd sit there taking breaks from running around the village, sharing treats if we had them, munching the nuts and mulberries we'd picked from the nearby woods.

"What are you smiling at?" Zohra breaks my train of thought.

"Nothing. I was just remembering how we used to play around that log," I say as my smile fades. "It looks so sad without us there."

"You're the one who looks sad over a piece of wood," Zohra

says. "Besides, I don't think we could all fit on that thing anymore. If you haven't noticed, our backsides have grown a bit." She smirks. "I remember when Rashid found that thing in the woods while we were picking berries and we all had to roll it up here. I think my back still hasn't forgiven me!" Zohra dramatically puts one arm on her back and slouches like an old *bibi*, and in fact, she looks a lot like her own grandmother when she does it.

I remember that day so clearly, even though it was a lifetime ago. Rolling that chunk of timber, all of us together as a team. It was a grueling task, and we didn't think we could make it, but Samiullah, whose family owns the well and the fields beyond it, he knew we could. Every few feet of progress, one of us would want to stop. But Samiullah wouldn't let us. He kept encouraging us to keep pushing.

He was always the leader out of our little gang of village kids. Some families didn't allow their children to play with us because we were a mixed group—Pashtun children playing with Hazara children—but our parents didn't mind. We were connected through the land and through our fathers— Samiullah's Pashtun father is the landowner, and our Hazara fathers are the farmers.

After we moved the log to its current spot, we all sat on it, picking out one another's splinters. We couldn't believe we'd done it, just like Samiullah said we would.

"Did you hear that Sami's back?" Zohra cuts off my thoughts of the past.

"What?" I don't think I heard the words correctly. Samiullah had left for religious studies—he was supposed to be gone for years. There was no way he was back.

"Yeah, I heard he's back from the *madrassa,* at least that's what my father told my mother and grandmother last night. He heard it from Kaka Ismail," she adds, throwing her empty plastic jug up in the air before catching it again, sending Afifa into a fit of giggles.

"Sami's father told your father?" I ask, still confused.

"Yeah, didn't your father tell you? Apparently he spoke to them when he came by to check on the fields." This time she misses the jug after her toss. "He didn't last long, did he?" She picks it up and slaps the dirt off the plastic.

"What do you mean?" I can't seem to process anything Zohra is saying right now. How is Samiullah back? Why haven't I seen him yet? Why didn't I know he'd returned? We used to be best friends, Sami and I. Could he be around here? We *are* near his house right now. He could be anywhere on these grounds.

"Most boys don't come back until they're adults with their scraggly beards, telling us all what bad Muslims we are," Zohra says, rolling her eyes. "Thank God he left early. Apparently Rashid is still there. Kaka Ismail said he's coming home soon, too, but just to visit. Knowing Rashid, once he finishes at the *madrassa,* he'll want to hang all of us for being infidels just because he can."

"Don't say that."

"What? We both know he's always been a little *dewana*."
Zohra shrugs her shoulders before crossing her eyes.

I cluck my tongue at her in disapproval while grabbing her jug. Samiullah's cousin has always been a bit rougher than the rest of their family, but he's not *crazy*. He was a part of our childhood. He was a part of what made us *us*.

As I walk down the path, My heads spins with Zohra's news. Is Samiullah really home? When he left three years ago, I thought I'd lost my friend forever. Could he really be back?

I look through the trees that guard their house from the well, and a stampede of questions race through my brain: Is he there? Can he see me right now? Is my dress clean? Why didn't I let Zohra braid my hair today? Why does it matter if I let Zohra braid my hair today?

But I know the answer to that last question. I know why it matters.

I always thought that by the time Samiullah came back, I wouldn't be allowed to see him anymore—that we would be at the age where a man and woman can't visit each other unless they're related. I figured they would find him a wife and marry him as soon as he arrived home. And I'd probably be married by then too. To someone else. My stomach stings at the thought.

Sami was always different from the rest of the boys. He saw me for who I was, not just as Ali's little sister. And he took care of me . . . but I guess he took care of everyone.

As we fetch the water from the well, I realize I'm conscious of my every movement, wondering if he's watching. It's so stupid. I know he hasn't missed me the way I've missed him. But I can't resist stealing glances past the foliage at his family's home.

I drop the bucket back into the water. When I feel the weight filling the plastic tub, I begin pulling the rope. I follow one tug with another. When the bucket makes it to the edge of the well, I pull it up and pour it into our containers, only to drop the bucket down again, repeating the tedious process.

Afifa eventually gets bored of our silence, and her little arms can't help pull the water from the well, so she runs back home. Zohra and I continue to work quietly, which makes us more efficient. The sun is starting to set over the mountains, painting the sky a bright maroon color, like my favorite tangerines. Before long it will be nighttime, and Zohra still needs to make her way home. I pour the last bucketful of water into the second container, watching some splash over the edges of the plastic mouth, making its way to my dress and turning the red fabric into a blood-burgundy.

"You think he can see us?" Zohra asks the same question that I've been wondering. She's staring at the Ismailzai property like an owl as she chews on the mulberries she keeps pulling out of the pocket she sewed into her dress for that very purpose.

"What? Don't be ridiculous!" I say to her, twisting the lid on the last jug. "Why would he want to look our way? He's probably busy with family." I sneak another glance through the thin trees, though.

"How am I being ridiculous?" She picks up the first jug as we prepare for the short trek back, this time slower and more grueling with the filled containers weighing us down. "That boy has been in love with you since we were sitting on pots! You don't think he wants to see how your breasts have grown?" she says, laughing.

I feel like I've been kicked in the gut and stripped of my clothes at the same time. In an instant, she has made me feel unclean. I suddenly hate Zohra for her words. Her openness about our changing bodies is embarrassing and disgusting. It doesn't seem to bother her that we are morphing into monsters. She even seems to like it.

"You are very uncivilized, you know. You have no manners at all!" I start walking faster. Sometimes I wonder if she's the same shy Zohra I grew up with, or if the girl I used to know has been replaced by the devil. I listen to her laughter. Definitely replaced by the devil. I slouch even more, trying to hide any indication of the swellings forming on my chest—the ones that are ruining my life by letting the world know that I am becoming a woman.

"I'm just joking, Fato!" Zohra is still laughing like the cow that she is. "I'm sorry! Besides, you should be happy. I wish I had them myself. I'm still as flat as the chalkboard we use during our lessons with Bibi!"

I can hear her feet scrambling behind me, and then she stumbles. "*Aaaakh!*" she yells in pain. I turn and see her on the ground covered in the dirt. The jug is on the ground too, lying on its side and pouring out water. I quickly run and set the jug upright before tending to Zohra. For a split second, I contemplate leaving her there, but I know I would never do that.

"Are you okay?" I ask, looking for the spot she injured.

"I'm fine," she says, holding her ankle. "I think I just twisted it. Maybe God was punishing me for talking about your breasts." She grins.

"I hope you learned your lesson." I can't help smiling back at her. I know she didn't mean to hurt me with her words. And I don't want to stay mad at her. She's my only friend left. "Can you get up?"

"If you help me," she says. I grab her elbow and pull her up. She takes a limping step. "It hurts a little, but I'll be fine. Do we have to get more water?"

"No, I got the jug upright before too much could spill out," I answer, looking for the lid. I spot the blue plastic covering and start to screw it back on, this time very tightly. "It's okay, my mother will send us back tomorrow anyway. As long as she isn't the one who has to go to the well, she'll use up any amount we bring her just so she can have us get her more. Over and over and over again! I sometimes think she only had children because she couldn't afford servants." I grunt, expecting Zohra to snicker too, but she doesn't. Whatever. I blow the hair out of my face and pick up her jug. "I'll carry both. I don't want you injuring yourself again."

I turn toward Zohra and suddenly notice a man standing nearby. He's hovering in silence, staring at the both of us. My heart stops for a second, and I take a step back, unable to think clearly but trying to focus. I've never seen this man before, which panics me. I immediately feel an icy chill racing through my body. We know everyone in this village—we're not used to visitors, let alone strangers.

But there is something about his ice-green eyes; they feel familiar, even comforting. The chill begins to melt. There is only one pair of eyes that gives me this feeling of warmth. And that's when I realize this isn't a strange man. It's Samiullah. My breath catches in my throat.

I look at Zohra and realize she's figured it out before I have, as she goes back to slapping the dirt off her clothes. "Welcome back, Sami!"

"*Salaam,* Zohra Jaan," he says. "Thank you." His voice rumbles. The sound is deeper than I recall. But it's not just his voice that has changed. He is almost as tall as his father now, and his skin on his face looks tighter and prickly, without the smooth, round cheeks I remember.

For the first time, I see the line of a jaw, chiseled like the men around the village. Except Samiullah's is different; it's not worn-out and tired-looking like the others, his bone structure is . . . beautiful. His perfectly arched eyebrows look darker and thicker, making his emerald eyes stand out even more. They hold the same sparkle I remember from years ago. But today it forces me to look away. I can feel my heart racing and my breath becoming heavier, and I don't know why. All I know is it gets worse when I try to look at him.

"When did you get back?" Zohra asks.

"On Saturday," Samiullah responds. "How are you both doing?" I know he's directing that question to me as well, but I'm afraid to speak. I feel nervous and out of breath, and I don't want them to know.

"We're fine, thank you for asking," Zohra finally answers him. "We were just getting some water, and I tripped and fell while I was chasing Fatima back to her house. It's getting dark, and we were scared to make my father wait too long to take me back home with him."

"Of course, I don't want to keep you. I just wanted to say *salaam* and see how you both were." I can hear his voice as I continue to focus on the yellow container holding the water.

"Thank you," Zohra says. "It's good to see you back home. I'm sure you have brightened your family's eyes, especially your mother's."

He nods. "Please send my regards to your fathers for me."

"We will. Fatima?" Zohra picks up one of the jugs and seems to be walking fine now. I follow her lead and carry the other jug with my head down. I use my head scarf to shield me from Samiullah and focus on not tripping as I walk toward my house.

I don't know what's wrong with me. This is Sami, our Sami, my Sami. Why can't I look at him?

Two

FATIMA

When I wake up, I realize I'm the only one left in the sleeping room. My father must be out in the fields with Karim, and my mother is likely milking our cow, with Afifa begging to help. As for my younger brothers, Houssain and Massoud, they are probably out playing with the neighbors' children somewhere in the village.

I rub the sleep out of my eyes. I barely slept last night replaying yesterday's events in my mind. I kept seeing Samiullah's face and hearing his new voice. But every time I remembered how I had acted, I buried my head in my pillow to keep from screaming. I'm just grateful Zohra didn't say anything afterward to make me feel worse about it, though to be honest, I don't think she could have, even if she'd wanted to. By the time we were out of Samiullah's earshot, we were within sight of our fathers and my mother, who had been waiting for us. I hope the encounter with him wasn't as embarrassing as I remember it being.

I follow my morning ritual, roll up my *toshak* and place it on top of the other mattresses that have already been stacked in the corner. I then fold my blanket, get dressed, wash my face at the stream and go to the *tandoor* room to have some green tea and *naan* that my mother and I made yesterday morning.

As I rip into the stiff day-old bread, my mother walks into the room carrying a bucket of milk.

"*Salaam*, Madar Jaan," I greet her. "I'm sorry I slept in. Why didn't you wake me?"

"*Salaam*, my life," my mother responds. Her hair has small pieces of hay in it. It looks like there may have been a wrestling match with Afifa, our *madar* and a frightened cow this morning. I wonder just how much of the milk actually made it into the bucket. "We thought we'd give you a day to catch up on your rest. We had enough bread left from yesterday and didn't need to make more for today. I hope you saw good dreams?"

"They were good, thank you," I reply looking down at my clear glass cup, not buying her reasoning, but I can't figure out why else my mother is being nice to me this morning. Usually she pulls me out of bed and has me slaving over the bread before I can even see straight. But today she is as sweet as honey.

Staring at my half-empty glass, I see one lonely little tea leaf floating at the bottom—it must have escaped the pot before I put the strainer underneath. The green leaf looks as alone and isolated as I feel. I can't help but sense the leaf's guilt at escaping its family of leaves in the kettle. "Madar Jaan, may I go to Zohra's house and see her?" I ask, quickly pulling out the leaf and dropping it back in the pot before my mother can catch me. I don't know how I would explain that to her. She already thinks I'm crazy.

"Of course, my darling," my mother responds without hesitation, pulling a piece of hay out of her hair and throwing it out of the room. "Have you moved past the alphabet yet?"

For the last several months, I've been going to Zohra's house to learn how to read. Her grandmother is one of the few literate people, let alone women, in this village. Her mother had been brought up in a time when the king of Afghanistan, a man named Amanullah, wanted women to excel and wanted the country to be one of the best in the world, at least that's the way Zohra's grandmother tells it. Zohra's great-grandmother had lived in the capital, Kabul, at that time, and the owners of the house her parents worked in taught her and her brothers for an hour a week before they convinced her parents to let her go to school. Then Zohra's great-grandmother taught her own daughters how to read and write. And now Bibi was teaching Zohra and had agreed to teach me too.

As a thank-you to their family, my father started giving Zohra's father, Karim, a little more of the share of wheat they farm together. My *baba* was thrilled at the opportunity, because my brothers aren't allowed to go to the one boys' school in our village, which is for Pashtuns. Samiullah's father, Kaka Ismail, says that my *baba* should send them anyway and that he would ensure their safety. But my father says Kaka Ismail is just being friendly and the boys are better off at home where they will learn how to provide for the family. Whatever I learn from Zohra's *bibi* I'm supposed to pass on to my little brothers when they get older. I think it's a pretty good trade, especially since it means I get to spend extra time with Zohra.

Plus, I really enjoy the lessons.

"We have the alphabet covered," I say to my mother, "but she likes to go over it every day and then add something new." I've been hiding the fact that I've actually learned more, because I want to surprise them when I get really good at it.

"Okay, well, make sure you send them my *salaam*s and take some of the cookies I made the other day," my mother responds as she heads to our sleeping area to grab some laundry to wash in the narrow stream. Hopefully she'll wash her hair too. There seems to be even more hay stuck in the back, but I don't feel like telling her about it. So I don't.

Before heading out, I grab the bag of week-old cookies that I know my mother is just trying to get rid of. I slip one out of the blue plastic bag for myself to make the trip to Zohra's more enjoyable. Luckily, they still taste good. I'd be so embarrassed if I gave Zohra's family stale cookies . . . again!

The crumbs make their way down my dress, but I decide not to wipe them away until I am fully finished with the cookie. What's the point? I'll just have brush myself off again. I've stuffed the entire cookie in my mouth when I hear something.

"*Psssht!*"

I turn around and don't see anything. I've begun to think it's an animal in the woods when I hear it again: "*Pssssht!*" I stop chewing my cookie and give all of my attention to the noise.

"Who is it?" I try to say, but my full mouth blocks the words.

"Fatima, over here!" I hear a male voice coming from the woods. I slowly make my way to the brush. As I get closer, his tall body emerges from the shadows of the trees.

The cookie falling from my mouth snaps me back to reality and has me mortified. I quickly wipe my mouth and chin and the crumbs on my chest. As if the embarrassment of yesterday wasn't enough, I can add this to my list of nightmares.

Samiullah laughs. The deep guffaws are sounds I've never heard from him before.

"What's so funny?" I snap. I suddenly feel very defensive. Who does he think he is?

"You were scared just now, weren't you?" He looks at me with his piercing emerald eyes.

"I was not scared! I was just wondering what animal sounds like a generator on full blast, rumbling, *tak tak tak*!" I am very happy with my response, but I suppress my smile the best as I can.

Samiullah starts to laugh again. His teeth are so straight, white, and from the looks of it, still real. That is something very rare in our village. Most people lose their teeth shortly after their teens. That's why my *baba* won't let us eat candy with our tea unless it is a holiday. He says the candy burns through your teeth, making them look like burnt sugar in a pan. But Samiullah used to sneak me candy from his house every week—and he ate a lot himself. From the state of his teeth, I think my *baba* was wrong about the candy. Samiullah's smile is perfect.

"What are you doing, hiding in the trees like a criminal?" I ask. It feels so good to be able to talk to him again. And I'm surprised at how easy it is, after last night.

"I've *felt* like a criminal hiding in these woods waiting for you," he answers. I feel my cheeks tingling. He's been waiting for me? "When I saw you with Zohra yesterday, I figured you two still see each other and that one or the other of you would pass this way." My stomach suddenly sinks—he wasn't waiting for me. "I was hoping it would be you who passed," he adds.

I can't meet his eyes. My gaze makes it to his chest, and all I can see are hard muscles through his thin white *payron*. My stomach starts to twirl.

"I just felt . . . strange after yesterday. We didn't even exchange one word."

"I know" is all I can say now, moving my eyes to his lips. They're deep red and thick. The top lip is perfectly curved and heart shaped.

"Look, I don't want to take too much of your time, but I wanted you to know how happy it made me to see you again."

His words bring me back. "And if you pass through here often—"

"I do, almost every day!" I sound far too enthusiastic.

"Well, then . . . maybe we can catch up more tomorrow?" he asks. His eyes start blinking rapidly, a trait that used to mean he was nervous. Is Samiullah nervous like I am? I can't believe how much that thought alone helps calm me. Still, I know I shouldn't be out here alone with him. And I shouldn't agree to meet him tomorrow. But my mouth betrays me.

"Okay," I say, as I start to leave.

"Before you go—" I turn around and see him reach into his pocket, pulling out a piece of folded paper. It's when he begins to unwrap it that I see the candies I missed so much while he was gone. "I thought you might like some."

"Thank you," I say. I take the candy. My fingers graze his palm, sending a bolt through my body. My heart races with excitement. And I realize, yes, I've missed the candy . . . but I've missed him more.

I reach Zohra's, not remembering any part of my walk there. All I see, over and over, is Samiullah's green eyes, hard chest, and deep red lips. My fingers still tingle where they touched his.

"Fatima!" Zohra comes running toward me and snaps me back. "My grandmother isn't feeling well!" she says with joy and a smile that catches me off guard.

"What? I'm sorry . . . what's wrong?"

"Oh, she's fine. Just old-people problems. But this is good news. Now we don't have to study, and instead we can talk!" Zohra grabs me by the hand and drags me to the room with the *tandoor,* where a kettle awaits us. Zohra pours us both a glass of *chai sabz,* not caring about the tea leaves, which pile into each glass.

I pull out my candies to share with Zohra over the tea and quickly ask her a question before she can ask me where I got them. "So are we supposed to study together without your *bibi*?"

She responds with laughter.

"Why would we do that? If *bibi* isn't around, neither is the work!" Zohra pops a small orange candy into her mouth. "My mother says she may have to be in bed for several days! That is several days of freedom!" Zohra's enthusiasm over her grandmother's sickness would almost be disturbing if I didn't know how much she loved her *bibi.*

"Are you sure she's okay?" I pick a red piece in the shape of a small slice of tangerine and savor the sugar as it melts on my tongue. I follow it with a sip of tea. The mixture of the sweet and bitter sends my taste buds into overdrive. I can't believe what I have been missing for so long. It's like fireworks in my mouth!

"Of course she is. She just has a little cold. My parents say it is harder for old people to recover, so she has to stay in bed longer." Zohra looks at me and then rolls her eyes. "She'll be fine! Stop worrying . . . Besides, we need a break from all this work. It's not like it's necessary anyway."

"Why do you always say that? We're so lucky, and I don't think you even realize it. We're being taught things other girls won't ever know."

Zohra rolls her eyes again, this time the other way to make sure I'm catching her reaction. As if it can be missed. "There is a reason why they aren't taught it—because they'll never use it!" Zohra says, taking a gulp of her tea, her hands surrounding her clear glass mug. "When we get married, do you think our husbands will have us sitting around reading books? Or do you think they'll have us cleaning, cooking and taking care of their family?" I know she's right, but it makes me so angry. "They'll probably be jealous that we can read. So why bother?"

"Then they're *khars*!" I say, already furious at the men we have yet to meet.

"Donkeys or not, they'll be our bosses," Zohra says with such ease it makes me even more agitated.

"Don't you have other dreams? Don't you want more than just to be married off to someone you don't know?" I ask. I'm confused at how simple it is for her to talk about giving up her life to a complete stranger.

"What's the point of dreaming about things we can't have? We'll only be disappointed. We might as well dream of the things that we're bound for, things already in our destiny.

Like dream that the man we marry isn't old . . . dream that he's kind . . . and dream that our destiny holds a mother-in-law who won't be horrible to us—"

"But what about love? What about the heart?" I know my question sounds foolish, but I can't stand how resigned she seems. In the poems Zohra's *bibi* reads us, there is always love, and it sounds wonderful.

"The heart doesn't count. Not with us. Forget about the heart. It's as useless as the rocks scattered throughout our country." Her words ring tragic and true, but I still hope to capture the rare gem in the pile of stones. "It's our destiny."

"Maybe we can change our destiny," I mumble quietly, knowing how absurd I sound. I know our fate as women in this country. But I would still like to fantasize about changing it.

"Okay. Fine. Let's play this game. If you had the power to do anything in the world, what would you do? How would you change your destiny?" Zohra asks with her dusty-brown eyes focused on me, ready for an answer.

"I . . . I . . . uh . . . I don't know. I was just trying to make a point." I always hesitate in sharing my real feelings with Zohra, at least when it comes to the secrets of my heart. She may be my best friend, but I am still afraid of telling her—or anyone. I'm afraid they'll all think I'm crazy. I mean, my mother already does, and I don't tell her anything.

"You can't say that. Not after yelling at me about not wanting to marry a donkey. Tell me. I want to know what else you think is out there for us." Zohra says, not backing down. I know I have to say something, because Zohra will keep pushing me until I do, and I am not in the mood for the game of back-and-forth.

"I hear there are universities in Kabul—universities that girls can go to. They can become doctors, lawyers, midwives and even artists! They can read as many books as they want, and no one is jealous. My father told me that the capital has changed so much since the civil war ended and the Taliban government was chased away. There are even women on radio and television—"

"Women on radio and television?" Zohra interrupts me. "They must be orphans! Their mothers and fathers would never let them be so exposed!"

"Just because a woman is in the public spotlight doesn't make her a whore!" I find myself yelling at Zohra.

"I am not saying she *is* one, but she will be treated as one," Zohra responds, unaffected by my tone.

"That doesn't make it right! Look at our friends—they can't even leave their homes anymore because their families are afraid of what others will say. They probably already talk about us just for walking to each other's homes."

"They do." Zohra looks at me with empathetic eyes. "And that's my point. We can't change that. Especially not in our little village. Those women have the protection of the capital; we rely on the protection of our families."

We sit in silence sipping our tea, then Zohra clears her throat. "Would you think less of me if I got married?"

"What? Of course not. Eventually that's what people are supposed to do." I look at Zohra, who is staring at her glass, sticking her finger inside and pushing a floating leaf down. "Zohra?"

"My parents were talking to me last night," she starts, hesitating. "They . . . they . . . they said that they want me to get engaged to a boy a few villages over . . ."

I'm speechless. Zohra's my age. She's too young.

"He's a distant relative of my father's. They say that he's looking for a wife, and he could take care of me. They're well-off too—they own a motorcycle." Zohra adds the last part as if to justify her parents' wishes. I can't believe my best friend's worth is calculated by whether someone owns a motorcycle or not.

"When?" I choke out.

"I don't know. My grandmother's not happy about it. She's told my father that they should wait until I'm older, but my parents are afraid the opportunity will disappear if we ask to wait a few years. His parents want him to marry soon."

"How do you feel?" I ask, not knowing what else to say.

Zohra just shrugs. "It's my fate."

I wonder if it will also be mine.

Three

FATIMA

The next morning, I do something even though I know it's wrong. I do it because I want to, ignoring the consequences. I do it because one day soon, I might not be able to anymore.

But because of it, I am now running.

I can feel the gravel against my callused feet, but I don't stop. The sun is beating down on my head, and sweat flows in rivulets down my back. I'm gasping for breath. But I won't give in, and I push harder.

I finally make it to the river—if you can call it a river. Right now the heat is so intense it has dried up to the size of a small creek. But still, even in the scorching late-summer months, the water is ice-cold. I imagine the snow traveling down the mountains behind me, melting as it gathers speed, turning into our river. I am like the snow as I race across the shallow part of the river, picking up my dress and the pants underneath, moving faster and faster. The water barely reaches my calves, but my feet are numb as I make it to the gravel on the other end.

I'm trying to catch my breath through my dry mouth. I can feel the thumping in my chest and the pulsing in my ears.

That's when I see it, the rock—*my* old rock. I run to it until I am out of sight. I curl up behind it. The rock will hide me, not just from him but also from the searing sun. It's a roofless cave, right next to the mountain, only one way in and only one way out.

He will never find me now.

Minutes pass, but it feels like hours. As I listen for his footsteps, I stare at my henna-stained nails. They look so pretty even as the color fades, like the orange-and-cream sherbet ice cream they sell in town. My mother made me color them last week. "Every woman needs to look her best, even if it is just for her own family, Fatima," she told me, for what was probably the millionth time. She has always felt that I needed to act more like a girl instead of yet another son, and never lets me forget it.

I wonder if Samiullah has noticed my nails when we've seen each other. Ugh, why do I care if he noticed? What's wrong with me?

Splash . . . splash . . . splash!

Oh, Khudaya, is he going to find me? I curl my body up tighter, praying for God to help me. I'm almost as round as the rock protecting me. I squeeze my eyes shut just as tight as I've squashed my body.

"*Salaam,* Fatima." I open my eyes, and he is there. He

is shadowed in darkness as the sun's rays glare behind him, straining my vision. Samiullah.

How did he find me? This is the third time I've hidden from him this morning, and the third time he's known just where to look. But perhaps I've been hiding in places where I knew he would find me . . .

I'm glad I chose to spend my day with him today, rather than head to Zohra's. I didn't think I should, but Samiullah put me at ease the second that he met me in the woods this morning. He said he'd protect me. That he wouldn't let anything bad happen while we were together. And I believed him. Or at least convinced myself I did. Besides, I didn't want to go back and hear more about Zohra's wedding.

"Did you really think that by closing your eyes you somehow could hide from me?" Samiullah says, laughing and mimicking my expression. He looks enormous from my crouched position. He's squinting, but I can still see the twinkle of his eyes. They make him look a little less fierce, more like the gentle Samiullah I've known since we were babies.

"No, I was just . . . just . . ."

"Praying? I don't blame you. If I were you, I would pray for the day you could win as well," he says with a smirk. At first I want to wipe that grin off his face, but then I realize that his smile makes the defeat more acceptable. I blink to block out his face. Why am I thinking these things?

Samiullah clears his throat. "Anyway, now that I've found you, what do you want to do next? I'm bored."

"You're always bored!" I say as I stand, slapping the dirt off my bright red *payron* and the green *tumbon*. "Well . . . I mean . . . you always used to get bored. I guess some things never change," I add, hoping to sound playful.

"Well, then stop being so boring," Samiullah quickly counters as he evens out my head scarf. I smack his hand off the brown fabric and march down to the river. Who does he think he is, convincing me to spend the day with him and then calling me boring?

Samiullah laughs again. "Oh, come on! You know I'm just joking!" He begins to run after me. "You're not boring, I swear!"

I have to smile—I can't stay mad at him; I never could. But I really shouldn't be here today. This could get us into big trouble. If our families find out . . . If the villagers see us . . . We are no longer at the age that they would consider this okay. I shouldn't even be talking to him. My smile begins to fade. I'm reminded of how unlucky my life really is.

The thought of Zohra being married off was frightening enough. But then my parents' conversation last night gave me bad dreams. I didn't think my simple questions about Samiullah's return during dinner would lead my mother to want to marry me off too. Maybe I shouldn't have said anything.

But I did. And then I overheard my *madar* talking to my *baba* as I was lying on my mattress pretending to sleep. I felt her eyes on me, even through the thickness of the wool blanket that covered my head. I could see her shadow as she leaned in front of the oil lamp and whispered, "Mohammad, she's too old to be seen with *that* boy again! And I know your daughter, she will want to play together as if they were still five! I didn't like it then, and I won't stand for it now! It will be hard to find her a suitable husband. They will think she has been tainted— and of all people by a Pashtun boy! It's time we think of her marriage. You even said that Karim has found Zohra a suitor. It's time we find Fatima one too."

They always talk about things they don't want me to hear when they think I'm sleeping. But they don't know that I'm usually faking sleep. I heard them the time my *madar* told my *baba* that it would be best to send my older brother, Ali, to Iran to make money for the family. She was wrong then, and she is wrong now.

I've been trying to ignore what she said all day, but I can't, and every time I think about it, my stomach turns and I begin to feel nauseous. God, I miss Ali. He would have told my mother that I was too young to get married. But because of her, I don't even have him anymore.

Anyway, my *madar*'s words won't matter. My *baba* loves me too much to send me away to a family I don't know, like Karim is doing to Zohra. But I can't imagine how even he would react if they knew I was out with Samiullah now. Alone. The thought sends a shiver down my spine. When my *madar* told my *baba* last night that she wanted to forbid me from seeing Samiullah, he said that I wouldn't be stupid enough to do something like that. I guess I am.

Samiullah has caught up to me now, and he's standing with his face tipped toward the sun. The rays hit his nose and cheekbones and throw the rest of his face into shadow. It makes him look older, somehow. I can even see his little prickles of facial hair. Right now he looks more like his father or even his cousin Rashid than the Samiullah I know.

"You want to see who can keep their hand in the water longest without freezing their fingers off?" I challenge him— because I know this is the one thing I can beat him at. He turns away from the sun, and he's my Samiullah again.

"Fine. But I don't want you to ruin your delicate hands in the ice water," Samiullah says, half joking, as he gets down on both knees at the edge of the river and dips his hands into the shallow river. I lift my *payron* and *tumbon* up slightly so I won't get them wet as I kneel by the water and follow suit.

It's hard to believe that this trickling river is our village's lifeblood. Farther downstream, manmade canals bring the water into some of our courtyards so we can all use it for cooking and bathing. Samiullah once told me that no other town he traveled to with his father while they delivered their farmed goods has water as delicious as ours. It has an icy sweet taste that pinches at the inside of your cheeks.

The tips of my fingers are going numb, and the rest of my

hand tingles from the cold, but I force myself to focus on the gravel digging into my knees and the sweat dripping underneath my head scarf—anything to distract me from the pain in my hand. I sneak a glance over to Samiullah, and his eyes are squeezed tight with determination. He can't beat me, though. He never did then, and he won't now.

"Do you hear that?" Samiullah's eyelids pop open, and he's staring directly at me, green eyes wide and frightened.

I'm about to say "hear what?" when Samiullah grabs my warm arm with his cold, wet hand and drags me toward my rock. He's holding on so tightly that I know it will leave a bruise. I can barely keep up with him.

"What's the matter? Why are we run—" And that's when I hear it too. The distant buzzing. I feel my heart start to race. That noise can only mean one thing: danger.

My feet are about to give way when we finally make it to the rock, falling hard behind it. I can taste the dirt flying up into my mouth. But the boulder is protecting us from the rumbling that is getting closer.

"Stay quiet until they pass." Samiullah whispers to me, short of breath. "Sounds like there's only one motorbike, but it has to be one of Latif's men."

This scares me more. No one else in our village uses motorbikes—he's right, it has to be one of Latif's criminals. They call themselves God's soldiers. Those words are like an evil pass to condone their wickedness. Instead, they should be called Satan's stooges. Shayton's henchmen. Some say they are the Taliban, but we don't know if they're connected to the real Taliban. All we know is that they are dangerous.

Whatever their label is, they are thugs who steal lives, money and spirits. I close my eyes and start to pray. I'm suddenly terrified. This wasn't supposed to happen. We were just supposed to enjoy the day like we did as children. No one was supposed to see us, no one. And especially not these thugs. My breathing intensifies. If they catch us, they will use God and religion as their excuse to do anything they want, including kill us. By being alone together, without any supervision, we're breaking the rules of not just our parents but of Taliban morality—it doesn't matter that we're young. I wrap my head scarf around my nose and mouth to quiet my breathing. They can't find us here. Like this. Together. *Please, God,* I say inside my head. *Please, God, keep them away. Khuda Jaan, please keep us hidden.*

I wonder if this is my punishment from God for meeting Samiullah today and lying to my parents.

The motorbike slows down a few yards upstream from our rock. I hear two pairs of boots crunching on the gravel. One set of footsteps gets closer and closer to where we are hiding before it stops. My heart races faster, and I start to feel dizzy.

"*Dilta rasa!*" a voice belts out in the Pashto language, calling his companion over.

"What? I need to pee!" another voice yells back.

"I don't care what *you* need to do, come here now!" the first man orders. "Look at this."

Oh, God. He must have seen our footprints. Will they lead him to our rock? If the men find us, they will accuse us of adultery. They could jail us. Murder us. I heard up north in Kunduz province just a year ago a young couple was stoned to death for being in love—not that Samiullah and I are in love, but they lie about everything. What's to stop them from lying about this?

"Those are donkey pellets." I hear the second voice say.

"Yes, genius. And if this water is good enough for donkeys to drink, it's good enough for you." I hear him slurping. "Oh, this is good water! Get me the jug from the bike. It will last us until we get home."

I can't help but feel some relief. This time they are just craving water, not blood. I let my breath out slowly and pull my scarf away from my mouth. Now that the initial fear has passed, I'm annoyed that he is savoring my village's water. His dirty lips shouldn't have the pleasure of our sweet water. Sensing my agitation, Samiullah holds me tighter to contain my anger.

"Look! *Mayan wogora!* Hurry, give me your gun. It's time to go fishing!" the first voice yells enthusiastically.

"Really? With a bullet?" the second voice says skeptically. His voice sounds almost familiar, but I can't place it.

"Well, how else are we going to get the fish?"

"I . . . uh . . . don't think a bullet. I mean, maybe we shouldn't

waste our ammunition on fish. It may enrage Mullah Latif."
The second voice sounds cautious.

"What do you know about *Mullah* Latif, young one? You
haven't even met him yet. Give me the gun." I hear a snort followed by bullets being loaded. "God, they're moving so fast,
those little devils."

Crack! Crack! Crack!

I've never heard a gunshot from so close before. My body
tenses. I squeeze Samiullah's arms as he tightens his grip
around my waist. What if they find us here? Will they shoot us
like they're trying to shoot the fish right now?

"Did I get one? Where'd they go?" The first voice sounds
confused.

"I think you scared them off," the almost-familiar voice
responds with a hint of annoyance. Why does he sound so
familiar?

"Good. The fish are like these villagers. We have to show
them who's boss! Maybe next time, we can chase some of the
human fishes here with my gun!" I hear him chuckling. "Grab
the water, and let's go so we can make it back before it gets
dark."

As I hear the men tying the jug to the bike and preparing
to leave, I'm suddenly very aware of Samiullah and how close
his body is to mine. I've never been this close to him—to any
boy—in my life. His heart seems to be beating as fast as mine.
He's still squeezing me tight, and I'm squeezing back, feeling

the muscles and veins on his arms as he holds me close. We listen as the roaring of the motorcycle fades away to a distant rumble, and still we don't move. I feel so safe like this, safer than I ever have before.

When the sound of the bike has completely faded, I turn my body around to find Samiullah staring at me. His green eyes look as unsettled as I feel. All I can do is stare back.

"Well, that was a close one," he says softly, his arms still cradling me. "Are you okay? I'm sorry for dragging you and—"

"Don't be sorry. You saved us," I tell him. I feel nervous again talking to him and avert my gaze. I know I should move away and undo the tangle of our bodies, but I can't make myself do it. We stay like that, quiet, listening to each other breathe for what seems like minutes, but is probably only a few seconds.

"You've got dirt on your face," Samiullah says, breaking the silence as he gently wipes his thumb over my right cheek. "Is that what's passing for makeup these days?"

All I can do is stare at him. The spot on my cheek tingles underneath his finger. I know it is wrong to be lying here like this, but I don't want to move.

"Come on," he says, finally pulling away. "I should probably get you home before someone sees us."

I nod, and we both stand up. I can't stop the shiver that runs through me. Even in the hot sun, I feel cold without Samiullah's body next to mine.

four

FATIMA

Samiullah says good-bye to me on the wheat fields in between our homes, out of the sight line of his mud house and mine. The land belongs to his family, but Samiullah and I are safe from intrusive eyes because my father and Karim have moved on to a different field, slashing away at the long strands of wheat on the other side of the property. The harvest is almost over, so they are making sure they've reaped the whole lot.

I walk the rest of the way back by myself, trying to gather my thoughts about what just happened. But I'm still confused.

Shouldn't I be terrified by the fact that Latif's men almost saw us? They could have killed us—they would have justified it by saying we were unmarried and alone. So why do I feel more anxious about what just happened with Samiullah? About the way he touched my face and held me close?

In no time at all, I'm home. I stand in front of our house. It's made up of many small dried-mud rooms spread out on a small patch of dirt, not just one building like Kaka Ismail's house. Like Samiullah's house.

I walk past the cooking room and the sleeping room to the chicken coop and take a seat on the patch of dirt next to it. As I lean my head back, I close my eyes and let the sun prickle my skin with warmth before it begins to set behind the mountains, bringing the brisk night air. I can smell the pile of dried dung patties stacked against the wall on the other side of the cage. Our village doesn't have enough trees to burn, so we rely mostly on cow dung for cooking and heat. The smell is so pungent you can sometimes taste it. But right now, I'm not bothered. I'm too distracted by thoughts of Samiullah, his eyes, his touch and his strength.

"Fato!" I'm jolted back to the present as I hear Afifa running toward me. Her fire-red hair darts at me like a cat chasing its prey. But her little body wobbles more like the chickens in the coop.

Afifa's entrance startles those dumb birds, who are now frantically cackling and running around the cage, sending dirt up in the air. The dirt makes its way into my mouth as Afifa jumps into my lap and smacks a tiny wet kiss on my lips.

"*Salaam*, Afo Jaan!" I greet her with affection.

Kissing her bubbled cheeks, I'm reminded of my own innocence, which I somehow feel slipping away after hearing my parents talk and spending the afternoon with Samiullah. I can't resist sucking in Afifa's small chubby cheeks after I've kissed them. And as if on cue, she giggles with delight. I finish my kisses by laying the last one on her forehead.

"How was your day, my *shadi gak*?" I ask, squeezing her tiny body to mine.

My burdens suddenly disappear.

"I'm not a little monkey!" Afifa giggles.

"You're my little monkey," I say as I start to tickle her.

"Okay! Okay! I'm a monkey!" She protests the tickles. "I'm a *shadi*! Where were you? Why didn't you play with me today? I mished you!"

I love the way she slurs her words. I love everything about her.

"I was out walking, my *shadi gak*."

"Where?" she says. *Allah tobah*—God forgive her nosiness. She must get it from our mother.

"What's it to you?" I say, tickling her again, and this time I don't stop. Her laughter is now mixed with tears as she begs for it to end.

"Fatima, is that you?" I hear my mother. "Come here, little woman. Where have you been? You're late. You need to help me with dinner."

"I was with Zorah," I lie as my mother approaches, holding a plastic bowl full of wet potatoes. That's where I was supposed to be, at least.

"Oh, really, with Zorah? How is Zorah? How is her grandmother doing?" my mother says, raising her right eyebrow. "Why did they send you home so late?"

"They're great! Both Khala Jaan and Zorah send their *sa-*

laams!" I pick Afifa off the ground and ignore my mother's last question. "I'll clean Afo up and come help peel the potatoes."

I can feel my mother's eyes on me as I walk my little sister toward the stream.

After I clean Afifa's face and hands with the cold flow of the stream, she runs off to find our father, who should be back from the fields soon.

I then begin to wash my own face. The cold water splashing the day's dirt off my skin feels so refreshing. But my mind starts to race with thoughts of Samiullah. They send me back to the moment he was holding me—so tight that I could feel his solid chest against my back.

I pull my sleeves over my elbows and rinse my arms. But even with the cold water on my skin, I feel the warmth of his body next to mine. The beating of his heart. His breath on the back of my neck. The touch of his hand on my face—

"Fatima!" I'm startled by the screeching of my mother's voice.

"I'm coming!" I yell as I jump up.

I quickly make my way to the dirt patch where my mother has already begun peeling the potatoes without me. Nearly half the bowl is skinned.

I guess I took longer than I thought.

"Where were you today?" my mother asks with a tinge of anger in her voice.

"Madar Jaan, I already told you I was with Zorah." I say, picking up a knife and a potato. I know there is no way she can prove otherwise, because she hasn't left our home. And if it came down to it, Zohra would lie for me even if she didn't know why.

"So you didn't go and see that boy?" she says, and I feel her eyes on me. But I won't look up to meet her scrutinizing gaze. "You asked so many questions about his return last night."

"Who? Samiullah? No. I haven't seen him since he left three years ago. I just heard from Zohra about his return the day before yesterday," I say, concentrating on my peeling but feeling my stomach tighten. "I guess he's back to working with his father and going out on their delivery trips?"

"No, he didn't go anywhere." Suddenly I feel my stomach drop. What does she know? "His father came over here to check on the crops. Ismail Khan said he was going to pick up some items on Saturday," my mother says.

"Oh . . ." is all I can respond, my eyes focused on my potato.

"Oh? *Tobah. Tobah.*" My mother shakes her head in frustration asking for God's forgiveness as she always does. Not for herself, of course, but for her wicked daughter. "You are forbidden from seeing him. You are not a child anymore, and I won't allow you to ruin our name by being seen with him or any other boy. Remember that." She carries the potatoes to the *tandoor,* where a pot is waiting with a half liter of oil. Underneath the pot, a steady fire is burning, fueled by two dried dung patties. She dices the potatoes and a small tomato, drops it all in the pot and lets it cook.

We hardly speak during dinner, except for the normal requests to please pass the bread, sprinkle some salt or pour a glass of water. My father fills the silence as he usually does, talking about his day with Karim, as my eight- and six-year-old brothers hang on every word.

"When he went to pick up the bag of wheat, a cat jumped out from behind the pile! That's when Karim shrieked like a little girl and fell backward, dropping the bag and landing on his *koonak*." My father chuckles with the boys. I glance over to my left and find my mother giggling quietly. My little sister is too preoccupied with her food or lack thereof. She's reaching her little bangle-decorated hands into the pot of potatoes, trying to dip her piece of bread. She comes out with just *naan* soaked in oil. But looking at her glowing eyes, you would think she had dipped her bread in gold.

"Fato!" my father says to me.

"Yes, Baba Jaan?" I quickly respond.

"I saw Samiullah early this morning. He came by to say hi. He is a good kid." My father quickly slurps up a handful of potato. "He sent his *salaam*s to everyone." He licks his fingers. "Were you helping your *madar jaan* today?"

"No, Baba. I was with Zorah and her grandmother today," I lie. Of all people, my father is the one I most I hate lying to.

"Strange. Karim said Zorah was taking care of her brothers

and sisters today because his wife was taking his *bibi* to the clinic in town," my father says with curiosity.

"Oh, yes. They came back early. I guess there was no line today," I lie again, feeling the sinking pit in my belly.

"Well, that's good," my father says, quickly moving on to another story and refocusing on my younger brothers.

All I can feel is the stinging gaze of my mother. Oh, God, does she know? Luckily it's dark, and all we have is one oil lamp dimly illuminating the dining mat, so it's easy to avoid her eyes and focus on my food.

After dinner we set up our sleeping mats. I tuck Afifa snug into her blanket. She looks like the little baby she used to be not so long ago.

"Fato, *dostit darom*," she says, rubbing her little hand on my left cheek.

"I love you too, my *shadi gak*," I reply.

"I'm. Not. *Shadi*," she slowly protests as her eyes desperately try to stay open.

"Okay, you're not a monkey. You're my little Afo. And I would do anything for my little Afo." I slide my hand on her cheek as I watch her give in and fall into a deep sleep. I'm finally beginning to feel the exhaustion of the day's events myself, and I let out a big yawn.

I get up and kiss both of my parents good night and head to my mattress, slipping underneath the blanket. I say the same prayers that my mother taught me when I was younger than Afo is now, and begin to doze off—I'm too exhausted to stay up tonight and eavesdrop on my parents' conversations.

I get lost in a dream not long after I snuggle into my pillow. Samiullah and I are running around the fields like we did when we were young children. A feeling of joy and happiness overcomes me; I think it's the feeling of innocence. I'm praying in my dream that it can last forever—

"*Baas!*" I'm awoken by the sound of my father's voice filled with anger.

"But, Mohammad, she's at the age," my mother pleads.

"I said enough! No more! I'm not marrying my daughter off to strangers. How do we know how these people will treat her? How do we know if we will ever see her again? I can't trade her to someone in another village for a little bit of money; just because it is in our culture doesn't make it okay." My father's voice begins to shake. "She isn't a sack of wheat. I can't just sell her for a few Afghanis and breathe easily for the rest of my life. Besides, she's too young. This conversation is over."

I keep my eyes shut, pretending to be asleep. But the pit of my stomach is turning. I feel sick.

"What about me, Mohammad? Didn't we marry when I was around Fatima's age? Things turned out fine for me. God is generous. We have to put our trust in God." Her pleas continue. "The boy comes from a rich Hazara family in the next village over. We can go and see her when we want. At least we will have the peace of mind that she is with our own people. They're not barbaric like those other groups!"

How can my mother say all this? Why does she want me to leave my home, my family and my life?

"They're not barbaric. What are you saying, woman?" my father slams back. "There is no innocent party in this country! You think just because he's from our ethnic group he'll treat our daughter like gold? Did the Hazaras not torture people through the wars too? Did *I* not kill people because of our ethnic pride?"

A jolt shoots up my spine, and I begin to tremble. My face tingles from the rush of blood. And I can hear my teeth clacking against each other, but I can't stop them. I suddenly feel so cold. The noise from my teeth is blaring inside of my head and it makes it hard for me to think. I can't believe what I just heard. My gentle *baba* has blood on his hands? The feeling in my stomach gets worse. I really think I'm going to be sick. But I try my hardest not to move; I don't want them to know that I'm awake. Or that my world has just turned upside down. It can't be true. The words may have come out of his mouth, but he must mean something else.

"Mossuma, I've done things, things I can never forget," he sighs. "And I can't pretend I'm not guilty. I fear every day that my loved ones will pay for my sins. Ali already has. I'm afraid that my greatest punishment will be to see my family suffer because of my past."

"But, Mohammad, it was a different place and time. And you were just following orders." My mother's voice softens, ignoring my father's mention of my older brother, who was killed by thugs years ago on his way to Iran. A trip he took at my mother's foolish encouragement to make the family money as a laborer. "God will forgive you; you were a young boy—"

"God can't forgive the things I did. What so many in this country did to *each other*! How can God forgive such atrocities?" My father's voice begins to shake. "God has cursed this country and our people. I'm afraid God will continue to punish my children for the things I did, the things I let happen. I've already lost one child, I don't want to lose another."

"Mohammad," my mother tries to interject but fails. I can hear her sniffle. They never speak of Ali. It has always been easier that way. But I still think of him all the time.

"I saw a man, one of *our* fighters, stick the head of a rifle in a baby's mouth. I can still see the baby sucking on it, as if it was his mother's nipple. The fighter couldn't stop laughing and pointed for all of us to look. They baby thought we were playing with him. It was just as his tiny mouth began moving again, in search of milk from the barrel that . . . the gun went off." My father's voice breaks. I hear him clear his throat.

Did he really allow this baby to die?

"Mohammad, that was the civil war, you were in Kabul. You had no other choice. That same baby's father probably would have killed you." My mother's voice is also shaking. I can tell she's trying to pacify him but is also scared.

Is this why my father never speaks of his time in Kabul? My brothers and I have always asked about what life was like in the capital city. But he will never tell us.

"My love, we don't know that." My father's voice is still so quiet and soft. "They just lived in the wrong neighborhood. And we had orders from the commander to send them all a message. I still don't understand why, to be honest, and I hope I never do. All I know is that I took part in that sin. I killed men, women and children. I allowed it to happen."

The thought of my father participating in atrocities makes me even more nauseous. I feel like I'm going to vomit, but I breathe deeply and try to will the nausea away. I don't want them to know I am awake and listening.

"But if you hadn't done it, they would have killed you! It was survival. You were just surviving."

"Sometimes I wish I hadn't survived. Now I am forced to live with those memories."

"Mohammad . . ." My mother says my father's name with such tenderness, and I realize for the first time that she does love him. Just like in Zohra's *bibi*'s stories. She loves him very much.

"This is why I want my daughter to live a happy life," my father says, his voice full of tears. "I've seen men steal women, keep them locked up as slaves—I've seen them sold, raped and killed. I've seen fathers crying on the streets, holding pictures of their daughters, asking if anyone has seen them."

I had heard these stories before, but I never thought they were true. I can barely believe them now, even though my own father has seen these things happen. Seen them, and done nothing to help.

"I've seen a man marry a woman only to torture her in order to make her family pay for a wrong they had done to his family. I don't want to take that gamble with my daughter's life."

"But some of our women are happy. Look at me," my mother says, almost pleading. "I was blessed the day that you came to this village. I was blessed the moment your family came to mine for *khastgaree* and asked for my hand in marriage. I thank God every day for you and the children. I want Fatima to have a provider like you. And I think she has a better chance of that with our own kind."

"What matters is his upbringing. His parents." My father's voice begins to rise again.

"Of course, ethnicity isn't *all* that matters. But this boy has a good upbringing. Good parents. He even went to a university in Kabul." My mother sounds desperate. "He is the reason why most of their village has electricity. And we both know that she will never be fully accepted by any other ethnic group."

"Mossuma Jaan, I'm exhausted right now. Can we discuss this later? My mind and my heart can't take any more tonight."

"Yes, *azizam*. But we can't put it off too much longer." My mother's words feel like a rope around my neck. "We knew from the moment our daughters were born that they wouldn't be with us forever, that one day they would belong to another family."

I can't help but think about what it would be like to be part of Samiullah's family, but then I feel worse, because even though they are kind to me now, I know they never would want me as a match for their son. My mother is right. A Hazara girl could never marry a Pashtun boy.

five

FATIMA

The temperature is still frigid as I wake up at dawn and head outside, but I can already feel the sun's rays slowly emerging, burning off the icy air. I splash water on my face from one of the jugs and let the cold water help me wake. I use more water to rinse out my mouth, swishing it and then spitting it back out on the ground. As I spit it out, I know I will be sent to the well again to refill the jugs, but for once it makes me happy because it means time away from home. All I can feel is dread as I head into the room with the *tandoor*, where I will spend the next two hours with my mother making bread.

By the time I get there, she has already pulled out the cooking *distarkhans*, placing the plastic sheets around the *tandoor*. "*Salaam*, Madar Jaan," I say as I walk in.

"*Salaam, janem*," she responds. "Can you start making the dough?"

"Yes," I say as I grab the small plastic tub and rinse it out with the remaining water from last night's kettle. I place it on a *distarkhan*, adding the flour, water, oil and some eggs. I mix the ingredients for the dough until it gets tough and hard. Then I start to fold and beat. The only thing that gives me strength is knowing that I will see Samiullah in a few hours, the way we'd planned when we said good-bye in the wheat field. We won't leave the woods this time, which will make it safer. Thinking of this gets my mind off my mother and her plans to ruin my life, and my father the fraud.

I notice her throw some plates of dung in the bottom of the *tandoor* and light them with matches and old news paper. She uses a long and thin metal rod to help the fire spread and build. We both work in silence like we usually do. But every now and then, I feel my mother's eyes on me; I don't dare meet them. I'm afraid it will lead to talking, and right now I don't want to hear anything she has to say. I don't even want to hear her voice.

She puts the kettle on a metal rack over the *tandoor* as I start patting out round balls of dough and placing them on the *distarkhan*.

My mother breaks our silence. "Maybe today we can sprinkle black cumin seeds on the bread and make it a little more fancy. It's what I used to do when I first got married to impress your father." I nod my head and continue to pat the balls of dough. "One day you'll do it for your husband too. The extra effort shows that you're a good wife and that you care for him."

I wonder if Samiullah likes bread with seeds? He's never told me. I've never asked him.

"Maybe we can make salty cookies today as well? I think

we can spare a few cups of flour," my mother says, smiling. "One day when you get married, you'll have to remember how to make all this food because I won't be around to remind you. You'll become the woman of the house, cooking for your husband, his family and, *inshallah,* your own children."

"I need to go to Zohra's today," I say as I pound my fist into the dough before ripping off another chunk.

"You can skip your lessons today. The cookies will be more important to your future than reading."

"They're expecting me. It would be rude not to go." I lie to my mother but don't feel the least bit guilty about it. She's betraying me by wanting to marry me off, so why can't I do the same?

"*Rafedara bitay?*" my mother asks with an annoyed tone. I hand her the small pillow used to put the bread into the *tandoor.* She begins to flatten one of my dough balls into a thin round. She uses her fingernail to poke holes in the dough, which will allow the bread to breathe as it bakes on the walls of the *tandoor.* "Put the seeds on like this," she says as she pats some of the cumin into the dough. When she's done, she takes the boiling kettle off the *tandoor* to expose the opening and slaps the dough onto the inside walls. She tosses me the *rafeda,* and it's my turn to follow suit. "You know, one day you'll want to be married, and you'll even enjoy it. It makes you a woman. I was so lucky that your father came for me. He has blessed me every day since, treating me like a friend, not a servant."

Samiullah had always reminded me of my father, his kindness and his gentleness. But last night's revelations made me realize my father is not the man I thought he was. Samiullah could never be like that. Samiullah would be a man who would treat everyone well, not just his wife.

My mother continues to talk, but I can't hear her anymore. I drown her out with thoughts of what a future with Samiullah would be like. Most likely in a home built by him and his cousins. It would have a big room for the *tandoor*. We could have tea in the living area and a courtyard for the livestock. We would eat candy, laughing and sharing stories . . .

I snap back to reality and realize how crazy I am for having those thoughts. Zohra was right, I keep dreaming of things that aren't possible. And a future with Samiullah is impossible.

Six

FATIMA

After we've finished with the bread, I leave my home, taking the route I use to Zohra's house. I feel bad about missing time with Zohra's *bibi*, but I promise myself I'll review the work in my head later tonight, before I fall asleep. Besides she may still not be well enough to teach us today. I walk through our flat fields until the tree line begins. We don't have much greenery in our village, but we do have spots where the pine trees grow. Children go there in the fall to gather pine nuts, but the area is ignored during the spring and summer.

I walk several meters forward, cracking and breaking the small branches under my feet. If I were going to Zohra's, I'd keep heading straight on the dirt path created by Karim walking to the fields every morning and home every evening. For a split second, it dawns on me that I can follow the path and actually see Zohra. I can read with her and her grandmother and save myself from the dangerous plan Samiullah and I have made. It would be the wise choice, going straight.

I don't. I turn right in an area where the foliage is sparse. Protected by the cover of the trees, I hunch over and whack away the branches and leaves. While I wait for Samiullah, my heart rate accelerates and my breathing becomes heavier.

I have rarely lied to my parents. I've never really had a reason to. But this seems worth it. And even though it frightens me, I can't stop myself.

I know that if I get caught, Samiullah and I could be in a lot of trouble, especially if we have a real run-in with Latif and his men. But what worries me more is that it will ruin my family's name and honor to have their elder daughter running around the village unsupervised. Not just unsupervised—alone with a boy. The more I think about it, the more my stomach drops. I feel the rush of blood darting straight to my face. I can't do this. It's far too risky. But just as I'm deciding to turn around and go to Zohra's, I hear him.

"Fatima?" Samiullah says, his voice deep and soothing. "Is everything okay?" Any anxious feelings I had suddenly disappear and I'm in a place of calm and warmth.

"Yes, everything is fine," I tell him.

"Are you sure? The color has drained from your face." His eyes look concerned.

"Yes, I'm sure." I smile at him and kick a small stone on the dirt below, trying to avoid his gaze.

"Good, then! So what do you want to do today? I should

probably teach you a little bit of reading just in case your parents want to test you soon," he says, smiling as he pulls out a notebook and pen from the pocket of his *payron*. I think he might be more worried than I am about getting caught. We both know his punishment would be less severe than mine, but he seems more alert than I am, ready to run at the smallest sign of trouble.

"I'm already a good reader, Sami," I tell him. "I'd be fine if my parents decide to test me."

He raises an eyebrow, and I think perhaps he's impressed. Then he laughs and says, "Well, what would you rather do?" as he puts the pen behind his ear, gently weaving it through his thick, wavy hair. I have an urge to touch his hair, just to see what it feels like, but instead I quickly look away and sit on the large rock behind me.

"How about we look for *toot*?" I say.

"That sounds perfect!" He actually seems excited. "I've missed the mulberries in this village. The fresh, juicy kind. I had dried *toot* while I was away, but I wasn't able to ever find the fresh ones."

"Good, then!" I'm happy my idea has been so well received. We head deeper into the woods, looking for the trees growing in the wild.

"I think I found one," Samiullah yells. I run over and see the wide tree with long branches and beautiful red and purple berries. I pick one and pop it in my mouth. The tart juices spark throughout my tongue. It's hard to believe these are the same berries that we dry and have with tea during the winter; the flavor is so different when they're fresh. "It's delicious, isn't it?"

I nod and continue to feast. Sami joins me. I find a branch thick enough to climb. I reach and feel the coarseness of the tree scratch the inside of my hand. I try to pull myself up, but I don't have the strength. Sami walks toward me and bends over. "Here, step on my back," he says.

"No, you'll get dirty." I'm looking at his white *payron*.

"I can have my clothes washed." He smiles at me with crooked lips before looking back down. I push myself up and am able to climb to an even thicker branch. Sami follows and sits next to me. He reaches out and pulls down a long branch, picking some berries and handing them to me before taking more for himself. We sit quietly eating our *toot* in the cool shade of the woods.

Thoughts of my parents' conversation last night keep popping into my head. I don't want to get married to a stranger in another village. I won't know him; he won't know me. And I won't be able to see Samiullah anymore.

"What are you thinking about?" Sami asks, breaking the noise in my head.

"Nothing," I lie.

"I don't think that's the truth," he says, making me smile. He has always been able to read my silence better than anyone else. "I see what we're doing—we're playing the guessing game! I like this game."

I can't stop grinning now and play along, pursing my lips together to show that I won't say a thing.

"Let's see. What can it be?" He snaps his fingers. "You've decided to lead a women's rights march in the village?" I snort, picturing my mother and the other women parading around. I saw women do that in the capital city back when our television set was working, before its battery died. "From the snot that just flew out of your nose, that is not it." I quickly touch my nose and realize he was teasing. And, of course, now he's the one smirking.

"Okay, then what can it be? Aha, you've decided to join the Afghan army. Not because you want to fight for your country, but because you want to get as far away as you can from your mother?" That's a thought. I should keep that in mind. But I press my lips together harder and shake my head.

"No, no." Sami gives me a long look. "Could it be that you're going to marry an old man with a long white beard and leave me stranded in this village without my dearest friend?" Sami-ullah says those words, obviously satisfied with what he finds to be a ridiculous statement, but it hits me right in the heart. Old or not, my mother does in fact want to give me away to someone. She's begging my father to give me away to someone.

As I look up at Sami, tears fill my eyes and distort my vision. I can feel them running down my face, and I am suddenly gasping for breath. I jump off the branch. I don't want him to stare at me when I look so foolish. I land hard on my feet and squat on the ground. The pain in my feet is nothing compared to everything else I am feeling. I hear Sami jump down after me.

"I'm so sorry. What did I say? Are you okay?" Sami kneels in front of me, his arms half outstretched, as if he wants to hold me but is afraid. I'm not afraid. Not anymore. I wrap my arms around his neck and bury my face in his shoulder, trying to hide my tears. He reaches his arms around me, holding tight. "It's okay," he whispers. "Just take a deep breath."

Our bodies stay enfolded for what seems like ages. I begin to catch my breath, and my tears stop streaming like the winter snow melting from the mountaintops; they instead become little droplets of rain. As we unwrap our arms and bodies, I immediately want that warmth and comfort back. I begin to feel silly for what I did and just look at the ground. "I'm sorry" is all I can say.

"For what? Don't be sorry." Sami sounds genuinely concerned. "But you're scaring me. What's wrong?"

I tell him everything, starting with my mother's plan to marry me off. I don't know if I'm just imagining it, but I think he looks distraught. I go on to tell him about my father and what he did when he was in Kabul. I tell him about the baby, but Sami doesn't seem surprised. And this begins to upset me too. "Why aren't you outraged?" I ask him.

"Fatima, your father is a good man," he says, picking more *toot* and settling on the rock beside me. "He loves you. He is even fighting your mother so she'll stop trying to marry you to a stranger. Not many fathers love their daughters that way."

"But how can you call him a good man? He killed people!" I notice my voice rising.

"This country, our people, that's all some of them know," Sami says. "Maybe that is all your father knew until he was taught something different. I'm not defending what your father did; it was wrong. I'm just saying that he probably didn't know better or he was forced to do it so he wouldn't be killed himself. I don't know. But I do know he isn't the only guilty person in our country." He reaches his hand out to offer me some of the berries, but I don't take them.

"What do you mean?" I ask, almost disappointed in Sami for defending such horrific acts. We're talking about taking lives! Taking lives of the innocent. Of a baby! "Do you think it's okay just to kill people? Would *you* kill someone?"

"Of course not!" Now Sami's upset too. "I'm just saying that maybe your father didn't want to do what he did. But he had to. Maybe he was forced to! Maybe he didn't know what he was doing!"

I'm suddenly caught off guard and become silent. I look at Sami and try to figure out his expression, but I can't. His voice is full of rage, but his face seems so sad.

"I'm sorry," he says, breaking the silence. But I still can't find the right words to respond to him. I feel like there's something I should be figuring out in the silence.

"It's okay," I finally say. But I don't know if it really is okay. He looks like a lost little boy; it makes me want to hold him the way he just held me.

"It's not okay," he responds. "I shouldn't have yelled at you like that."

"So why did you?" seems like the best question I can ask right now.

"I'm just saying that life isn't always what we see in our small village," he says. "There is a lot going on out there that's scarier than what we experienced yesterday, and it's scarier than what we face on any day."

I know Sami has seen and experienced more than I have and has been to more places than I have been. Even before he went off to the *madrassa,* he and his father would travel from village to village delivering goods. But he, like my father, barely talks about it. And when they do, it is all about how great our village is compared to the rest of the country. I'm beginning to feel the distance between us.

"There are people out there who don't value life," Sami says. "They have no sympathy for the innocent. They care only about power, control and money. And I'm just trying to say that maybe your father became a puppet for one of those men."

He snaps a branch he has picked up from the ground. "Our village protects us from all of that. And your father is protecting you from that. That ugly world is for a different type of person, it's not for you."

Even if it's ugly, even if it's terrible, I wish someone would let me see the world for myself. Then maybe I would understand. Then maybe I could have this conversation with Sami without feeling small, stupid and simple.

"I want it to be for me," I say. "I want to see the world outside of our village. I just want . . . to know what else there is. It can't all be ugly if girls are going to school and working in other places. I still don't understand why you came back."

"I love this village; I love the people in it." Sami sounds sincere and sad. "I'm so lucky I was able to return. All I wanted while I was gone was to return. I begged and pleaded with God every day."

I am more than baffled by this confession. I can tell by the softness in his voice that he's telling the truth. But I still don't understand it. How could he give up the opportunity he had to see other villages? Maybe even the capital? Get an education? Although I feel guilty for making him feel so sad, I have to ask, "Did you miss your family? Did you get homesick?" I know from his eyes that it's not that, but I don't know what else to say. And I have so many questions I've wanted to ask him about his time away, but I haven't had the courage to hear his answers. I was afraid I would be jealous of his other life, a life I wasn't a part of and never could be.

"Yes, I missed my parents and my brothers, sisters, cousins, you—I missed everyone," he says. I can't help but feel joy in knowing he missed me, because I missed him too. When he first left, I used to lie on my *toshak* at night wondering if he thought about me. "But that's not it. I honestly thought I would never come back. Being there was like my body and soul were stuck in darkness. Remember that day, years ago, when that horrible storm hit our village?" I know exactly what he's talking about. I never saw a day or a storm like it again. The sky turned black, and thick clouds rumbled with the anger of God or the unforgiving laughter of the devil. But I can see that Sami remembers something more. "Do you remember that frightening feeling when the storm built up, and it was so thick, so dark, and suddenly the angry clouds were no longer just in the sky? They formed a moving wall from the ground to the sky, raging, tumbling and twisting toward us—almost as if the devil had come to take us away."

Although I was young, I remember it all clearly. I had never seen my family so afraid. Kaka Ismail told us to come to his house with Sami's family. Many of the villagers made their way there too. We shivered in both fear and cold from the downpour. Sami's mother made tea for everyone, trying to be hospitable and likely just trying to keep busy. No one had ever seen the clouds that way before. The men stayed in the *maymon khana* just outside the house because they're not allowed to see women who belong to other men. But I was with the women and girls, sitting in the kitchen inside the home. Samiullah's mother kept brewing tea over the *tandoor,* and out of courtesy, we all continued to drink and nibble on bread as we heard the thunder and lightning in the distance.

The younger boys were allowed inside the mud-walled home, but they kept playing in the courtyard, getting wet to show how brave they were. Every once in a while, when the thunder roared, the boys would jump. I remember watching my brother Ali playfully taunting the younger boys who were afraid. He was the oldest of the group, but probably the most lighthearted, trying to make them all smile.

I can also see Sami, much younger then, sitting on the roof of one of the mud rooms, drenched by the rain, his face lost in whatever he was looking at. But it was easy to see his expression turn to terror as his eyes locked on to something in the distance. He looked down and caught my eye before yelling at all the kids to squeeze into the small space with the rest of us. "Do not leave this room!" he shouted, frightening us even more, before he ran out to the guesthouse, where the men were waiting. That was when we heard it. The rumbling sounded as if it were coming from below the ground, a thundering noise that I can still hear inside my head. The wind picked up, and debris began flying everywhere. We moved away from the door when we saw cups and brooms flying as the air outside sucked them from the house. We all held on to one another, and the small children began wailing. Looking around, I also saw tears of panic in the eyes of the adults. My mother held on tightly to my newborn baby brother, who was sleeping and unaware of any trouble. She pressed me against her body in an attempt to hold me as well. I could see the storm from a distance through the small window. It was a dark cloud twisting outside of the house and carrying objects as it passed, I thought I even saw cows and chickens being carried away.

They called it a *toophan*. It damaged some homes and properties, but shockingly and luckily, no one died, surprising all of us after we saw the damage it left behind. Many animals were missing after the storm. Sami's *bibi jaan* said that when a storm like that hits, it's because an innocent person has been murdered. My father told me that was a superstition among the older people. He said, "If what she said were true, Afghan skies would always be black." He told us that these types of *toophans* are rare in Afghanistan. In fact, he had only heard about them from a foreign movie he had seen in Kabul, but in the movie they called it a "tornado."

I remember the darkness and the fear, but I don't understand why Sami is comparing this storm to his time away at school, a time I imagined he was meeting new friends and forgetting his old ones.

"That feeling of impending doom," he says. "That's how I felt every day at the *madrassa*. That place was . . . a nightmare."

His confession catches me off guard.

I reach my hand out to Sami, and he grabs my fingers tight. I'm about to ask him why it was a nightmare, what was so terrible about the *madrassa,* when we hear branches cracking. I look at Sami and see my own panic mirrored in his eyes. He drops my hand. My heart races—not from what we've been talking about or how it feels to be with Sami, but from pure, unadulterated fear.

Part Two

Seven

RASHID

Look at them scatter like mice. Proof that they know they're sinning. Just the noise of my sandals stepping on some sticks has them running for their lives. This is the deed of a *kafir*. May God punish both of those unbelievers! Better yet, I can help God in that mission. I can be his vessel. Why else would God have me witness this blasphemy?

I'll teach those two a lesson they'll never forget. But not right now. I have plenty of time to punish those donkeys.

I pick up my bag of belongings and gifts and head to our house.

Walking by the base of the mountain path sends me back to the time before I left for the *madrassa*. I used to race the other kids up the rock-strewn dirt. I'd always be in the lead, pebbles flying from my heels as I ran, spraying anyone who was on my tail. Out of breath and panting, I'd make it up first. I was the best; I still am. Just thinking about it, I can taste the sweat sliding into my mouth—the flavor of victory and greatness. I lick my upper lip to capture it again.

I stop at the rusty, light blue gates of our front door. The fallen tree we rolled over here from the woods years ago still sits outside the house—a place for resting and watching the village. There was never much to see except the peasant neighbors walking over here with their clay jugs, mooching off our well. The only exciting change was when they swapped the clay containers for plastic ones. My uncle has always been far too generous to those bastards of Ghengiz Khan. His misguided generosity still stirs my blood.

Taking a deep breath, I knock on the metal door—the echoing noise sounds like the banging at an ironsmith. I listen as the soft squealing of women running toward the door gets closer. I smile. They must miss me so much.

I hear the door unlock and my aunt yelling at one of my cousins to let her do it, which makes me laugh. I love it when they fight over me. The door slides open slowly, and my dear aunt is standing there with a cluster of smiling girls behind her. At least I think they're all smiling. The cousins' wives are covering their faces, so I can't actually tell. I run up to my aunt, who is looking frailer than before, and kiss her hand as she starts crying and kissing the back of my head. I've always had a soft place in my heart for two of my aunts. Uncle Ismail's sisters never married because there was never a good enough suitor. As the leader of the tribe it would have been beneath him to give them away to just anyone. And although I agreed with that decision, I always wondered if they were happy living with their brother and watching as their nephews and nieces got married and had children.

"Aday, I've missed you so much," I say as I continue to kiss her wrinkled skin, more withered than I remembered it. Aunt Gul Babo gently pats my face. I look up and see her eyes welling with tears. I give her a wink and then look to the other ladies. "*Salaamona, mainday, aw, peghlo, singa yasti?*" I ask them how they are, and the response is just a bunch of giggles and a couple of them running off.

It's good to be home.

My first stop is the room with the *tandoor,* since the little children have found a way to glue themselves to my legs. I find my aunt Gul Bashro, Uncle Ismail's other sister, and the young girls making one of my favorite meals, *aush.* There is flour everywhere, including on the cheery faces of the girls greeting me. They're rolling and kneading the dough before they slice it into long lines and mix it in a giant cauldron of boiling water with diced leeks. I'm touched that they remembered how much I love this soup. Although I am a little insulted they haven't sacrificed a goat for my arrival. I'm sure they'll do it later.

"You finally made it!" my aunt says. Gul Bashro isn't as emotional as Gul Babo. She's definitely got some Pashtun male charm in her. "Look at all this effort for you. I hope you know how hard it is to make *aush.*" She says this with a half smirk, as I go to kiss her hand, whitened by flour.

"*Kor mo wadan,* may your house always be safe. It smells

73

delicious!" I say. That's when I catch a glimpse of her: Sami-ullah's sister, looking as beautiful as ever. Her name matches her presence, Nur—she's a light glowing upon all of us. She has averted her gaze like a good young woman should. Even though she's two years younger than Samiullah, she has obviously hit womanhood.

I don't stare. Instead I quickly grab some raw dough and stick it in my mouth before running off, barely in time to save myself from a swat from my aunt's rolling pin.

That's when I see Gul Bibi, Sami and Nur's mother, my father's younger sister. When my father was murdered, it was Gul Bibi who convinced my uncle to bring me into their family. Gul Bibi and my father had a bond even stronger than most siblings. When they were children, they were inseparable. My grandfather used to tell us that if my father wasn't around, my Gul Bibi wouldn't eat, not until she knew that her big brother was eating too. After my father's death, she said that what kept her alive were her children and her *lala*'s son. My eyes well as I see her frail, bony body, so I bow my head and go to kiss her hands before she can see the tears. Pulling her hand away, she brings me up and squeezes me to her chest.

"My boy, my sweet, sweet boy," she says gently. She touches her damp hands to my cheeks before she kisses them, followed by my eyelids, then my forehead. I don't mind.

"It's good to see you, my sweet mother," I say, and I mean it. I didn't realize how much I missed her until this very moment.

"Enough, enough. Let the boy go." My great-uncle's voice surprises us from behind. Jaan Baba is the only male elder in our house right now, and he has made his way out to the court-yard to greet me. As soon as the kids see him, they scatter. I guess he still has his charm with the children. He is leaning his frail body on a walking stick and has already put his arm and hand out for me to kiss. I quickly run and bring my lips to his fingers. His hand is shakier than a generator on full blast.

"*Salaam aleykum,* my son; your arrival brings us joy," he says, pulling his hand away. "The men are out but will be back before the sun sets. For now, come sit and tell me everything about your new life." He shoos my Gul Bibi away as he turns to walk inside and barks at one of the girls, "Jamila! Bring us some tea!"

Waiting for the sun to set and the men to arrive feels like waiting for clay to dry. I tell Jaan Baba nearly a thousand times about the school and how they are thinking of making me into one of the teachers. His sleeping bouts and the rumbles of his snoring keep interrupting my stories. Every time he wakes, I find myself repeating everything over again, which is beginning to annoy and frustrate me, but I pretend like it's fine, even adding some forced smiles and laughs. I know we have to respect our elders, but how about they show some respect in return for our patience in sitting with them! If only Jaan Baba and the rest of them knew what their precious nephew Sami has been doing all day, then they would respect me even more.

While we wait for the men to get home, some of the kids run in and out of the room peeking at me. Some remember me from when I lived here; others don't because they were too small when I left. At first it's cute when they pop their tiny heads in, but after a few hours, they are annoying me as well. "*Za larsa!*" I finally yell at them to get out of the room. Their eyes pop with fear as they run out.

When the men arrive, I can hear my uncle Ismail being greeted by the women. I get up and head out to the courtyard, and I see my uncle and my cousin the infidel lagging behind him. Sinner! He's so smug, trying to act sweet as he picks up the little kids, who are giggling like goats. Even his lovely sister Nur kisses him after she's greeted her father. Sami doesn't deserve her respect and admiration. He lies to everyone and acts as though he is a man of virtue. I don't understand why he's so loved. He's a pathetic fool and a dropout. A failure! He may be my uncle's oldest son, but I've done more to make them proud. I'm the one who stayed in the *madrassa*, who learned to recite the Quran. I'm the one they should be the proudest of. Not that little ant.

"Ah! My son! So good to see you!" Ismail Aaka finally directs his attention to me. As we hug, I see Sami smiling at me. I play along in this charade and smile back.

"*Salaam aleykum*, Rashid," Sami says coming in for an embrace. "I've missed my uncle's son. Have you been well?" I'd almost think he sounded concerned if I didn't know him better.

"Very well, cousin," I respond. "Life is good, learning all

of God's splendid instructions and hoping to share it with our loved ones." I look at him, waiting for a reaction. We both know he has lost any standing when it comes to the glory of God's teachings.

"I'm glad you're well," he says, slapping my shoulder. "I hear the ladies made you a feast tonight! I think they may have even sacrificed a chicken in your honor."

A chicken? That's it? Well, it's not a goat, but it will do.

The men gather in one of the rooms, and a *distarkhan* is laid out for us to place our food on. One of the young boys brings the *quza* and *chilemchi*. He pours water from the metal pitcher, and we rinse the dirt off of our hands to prepare for dinner. Tonight they brought the glass bowls and metal spoons out for the *aush*. As for the chicken, we rip it apart with our hands and devour it.

I can tell it's been a long time since some of the men have eaten meat by the way they are savoring every bite, pulling every last bit off the bone and sucking it clean. I do the same, but it hasn't been long since I've eaten meat. Just last week. after the instructors from the *madrassa* sent me to help Mullah Latif and his men, we took some chickens and roosters from a home in a nearby village. We told the villagers it was their duty to pay us with their poultry that night for protecting their village. It was the least they could do for us.

But I don't want my family to know yet that I have been trusted to take care of these villages as a part of a group of

God-fearing citizens. I need to ease them into it. They don't have any concept of good and bad, God and the devil. At least not like I do. I'll teach them as much as it is possible for them to learn. But not yet. I know how much my uncle hates Mullah Latif. He calls him a fraud and a thief, but that's only because Ismail Aaka doesn't know better yet.

"So, Samiullah, where were you all day? I was hoping to see my dear cousin when I arrived," I say as I stuff my mouth with some bread soaked in the oil and tomato sauce from the chicken.

"I'm sorry for missing you, but I went into town to help Father in the shop," he responds. I can't believe he has the nerve to look me in the eye when he says that. "We were trying to sell some of our wheat to one of the villagers, but he looked so poor and desperate that father just gave it to him. This drought has hurt a lot of people, but I feel it's the same every year."

"Because it *is* the same every year." No wonder he dropped out of the *madrassa*—he's an imbecile. "That doesn't mean you should be giving handouts to every villager who says he's poor!" I quickly catch myself before my temper rises any higher. "Did you see anything else today?"

"No, that was it," Sami says quietly. He stuffs his mouth and begins to chew. Finally, he feels the shame. He is beyond helping. He lost God long ago. And today I find him holding the hands of a peasant girl? The devil has a hand in this. It will be up to me to fix my little cousin.

Eight

RASHID

The next morning I catch Sami trying to leave the house like a snake slithering out of his hole. I rush out after him, ignoring the calls from the ladies to have tea and bread. He is making his way in the opposite direction of the wooded area where I saw him yesterday. Who is he trying to fool?

"Hey, cousin!" I run up to him. "Where are you going?" I give him a fake smile.

"Good morning, Rashid. I'm just heading to town to get the store ready for my father," he says rather convincingly.

"Can I come with you? I haven't seen the store in ages," I say. *And I don't really believe you want to go there*, I want to add but catch my tongue.

"Of course, but there hasn't been much of a change. I hope you're not too disappointed," he says, still walking. I catch him making some glances toward the Mongol peasants' house. Pathetic cow.

My presence is saving him from the mistake of seeing Fatima. God will reward me for my good deeds. I want to hear from Samiullah's mouth that he has sinned. Maybe if I spend the morning with him opening up my uncle's shop, he will let it slip.

When we finally make it to town, I take a look around. Sami was right—not much has changed. There are still the same shacks lined up along a dirt path. They look like houses made of oversized playing cards, but instead of paper, they are constructed from ribbed metal siding and roofing. Only about half of the twenty or so square boxes look like they're being used; the others lie empty with doors open, abandoned. Relics like these are found all over the village, empty huts that once housed entire families, now forsaken and left behind. So many people are abandoning their land and heading to major cities, as if that will help their financial woes. The more the Afghans head to the cities, the more they are exposed to sin, scandal and greed, elements of Shayton that are being spread throughout our country by the foreign invaders and the unbelievers.

"Do people even bother coming into town anymore?" I ask, kicking an old empty can lying on the dirt path.

"It's still early," Sami says while twisting the key in the hanging lock. "As the sun fully rises, the remaining store owners will open up shop. But truthfully, there aren't many people here who can purchase or trade anything. Everyone is struggling. And the Taliban come and harass the shopkeepers, demanding a tax on their goods. Most people decided it wasn't worth keeping their shops open because they couldn't afford the taxes and penalties."

I clench my fists at my sides. These villagers should be happy to support the Taliban. They owe groups like mine for keeping them safe. If we didn't, infidels would steal our land and convert our people.

"And what about your father's land that the Hazaras farm? Are they producing anything?" I ask, changing the subject as I help him open the doors and latch them to the side.

"The land Mohammad Aaka and Karim Aaka are farming is producing the most wheat of all the grounds," Sami says. "The remainder after they keep their share is sufficient but not as much as it used to be."

"How do you know they're not holding out on you and keeping more for themselves?" I am disgusted by the fact he calls them *aaka*. They're not his uncles, and they don't deserve to be treated with such respect!

"You know them better than that." Sami looks at me with disapproval.

"I do know them, Sami, and I also know their kind," I respond. "You can't trust those people. They'll smile to your face and tell you what you want to hear, but they'll be the first to stab you when you turn around. They don't have the honor of a Pashtun. They're the descendants of barbarous monsters, and they haven't changed, no matter what they want you to believe."

Sami drops the sack of wheat he was pulling out of the store. I stare at him as he slaps the dust off his hands.

"That's not fair, Rashid," Sami the traitor says to me. "If we judge them on their ancestors, what about ours? Don't we have criminals and barbarians in our blood as well? Haven't we killed for reasons as stupid as an insulting word? Or how about our land? The land that belongs to us probably belonged to their forefathers first." He's raising his voice in obvious defiance, the little ant. I should crush him now. "Generations ago, before this land was stolen by the king and given to us, we were just simple *kuchi*s, nomads going from one place to the next. Who's to say it isn't already their land?"

I'm disgusted at how he can so easily defend people who aren't even family, who aren't even from our ethnicity, let alone our tribe! But I'm not surprised. He's too weak to see what's right and what's wrong. "This land was given to us by King Abdur Rahman Khan, who wanted to spread the Pashtun power throughout our country! He kept Afghanistan from breaking up into separate states! Besides, the land wasn't even being used when it was given to our tribe!" I retort.

Sami ignores me as he begins to pull at the sacks of wheat.

"Can you help me carry these bags and put them outside the store?" he asks, pointing his grubby finger at a small stack of wheat bundles. He's obviously avoiding an argument because he knows I would win. "So, how is the *madrassa*?" I'm shocked at the nerve of his question.

"It's good," I say, helping him with the sack he is tugging. Truth is I don't really know, because I have barely been at the *madrassa* lately. "My skills are now being utilized to help the young boys. I've mastered the Holy Quran to the point where I am able to teach others the meaning behind the words." I try not to let my pride show on my face. He must be so jealous.

"That's great," he says. "I hope you're able to teach them the true word of God, not the way it's been manipulated." Sami and I drop one of the bundles on the ground, and he heads in for another, but this time I don't follow him. All I can do is stare at the back of his stubby head.

Manipulated? The nerve of this imbecile. *You may have the rest of our family fooled, but I'm on to you, little cousin. I'm the honest one! I'm the good one! I'm the one who believes in God, the only one here who knows what God wants from all of us. I'm the one who doesn't dishonor women in the woods. For you to act like you know better is insulting!*

"How would you know what's manipulated or not?" I say to him through the door. "You left, remember?" Sami looks out of the door, his eyes lock on to mine, and I know my words are daggers to his pride. "You dropped out. You couldn't handle the fact that I was better at something."

"Rashid—" Sami begins to say something but stops. He then walks out of his cubbyhole and faces me. "Do you really believe that's why I left?" he says. He looks like he's examining me. His eyes are making me uncomfortable and even angrier. "If that's what you believe, you're mistaken."

"Why else, then?" I respond. "Tell me why you left. You act

like you're so much better than all of us, but you are nothing. You don't know the meaning of God and Islam. I know who you really are: a Godless sinner who runs around with those horrible Mongols. Have you forgotten how they killed my parents? They were your family too!"

"My brother, they weren't the ones who killed your parents," he says, fake sympathy in his eyes. What a condescending bastard.

"It may not have been Mohammad or Karim, but it was their people! The same filthy blood runs through all of their bodies!" I kick the bag of wheat and see particles fly up in the air. "The nerve you have to act like you're so special while you run around with that peasant whore in the woods! Soon everyone will know what a disgusting little vermin you are. And if they don't punish you, I will!"

"What? What do you mean?" he asks, clearly frightened. "What will you do?"

"Are you more afraid of what I will do than what God will do?" I ask. I can't believe how far away from God he has fallen.

"Rashid—"

"Don't worry, dear cousin, I don't have any plans to tell anyone. It will be God who will punish you with the most might—not our family. You'll see!"

I turn my back on the scum and walk away.

Nine

SAMIULLAH

As soon as my father arrives, I leave. Luckily, he doesn't take much notice of my swift departure. I'm walking fast, but I have no idea where I need to go. That's not true—I know I need to go see Fatima and warn her, but there is no way of going there without someone spotting me, and we both agreed to be careful about seeing each other after the incident in the woods. I stop and turn toward her house, but I feel paralyzed as I stare at the empty fields before me.

What if Rashid is already there telling her family? Oh, God. What if he's telling mine? No, he can't be, at least not yet. He said he wouldn't. And I believe him. For now.

But how can he hate me so much? We're like brothers. At least I thought we were. It must be that horrible *madrassa*—it has to be because of that *madrassa*. I know we thought differently about the school, and I know he was upset when I left, but I had no idea he was so mad at me.

Oh, God, those must have been his footsteps we heard cracking in the woods. What did he hear? What did he see?

Poor Fatima—this could ruin her. I have to protect her. But how do I do that?

I close my eyes, but all I can see is Fatima's gentle smile with her perfect teeth and that little beauty mark just above her lip. When we were younger, she called it her ugly mole, but I think God placed it there by design to complete his beautiful piece of art.

Fatima, what have I gotten you into? If her parents find out, would they marry her to that boy in the other village right away? Thinking of this makes me drop to my knees. I know a sharp piece of stone has just ripped through my *tumbon;* my knee is likely bleeding, but I can barely feel it. I am numb, except on the inside. My heart has fallen into my stomach, and I'm overcome by nausea. I lean one arm in front of me and hold my head down. I can feel the sun striking the back of my neck as sweat drips into my clothing. I dry heave, hoping to get whatever is in my stomach out, but it isn't working. Instead I find my vision obstructed by tears filling my eyes. I turn and drop my entire body to the ground, feeling defeated. The sun's piercing rays heat my face, arms and feet. It's God's blanket of warmth, and I suddenly begin to feel, at least for a few moments, at peace. Right now it is just God, the earth and me.

Please, oh Gracious one, help me. I can't let anything happen to Fatima. I must protect her. You are the all-knowing and most merciful. You and only you, my Lord, can help us. Please, God, give me the strength to fix this and, most important, to keep Fatima safe.

I close my eyes again and see her before me. I feel my face creasing into a smile, cracking my chapped lips. I can't believe just the thought of her can make my heart swell and my skin tingle. Such a foreign feeling—so joyous that it's almost painful. The thought of touching her face sends a jolt of excitement through my body. I want to feel the smoothness of her skin on my fingertips. I wonder if her lips are as soft as they appear.

I move my own lips in prayer: *Please guide me in what I should do, most merciful and generous God. I know what I'm feeling can't be wrong. I know it in my heart and in my mind. I don't believe you would have me feel this way, so deeply and so purely, if it wasn't right. Thank you for blessing me with this feeling that I can only describe as love. And if it is love, this means I have always loved her. All I ask, dear God, is don't let me lose it. Don't let me lose this feeling and don't let me lose her. I know her family and my family will be against any kind of union, but I believe it is possible with your help and will. I just need time to figure it out.*

Please, God, help Rashid. Protect him from himself and the evils that surround him. Please stop him from the evil thoughts that darken his soul and please give him the strength to find the goodness I know is in him. Oh most merciful God, stop him before it is too late, before his soul can no longer be saved.

The brightness of the sun through my closed eyelids disappears, and I feel my face cooled by a shadow above me. For a second I'm afraid to open my eyes but then I realize if it were

Rashid, he would have already said something. I open my eyes. It takes a moment for my vision to adjust to the bright world in front of me. I hear the giggles before I can even make out who it is. It must be little Afifa, Fatima's sister. She looks just like Fatima when she was younger, except with red hair. Afifa falls next to me, laughing. The bangles on her right wrist jingle as she hits her hand on the ground, laughing harder. This makes me smile too. The innocence, the amusement.

"What's so funny, silly girl?" I ask.

She can't answer because she's too busy gasping for breath. "You're . . . sleeping . . . on the ground" is all she can muster before dissolving into a fit of giggles again.

I begin to cluck my tongue and shake my head. "Do your parents know you've roamed this far out?" Her little face suddenly looks terrified. "Do I need to tell them?"

"*Nay!*" she screams in defiance.

"Okay, okay. But you shouldn't run so far from your house. There are scary animals that eat little girls like you," I say. She doesn't look as scared as she did before. Instead she seems intrigued, as if she might want to meet those animals. She rolls her body off the dirt, picks up a small stick, and grins at me before she toddles off. Her smile tugs at my heart; it's so similar to her sister's.

But if Rashid follows through with his threat, I don't know if Fatima will ever smile again.

I stand up.

• • •

I know there is only one place I can go and only one person I can ask for advice. He is the only one, besides Fatima, I can trust. I ask God one last thing—to keep Rashid quiet until I can get back, until I have a plan. I know Rashid said that God would punish me, not him, but I don't trust him to stay silent for too long. He's never been able to keep a secret—especially not one that makes me look bad.

I don't even bother lying to my family about where I'm going. I tell them I'm heading to a nearby village to see Mullah Sarwar. But I don't tell them why. I just say I want to check in on him and make sure he is okay. They don't question me. They know Mullah Sarwar is getting older and is in dismal health and that we became close when I left the *madrassa* and stayed with him for a little while. My mother won't let me leave until I finish my bread and tea, so I quickly stuff it all in my mouth as she disapprovingly clucks her tongue.

"You'll get a stomachache by eating that fast," she says. I smile and kiss her hand before leaving the house. I pull out my father's bicycle, and before I can start pedaling away, my mother rushes over with a bag full of bread, cookies and fruit. "Here, take this with you. You might get hungry along the way." I try to explain that I couldn't even finish what she is giving me in a week. "Good, that means you won't run out, then! Send our *salaams*." I allow her to kiss my forehead, and I begin my bumpy journey.

It takes a few hours, but I finally make it to his village. Their village is bigger than ours. It even has a small *masjid* where Mullah Sarwar often gives a sermon on Fridays after prayers. He's been in charge of that *masjid* for almost sixty years. He says he can always tell that the situation in Kabul has gotten really bad when whatever force is shaking the capital reaches his little village. The Soviets even bombed the *masjid*, but the villagers got together and rebuilt it. About a decade later, when the Taliban were in power, they also made it to his *masjid*. They threatened to beat him and all the men in the village for not being pious enough and not growing their beards to the proper length, but ended up leaving the village alone because the men were Pashtun.

Mullah Sarwar never backed down from his teachings and was very loud about his beliefs, but he's always gentle and kind. I think that Mullah Sarwar would be able to calm even the devil if they were ever in a room together. He was the one who saved me from myself and that *madrassa* when I decided to leave. He taught me to love God in my own way and not by the teachings of people who don't understand Islam.

I knock on the door, and someone slides open the peephole and quickly shuts it. I know it's one of the women in the family. So I just wait. A few minutes go by, and the door opens slowly. There is a little boy, probably about four, straining as he pushes the metal gate open with one hand while keeping his balance with the other. This has to be Sarwar's great-grandson from another village. "*Singaye?*" I greet him, pinching his cheek. He giggles in response. "Where's your grandfather?" The boy grabs my hand and escorts me outside to the guest-house, where the men meet.

"*Kena,*" he says, directing me to sit before he runs out.

I wait in the large room decorated with carpets, curtains and long cushions. The curtains look just like the ones at my home. White cloth stitched by the women of the house with little designs, like green trees and pink birds. I sit down and stare at the patterned, handwoven rug, trying to concentrate on the floral design instead of the thoughts that bothered me on my entire trip out here. The carpet was probably made up north somewhere, maybe in Mazar-i-Sharif, the heart of car-pet making in Afghanistan. For the size, it would seem maybe five people worked on this rug, flicking and pulling wool and silk for months, possibly even years. I wish I could tell them that it's in the home of a good man.

A little more time passes, and I'm imagining what the lives of those carpet makers are like when Mullah Sarwar makes it to the guesthouse. He is weaker than he was the last time I saw him and is being helped on one side by a teenage boy and on the other side by a walking stick. His beard seems even whiter than it was when I left him a few months ago. It took me some time, living with distant family a few villages away, to find the strength to go home. The few darker hairs he had are now as white as the snow-covered mountains in the winter. I jump up to greet him, leaning down to kiss his hand.

"*Singaye, zoya? Kena, kena bachi!*" he greets me but waves me down to have a seat. "*Walid, chai rawra.*" He tells the teenager, who is apparently named Walid, to bring us tea. I don't remember him from my time here; he must be visiting along with the child. I give Mullah Sarwar the bag of cookies my mother sent with me, and his patchy eyes light up. "Ah! *Khajoor,* my favorite! Please send my thanks to your family. May God bless them and the hands that made this."

He sets the bag down and begins to untie the knot, the plastic crackling as he unravels it. Mullah Sarwar pulls out a *khajoor* and takes a bite of the thick oval cookie. He moans with delight, unaware of the crumbs that have landed on the slopes of his beard. "This is delicious! My family is trying to limit my cookies, but what they don't know won't hurt them." He gives me a wink, and I respond with a quiet laugh. "So what brings you here, my boy? Are you checking to see if I am dead yet?" He chuckles.

"God forbid, Mullah Saib. Please don't use such words," I say. "I came to see how you were and if you needed anything." Which isn't technically a lie. I really did want to know how he was doing, and I've been meaning to take a trip out here to see him anyway.

"Well, I'm not dead, my boy, and I am happy I'm not dead

because I get to see you here and share cookies!" He smiles and pats me on the back. Walid comes in holding a large thermos in one hand and two clear glasses for tea in the other. Trailing behind him is the four-year-old concentrating on a plate full of nuts and candy, obviously afraid of dropping it. Walid begins to push at the top of the thermos, pumping steaming green tea into the glasses. Mullah Sarwar kisses the four-year-old after he successfully sets the plate down in front of us. "Good job, Saleem!"

We start sipping our tea as the boys make their way out of the *maymon khana*. "I am sorry for not coming sooner. I should try to come every few days," I say, breaking the silence.

"Don't be silly. For me, not seeing you was a good thing," he says. "It meant you were moving on with your life and settling into what I hope is a good one. I don't expect you to visit me often. Let go of these formalities. Yes, I am an old man, but that doesn't mean everyone has to stop living to make me happy. I wish more people with my color beard would realize this. Maybe there would be less blame and fewer hurt feelings." He shakes his head disapprovingly while sipping tea. "But now that you're here, I'm beginning to worry, my son. Is everything okay?"

"Please don't worry. I don't mean to make you worry," I say, and quickly sip my *chai*.

"There is something wrong, isn't there?" Mullah Sarwar asks. He leans in closer, and it feels as though his hazel eyes can see through my own and straight into the depths of my soul.

The secrets I hold there suddenly feel exposed. "What troubles you, my son?"

I want to keep quiet out of fear. I can't take my words back once they're released. But I also know he's the only one I trust to help. So I open my mouth and begin to speak. My emotions are hard to confine, and I explain everything to Mullah Sarwar. I emphasize the fact that Fatima just sees me as a friend—it is I who sees her as something more—though as I say it, I wonder if I'm lying about her feelings. I tell him that I don't want to taint her name in any way, but I fear it may be too late. And that it is all my fault, for asking her to meet me alone, for spending time with her when I knew what it would mean.

"Do you love her?" Mullah Sarwar asks.

I flinch. For some reason, I didn't expect that question. I suddenly feel even more uncomfortable, not because Mullah Sarwar is asking it, but because I've never really spoken about love to anyone. Not about Fatima, not even about my own mother. But I think about what I said to God this morning. About the way seeing Fatima can brighten my day. About how I dream of the next time we can be together. About how I want to protect her and keep her safe and make her happy.

"I think so," I finally respond. "Because of her, I enjoy waking up every day—it's been like that since were children. I feel so alive when I'm with her, and even the thought of seeing her again fills me with happiness. Is that love?"

Mullah Sarwar smiles sadly. "I think you've just answered

your own question," he says. "I'm not saying that what you're feeling is wrong. In fact, if it feels as pure as it sounds, it is probably right. God has blessed you with something beautiful and rare. But that doesn't mean it won't be very difficult, for so many reasons. You're worried for this girl, as you should be, but you should also be worried for yourself."

I know he's right—it will be difficult, and we should be worried—but the fact that he doesn't say that being with Fatima is impossible gives me hope.

"There are many in our culture who will see this as an offense to our faith. And they will want to take it out on you and this young lady. You have to be very careful, my son." Mullah Sarwar is quiet before releasing a poignant sigh. "*Zoya*, the gift God has given you is precious."

"Is it truly?" I ask, already knowing the answer deep inside.

"It is," he answers. "But it's not always easy. You have the choice to accept this gift from God or ignore it. I know how blessed I am to have loved my Aziza. She and I created a home and a family together. We raised them together, and now have beautiful grandchildren and great-grandchildren. All that started with the seed of love God gave us. Our only responsibility was to nourish it and treasure it."

I hang on every word, still unaware of what I should take from this. Is he encouraging me to pursue my feelings for Fatima? And if so, how?

"So do I do the same?" I ask, feeling as lost as I have from the start.

"That's difficult to answer," Mullah Sarwar says, looking away. "We don't live in a society where we can love freely. Even Aziza and I were an arranged marriage, but we turned the unfamiliarity to friendship and then eventually love. Our society does not allow us to cherish God's gift publicly. We have to be careful with our heart, who we express it to and how open we can be with it. You have many obstacles to overcome. Do you want to be with her?"

"Of course I do," I answer.

"What I mean is do you want to marry her and be with her for the rest of your life?" Mullah Sarwar asks. "You're still a boy entering adulthood. Are you ready for such a commitment?"

I think for a moment about Fatima. I see her sweet smile as it creases her cheek and lifts the beauty mark above her lip. My stomach quickly jolts with a feeling of happiness and just as quickly drops.

"My life would be empty without her," I respond. "At this age and at any age."

Mullah Sarwar stares at me. He almost looks like he has a smile on his face, and then he nods.

That's when I finally know what I have to do. I just have to hope I can do it before Rashid shames me and Fatima in front of our families and the village.

Ten

SAMIULLAH

On my way back home, I decide to take a quick detour. I make my way to the Suleiman *ziyarat* by riding my bike through dirt and pebbles, passing two mountains, one luminous red and the other a lush green, just as Mullah Sarwar said they would be. It's just past the gently flowing stream, which sparkles from the sun's rays as if there are thousands of small diamonds scattered at the bottom. The *ziyarat* is a small but intricate structure constructed with blue tiles and colored glass, just outside Mullah Sarwar's village. I can tell the glasswork has been used in place of the jewels that once adorned its walls. Verses of the Quran-e-sharif have been delicately painted throughout the entire structure. It looks as though the holy book in its entirety is written in the exquisitely complex gold-and-blue designs.

For centuries, this shrine has been known for its spiritual powers when it comes to relationships and love. I first heard about it when I was at the *madrassa*. At the school, some saw it as a sin that people would pray at such a "blasphemous" place. They would say that the Sufis, the Muslim mystics who used to roam our lands centuries ago, glorified saints in Islam and created these shrines. It never bothered me, though; *ziyarats* have always been a part of our culture—even before Islam—a part that the zealots haven't been able to wipe away. And one that now, I hope, will give me strength.

I make my way inside the ornate shrine and find two tombs. They are said to be of the old Afghan poet Suleiman and his wife, Banafsha. A woman completely covered in a blue *chadari* sits near the tomb, squatting as she rocks back and forth. She's mumbling some prayers. Behind her is a man with a long dark beard, wearing a gray turban and flicking around his prayer beads. He doesn't seem to be interested in the tomb of the ancient lovers—he's busy looking around the complicated structure. When he sees me, he nods his head in greeting. I nod back and then he returns to his wall gazing.

As I pray, I recall the story my classmate told me about Suleiman and his wife:

Suleiman was just a baby when his parents left him inside a basket, snugly wrapped in blankets, outside a carpenter's shop hundreds of years ago. The next morning, the elderly carpenter, Wahid, saw the basket and read the note that explained the parents were poor and could not take care of their baby, Suleiman, but that he was conceived with love and affection and that they hoped he could live a better life with a wealthier family. Back then, to be a village carpenter meant you had wealth, which is probably why the couple dropped the baby outside the old car-

penter's shop. But the old man did much of his work for free, to help those who couldn't afford his structures. He didn't make a profit off of his merchandise and was not a wealthy man. Still, because of the Muslim teachings to help those less fortunate, Wahid the carpenter decided to keep the child and raise him to be honorable.

That little baby eventually turned into a handsome young man who helped the carpenter with his business and was well known among the villagers. Despite his past as an abandoned orphan, many families wanted Suleiman to marry their daughters. They knew him, trusted him and saw him as Wahid's son. But Suleiman was committed to taking care of the old carpenter, no matter how many times Wahid encouraged him to start a family of his own.

One day at the shop, Suleiman overheard Wahid speaking with a customer. They were talking about building his daughter a wooden chest to hold her "jayz"—the curtains, towels, table-cloths and other things she would sew to take to her husband's home. The customer told the carpenter that his daughter's dream was to get married, but she had been disfigured in a house fire when she was a young girl, and the family did not believe anyone would marry her. Still, since she held on so tightly to the dream of finding her true love, they couldn't break her heart and wanted to buy her a beautiful chest for her jayz.

It was left to Suleiman to build this wooden chest that would hold the dreams of the young girl. It took him a week of *hammering, chiseling and nailing to complete a beautiful trunk that he painted red and pink. During that time, all he could think about was that disfigured girl he had never met and her dream of love. When he presented the chest to the old carpenter, he told him that he wanted to marry the girl, sight unseen. He knew he could take care of her and would do his best to make her happy. The carpenter made no objections and spoke to the girl's father. The family was happy with the match, and the girl, Banafsha, came to live with Suleiman and the carpenter.*

Banafsha took care of the carpenter when he was old and frail and quickly became Suleiman's best friend and companion. They shared stories of their pasts, their hopes for the future and the fears and joys that they held deep inside. In time, their friendship turned to love, and that love grew into something neither had expected. Time went on, and they had children, the old carpenter died, and Suleiman continued working with wood. But in his spare time, Suleiman began to write poetry, beautiful poetry. In his lifetime, he wrote thousands of poems, most about Banafsha and the beauty of love, some about the old carpenter and a different kind of love and admiration.

Suleiman and Banafsha lived and loved together until they became old and gray. Their story became that of legend, at least in this part of Afghanistan. This shrine was created first by their children as a final resting place for their parents. And then the villagers decorated it with the Holy Scripture. In time, it became a place for lovers or those hurt by love to come pray for love and affection.

I think of my classmate who told me this story. And I think of all of the people who have visited the shrine before me, praying for love.

I sit by the tomb covered with a beautiful azure silk cloth with embroidery of the Holy Scripture on it. *Dear God, I need your help and guidance as I try to tell Fatima how I feel about her. And I will need your help as I try to convince Fatima's family and mine that, no matter our differences, we belong together.* I sit and recite passages from the Quran before I finally ask God for my one true desire. I ask him to help make Fatima my wife.

Eleven

RASHID

From a distance I can see them, pushing their old *karachee* through town. It's surprising the old wooden cart hasn't crumbled yet. Mohammed and Karim look older since the last time I saw them. Their bodies are thinner and their skin rougher. They are greeting the shop owners as they pass, and I decide to go into the shop so I don't have to talk to them.

"Your farmers are here," I tell my uncle. It's too bad that my foolish cousin isn't here as well. I have come up with a plan, but I need Mohammad, Sami and my uncle all in the same place to make it happen. Even though I told Sami that God will punish him, I have figured out a way to help God along.

Sami has always been the favorite, the angelic son. It's time my family finds out he isn't as pure as they think he is. I know it, and God knows it. Soon they will know it too.

"Oh, wonderful," Ismail Aaka responds and heads out of the shop. "*Asalaam aleykum*, my brothers!" I can hear him greet the scum.

"*Walaykum asalaam!*" they chirp back.

I hear mumbling until my uncle shouts out to me, "*Zoya,* Rashid, *chai rawra!*" I roll my eyes. He is ordering me to serve the peasants. I am tempted to tell him about my time with the local Taliban, but I am waiting for just the right moment, so I bring out the thermos with green tea and place it on the small metal table we sit around. They nod their heads at me, and I look away; they don't deserve my attention.

"*Zoya,* where is the candy?" Ismail Aaka asks.

"Really, there's no need for candy," Mohammad, the father of the whore, says. "We just came to drop off the wheat."

"Don't be silly . . . Rashid, bring us some candy," my uncle orders again. I nod. If I speak, I will scream at him for making me serve these people. I head into the shop, grab the candy and drop it on their table.

"Be careful!" Ismail Aaka barks. "Is something wrong?"

"No, uncle, I'm sorry. It slipped out of my hands," I respond.

"Okay, thank you for the tea." Ismail Aaka turns his attention back to the men and shakes his head. I walk back into the shop and wait out their visit. I can hear them talking about their sons and the land. It's all quite boring. I lean back on my plastic chair and decide to take a nap when I think I hear . . . is that . . . it is! Is this my lucky day? Sami, Mohammad and my uncle all here at the same time?

"I went to go visit Mullah Sarwar a couple of villages over. He's getting frail, and I wanted to check up on him," I hear Samiullah tell the men.

"How was the mullah *saib*?" Ismail Aaka asks. "I hope you passed on our *salaam*s."

"I did, Father. He was very grateful and also sends his good wishes," Samiullah says.

I step outside, trying to keep the grin off my face. Now is the time. "Did you speak of anything else?" I ask, walking into the open air. "You've been gone all day. Surely you had lots to talk about."

Samiullah looks up. I see the fear in his eyes at the sight of me before he turns and looks at Mohammad. The look on Sami's face is priceless. And now it's time to expose him for the slime that he is.

"Well, my dear cousin, what else did you talk about?" I ask.

"Samiullah, are you okay?" Ismail Aaka asks his pathetic son.

"Yes, is something bothering you?" I ask.

"No, no. I'm fine. I'm sorry, I'm just very tired," Samiullah says.

There is silence again. And the peasants now look uncomfortable too. They glance at each other, as if practicing mind reading. Fatima's father speaks up. "I think we should start heading back. It's getting late; we've stayed far longer than we should have."

"That's true, you have stayed too long, but I think you should stay a little longer," I say. "I think you would be very interested in what has been going on in Samiullah's mind lately."

"Rashid!" my uncle yells.

"What do you mean?" Mohammad asks. I can see that question in the eyes of the rest of the men as well. Except for Sami. He knows exactly what I am talking about.

"I think it is better if it comes from Sami," I say. His eyes are pleading with me to stop. "It would be quite improper for me to say anything. Right, dear cousin?"

"Why are you doing this?" Sami asks.

"What is going on?" Ismail Aaka demands.

"Will you tell him, or should I?" I ask Sami.

"I really think we should leave," Mohammad the peasant says.

"No!" I respond. "This involves your daughter."

There is sudden silence. Mohammad looks as if he has just been slapped. I almost feel sorry for him, at least for a moment. No one wants to be put to shame by a dirty daughter. Karim looks away. He must be embarrassed that we are speaking of the other peasant's female family member. Ismail Aaka looks shocked; his mouth is open, and he is staring at his son.

But Sami's face is the best. He seems on the verge of tears. I think I might be smiling, so I try to control my facial muscles. I have to pretend I'm not enjoying this.

"What is going on?" Ismail Aaka finally says. He looks back and forth between Sami and me. His voice is quiet, but I can hear the anger. He then comes to me. "What are you saying? How dare you speak of your uncle's female family members!"

"He's not my uncle! And they are not our family!" I find myself yelling. But I cannot believe Ismail Aaka is directing his anger at me and not his filthy son.

"You are forbidden from disrespecting Mohammad and his family!" Ismail Aaka says. "Do you hear me?"

"I'm not the one disrespecting them," I say. "It's your son who is disrespecting him, his daughter and *our* entire family!"

That's when I feel it. The sting sends a rush of blood to my face. I can't believe Ismail Aaka just slapped me.

"Shut your mouth right now! Or I will show you how I punish my *own* family!" Ismail Aaka says. I can see the fury in his eyes. It scares me for a second before I realize that I am the one who should be furious. I didn't do anything wrong!

"I'm not the one who you should want to punish. Your son is the one who needs discipline!" I say.

I give Sami a snicker and start clucking my tongue before leaving them to drown in the mess I have exposed. I walk straight toward the orange skyline. This is not the last they will see of me.

Twelve

SAMIULLAH

I can't look the men in their eyes. Not my father, not Fatima's father and not even Karim. I have shamed us all, and I have humiliated Fatima the most. She is blissfully unaware of the hell that is about to hit her, and I feel so guilty because of it.

"I-I-I'm sorry for all of this," I finally find the courage to say. My father and Karim turn to look at me, but Fatima's father is still looking down with an expression that I cannot read. "I don't know what to say. But you can't believe Rashid. He is not right in the head."

"What does he mean about my daughter?" Mohammad says. His voice is quiet, but there is no ignoring its forcefulness. He finally looks up at me. His stare sends a shiver down my spine. "What involves my daughter?" His anger seems to be building.

I'm frozen. All I can do is look into his stern eyes. I want to bring back the gentleness that I am so used to. I don't know how to respond to this ferocity.

"Tell me!" he yells, making me jump. I think it makes all of us jump.

"Kaka—" I say before being interrupted.

"Don't call me uncle," he snaps.

"I'm sorry. I really am sorry. Rashid is just causing trouble," I plead. "He wants you to be angry with me. He wants my family to be angry with me. And he wants to use my friendship with Fatima Jaan as a tool in doing just that. He wants to rip our relationship apart."

"What do you mean by friendship and relationship? What relationship?" Fatima's father retorts.

"Please don't misunderstand me," I say. "There is no relationship except that of mutual trust and admiration between our families. And Fatima has been my dearest friend since we were children. You all know that." I look around for affirmation, but everyone stays quiet. "That is the relationship I speak of. I would never disrespect you, your family or my family. We are all one family. I grew up with you as much as I grew up with my father. You are like a *baba* to me. I listened to your advice and even to your scolding when I did something wrong. You knew me before I took my first steps or said my first words. You know me as well as my family does. Please don't listen to the words of a raging lunatic. Something has happened to my cousin at that *madrassa*. He has become an unforgiving man. One who looks for trouble and wants to divide everyone even more."

The men are perfectly still, all staring at me. I swallow hard.

"Why would he say all that?" my father says. "He seemed to know something that he wanted you to share."

I look at both my father and Mohammad. I realize I need to say something about wanting to marry Fatima. I didn't expect it to come so soon, and I should really talk to my father first, alone, and have him talk to Mohammad. But I don't think there's time for that now. My palms are sweaty. I know my request won't be taken well, at least not in the beginning, but it is time to tell the truth. My throat is scratchy and dry. My breathing feels shallow, but I fight through it.

"I in no way mean to bring shame to you or to my family." I direct my attention to Fatima's father. "I love and respect you like my own father. I have seen your love and adoration for your children and your family." I look at him, but I can't see anything other than the words I am trying to string together. "You and my father have both been examples of the kind of man that I one day want to become. From your examples, I see the possibility of being a good person despite all the bad that surrounds us. I see it in you, and I see it in your children."

I'm afraid to move on to the next part, but I know I have to. I can feel all their eyes on me as my head pounds and droplets of sweat stream down my back. "Ali and Fatima were as close to me as my own brothers and sisters growing up. We ran in these fields together." Mohammad Aaka's eyes shimmer with tears at the mention of his son. "I ate at your house; they ate at mine. We shared memories that only families share together. And I hold them, as I hold all of you, dear to my heart. I miss Ali every day, as I know you do. And my eyes brighten every time I get to see Fatima, as I know yours do. I care for all of you—including your daughters—and would protect them with my life."

"What are you trying to say?" Mohammad asks.

"Yes, what *are* you trying to say?" my father adds more sternly.

"I didn't want to do it like this—not this way and not at this time," I say as I get down on both knees. I'm feeling a bigger knot in my stomach. "I promise you that Fatima has no idea what I am about to say, so please do not take this out on her, I beg of you. I am trying to say that I want to be a part of your family for a long time, if you will allow me. I know this is not the traditional route, but I have to say something, because I cannot lie to you."

"Samiullah?" my father manages to say in what seems to be a state of confusion.

"I don't think I understand you." Fatima's father interrupts my father. "It almost sounds as though you are asking for my daughter's hand."

We're all silent, and I look at the dirt next to his sandal, afraid to face them. I'm prepared for fists and anger, I just want to brace myself before they arrive.

"Did you know about this?" I hear Mohammad yelling.

"My dear friend, I have no idea what is going on!" my father responds. I look up and see the rage in Mohammad Aaka's face and the confusion on my father's.

"He is speaking of my daughter!" Mohammad yells at my father. "*My* daughter!"

"Calm down, brother." Karim goes to hold Mohammad back. "Calm down."

"Calm down?" Mohammad looks at Karim in a state of shock. "How would you feel if he was talking about Zohra in this manner? Would you not feel disrespected? This is my daughter! They are shaming my daughter!" His voice cracks in a mixture of sadness, anger and shame.

"Please, that is the opposite of what I am trying to do," I interrupt, jumping back in. "I never want to shame her or you. I am just trying to tell you that I will take care of her. I will treat her the way you would want her to be treated."

"Stop talking now!" my father yells at me. "This is enough! You don't know what you are saying. What kind of disgrace is this? You keep disgracing us and them."

I should have spoken to my father about this. Convinced him about my feelings. Had him go to Fatima's house and meet with her family and ask for her hand. That would have been the proper way, the way Kaka Mohammad would respect. But that would have taken time, a luxury I don't have.

"But, Fath—" I try to speak.

"I said shut up!" my father roars.

"But—"

"Enough!" he yells. The rage in his eyes is piercing. When he turns to Mohammad, he looks more apologetic. "My dear friend, I-I-I don't know what to say about what just happened. I'm very sorry. Can we please talk about this when we have all calmed down and have had time to think about it? I don't want us to say anything that will damage our friendship. Let us just wait until our blood is no longer boiling. You have every right to be angry, but I beg of you, let's wait and let it simmer down. I too am shocked. But let's allow our rage to settle before we speak again."

Mohammad looks at my father and just nods, his eyes still burning. He turns around without looking at me. He and Karim take hold of their *karachee* and prepare to leave. I try to take a step toward them, but before I do, I catch my father's eye. He doesn't move a muscle, but I can tell I am forbidden to move. So I wait, and I watch as Mohammad and Karim fade away from the horizon. Once they have disappeared from our view, I turn my face to my father but stay quiet. I know him well enough to see that this is not the time for me to speak first. I feel like a child again, waiting for my punishment for disobeying my father, but this is much worse.

"What is wrong with you!" my father shouts. He picks up his hand, and I brace myself, but he doesn't hit me. "Who do you think you are? Who raised you? Do you not think anymore?" My father puts his hand down. "You have dishonored us in so many ways. How could you not think of your father, your family and your tribe before saying those words? How could you not think of the women in our family? Our honor has been violated." He sits down on the dirt-ridden white plastic chair outside of our shop, shaking his head as he stares at the ground.

"But, Father," I try to speak but stop at the sight of his finger pointed in my direction signaling me to stay quiet. He's still not looking at me.

"What would you have done if someone asked for your sister Nur's hand in this way? Did you think of that? What would you have done?" he asks. This time he looks at me, and I know he wants a response.

"This is different, Father," I say, hoping that I can end it there, because I know how I would react if anyone spoke about my sister the way I spoke about Fatima. The thought of it makes my insides churn.

"But how would you react if this were about Nur?" he asks again.

"I wouldn't be happy," I say as I look down. "I would be enraged." The thought of any man looking at my sister or thinking about her in a sexual way makes my head spin. I wish Mohammad and my father would realize what I feel for Fatima is not lust but love.

"If you would be that upset about your sister, think about how upset Mohammad is right now after you spoke about his *daughter* in that way. I know," he says as he hits his chest. "I'm a father of several daughters, and I would kill anyone who tried to dishonor any of them! I would shed blood for their honor and our family's honor. You don't understand this, and you won't until you have your own children. What you have done is shameful."

"Father, I understand what you are trying to say." I tread carefully. "But I want you to also understand what I was trying to express. I know I failed in conveying my intentions clearly and in a respectful manner, but I care for Fatima. I want to marry her." I pause to look at my father's face, and I am unable to gauge it. He is just staring at me. I was expecting anger, shouting, even a strike—but all I have is silence. "Father, do you understand? I want to marry Fatima. I'm sorry for not approaching you first and going about this in an unsuitable way, but I want to marry her; I want her to be your daughter-in-law."

"Stop it," my father says softly as he rubs his head. "Please, stop." He takes a deep breath and lets it out and looks at me again. "Impossible. There is no way this can happen, no way. You are a child! You are only seventeen years old. And even if you were of age, you are my son! The *khan*'s son! You will marry the girl we feel you should marry. Not the daughter of a farmer . . . a Hazara girl! You haven't just insulted Mohammad, you've insulted us."

"But, Father . . ." I try to speak, but I can't find the words.

"*Zoya*, this is not a world where you can do whatever you

114

want," he says. You cannot dream of something and think you can have that in reality. You have a life, a family and responsibilities. You can't just change everything in your life and lineage because you *want* something. My son, you must grow up." My father stares at me with what seems like pity before he looks back down to the ground. "Now we need to fix this. Do you understand?"

I stay quiet, taking it all in before I respond.

"Yes, Father. I understand, it needs to be fixed."

Part Three

Thirteen

FATIMA

I haven't been able to concentrate on anything Zohra has been saying all day. My mind has been on Sami. He didn't come to meet me in the woods this morning or yesterday. I know he was scared when we heard those footsteps—I was too—but it could have been an animal. Likely a deer or maybe even a leopard—we spotted one here when we were kids. Instead I've been meeting Zohra; her *bibi* is still sick but feeling a little better. She pops her head in every now and then to see if we have our books out. "If you don't learn this now, you will never learn it!" she barks at us when she sees us lying around not reading. "When I was your age we were excited to learn!"

Zohra still doesn't know if she will be engaged for certain, but seems to jump from being excited to sad at every turn in our conversation. "I wonder if he will be handsome" will turn to tears followed by "Will I ever see my family again? Will I ever see you again?" And as much as I feel for her, I wonder about Sami. Is he staying away to protect me, or is he already tired of me? My mother always told me about boys who trick girls into thinking they like them so they can use them, ruin them and then marry someone else. But Sami isn't like that. Is he?

Suddenly we hear Zohra's father. "Where is she?" Karim is yelling. And he's home much earlier than usual. "What? Where?" He then comes into the room where Zohra and I are sitting. We both jump up.

"*Salaam, Baba Jaan,*" Zohra says.

"*Salaam, Kaka Karim,*" I follow.

"Go to your home . . . now!" he yells at me. He looks more agitated than angry. But I don't dare stay a second longer. I've never seen Kaka Karim this way. His wife and mother come running into the room as I scurry to gather my supplies.

"What's going on?" Zohra's mother, Zainab, says.

"Nothing, but Fatima needs to go home," he says loudly.

"Is my family okay?" I find the courage to ask as quietly as possible. Why else would he be here so early and look so frantic? I'm feeling more frightened than before. "Is it my *baba*? Is he okay?"

"No one is injured, but you need to go home!" Karim yells again. We all jump at his ferocity, and I run out of the room. I can still hear him yelling at Zohra when I get outside. "Do you know about her and Sami?" I can hear the women gasp, and my stomach drops as I fall behind the back wall outside of the room.

"What? No . . . ," Zohra says. I hear a slap that makes me

flinch, and it's followed by the sound of Zohra crying. He hit her because of me. I crawl on the dirt so I am sitting under the window and can hear better. How does he know? Does this mean my father knows?

"I'm going to ask you again, do you know about Fatima and Sami?" Karim says.

"I swear on the Quran-e-sharif, I don't know what you are talking about," Zohra manages to say through tears. I can hear the sound of him slapping her again, followed by her wails.

"Karim!" Zainab screams for mercy. "Why are you hitting her, and what are you talking about?"

"Mohammad and I went to town today to drop off supplies to Agha Ismail, and Sami came by, and he ended up saying he wanted to marry Fatima!" Karim responds with anger. "I felt sorry for my dear friend—he was humiliated!"

The women gasp again.

Sami asked to marry me? I can't believe it. Can this be true?

"Why are you hitting Zohra?" Zainab pleads, breaking me from my thoughts.

"Fatima is her friend. She must have said something to her!" Karim barks.

"I swear, Baba Jaan, I don't know anything about this," Zohra cries. "Fatima has not told me anything, I swear!"

"Being friends with her could ruin your chance of getting a suitable husband," Karim continues to yell. "Do you under-stand that?"

"God forbid," Zainab says. "How do we know Fatima even knows about this?"

"Why else would the boy have the nerve to ask without his family's knowledge or approval if they don't already have a relationship?" I hear tongue clucking.

"Leave the girl alone." Bibi's talking now. "Come on, Zohra, *janem*. In my day it wasn't uncommon to marry a boy you liked. Look at how far backward this country is moving."

"You lived in the city, Madar," Karim responds. "It's easier to hide shame in cities! Besides, you married the man your parents wanted you to wed."

"Yes, but I thought by my old age my granddaughters would be living a better life than I did. Come, my darling."

I decide to run before someone sees me. I'm afraid to go home, but if I don't, they will question where I've been. If Karim slapped Zohra simply for being friends with me, I can't imagine the punishment I'm going to get. I run home with thoughts of Sami and my father in my mind. What happened in town? Why would Sami do this without telling me? There must be a reason.

I reach my home and change my sprint into a slow walk, dreading what lies ahead. I look to see who's around. There is an unnerving calm. I notice my mother at the stream washing Afifa's hair. Afifa has fallen asleep standing up, with her little head leaning on our mother's knee as she combs the red strands. And if I'm seeing this correctly, it looks as though our mother is humming a song. How can this be happening? She must not know yet. I look around again, but still see no sign of my *baba*. I breathe a little easier as I make my way into the *tandoor* room and start peeling potatoes for dinner.

Maybe this is all just a bad dream.

fourteen

FATIMA

It's been two days since Sami asked my father to marry me, but we have not yet talked about it. In fact, my *baba* has barely spoken to me at all. My mother has been eyeing us, but the children haven't noticed that I'm the cause of the uncomfortable silence. I haven't been allowed to go to Zohra's house—my mother said that I need to do more chores, and my *baba* agreed. But I know the only person who can tell me what is going on is Zohra. I still feel guilty for the beating she received because of me. I know her father must have felt guilty about it later. We've known him a long time, and I've always thought him to be a gentle man. I don't dare bring the subject up with my *baba,* so I continue to pretend I don't know what's happening. All I know is I have to find a way to see Zohra.

"Is everything okay, Madar Jaan?" I ask my mother as we prepare dinner. The silence in the room is agitating me, and I need to break it.

"Everything is fine," she responds as she continues to dice potatoes, not meeting my eyes. I know everything is not fine.

My parents stopped their nightly conversations. My mother has tried to speak, but my father will not let her. Our meals are silent. The boys have tried to get our father to tell stories, but he stays quiet. Even Afifa has sensed something is off and finds comfort in sitting on my lap during dinner, asking me to feed her.

"Okay . . . ," I say as I scoop up the onions I've been chopping, using both hands. I drop them in the pot of oil. Immediately the oil starts crackling. I stir the pot with a wooden spoon, and the oil splatters, landing on my hand, burning it a little. I continue to stir the onions before daring to speak again, afraid of what the reaction will be. "Madar Jaan, I was wondering if I could go to Zohra's house tomorrow to practice our studies." I don't dare look up as I say these words, continuing to concentrate on the onions as they begin to brown in the pot.

"No!" my mother says firmly, walking over with the plastic bowl of diced potatoes and dropping the pieces in while staring at me. The pot sizzles, shooting up burning droplets of oil.

"But, Madar, Bibi must be upset that I haven't been coming." I try one last time.

But my mother ignores me this time, walking out with the *distarkhan* and setting it up for dinner outside.

It's another meal of silence. Except for the sounds of chewing, slurping and finger licking. Everyone eats but my *baba*, who just stares at the food.

At the end of the night, we all head in and make our beds, and my father finally says something to me.

"Fatima," he says sternly.

"Yes, Baba Jaan?" This is the first time in two days he has been able to look at me.

"Don't go to sleep yet. We need to talk to you after the children fall asleep," he says.

"Okay, Baba Jaan," I respond as he turns to go back to his sleeping mat. My mother is sitting on her mat staring at us with angry eyes as she knits yarn booties for the boys.

I tuck the boys in and give them kisses. Afifa waits for me.

"Sing a song," she says to me. I look at my angelic little sister and long to be her age again—to be so innocent and unaware of the world. She curls up in my lap, and I start humming a tune I learned years ago from Zohra's radio. I start rocking my little sister, hoping it will take her a while to get to sleep. But she falls asleep as fast as she does every other night. I slowly lay her down and cover her with a blanket. I kiss her forehead and cheeks and brace myself for what's next. I stare at my sleeping sister and stall as much as I can.

"Fatima, come here," my *baba* says, and I know I can't put it off any longer. I can feel the thumping of my heart as I approach my parents. My mother puts down her knitting and almost looks excited.

"Sit down, *azizam*," my *baba* says with gentleness in his voice. The tone is so surprising that I can't help but look at him. I sit down in front of the lamp, casting a shadow on their faces, but I don't dare move. My eyes bounce between my parents.

One who looks so tired and drained, and the other who seems to have found new energy as she stares at me.

"Is something wrong?" I ask, still pretending not to know what happened.

"Fato, we have something very important to speak with you about," my *baba* says and then lets out a breath. I nod my head. "We've decided . . . your mother and I have decided . . . it's time for you to get married."

"What?" I say, wondering for a brief moment if he has agreed to let me marry Sami. Perhaps that's why he has been so quiet—he's been making a plan with Kaka Ismail. I feel hope fluttering in my chest.

"We know about your strong friendship with Samiullah," my *baba* says, and that tiny flutter grows larger. "He approached me in town the other day and expressed his feelings for you. He said that he cares about you and would like to marry you." Could it really be true? Have my parents agreed to Sami's proposal?

"He spoke with you?" I manage to whisper.

"Yes, and he told me that the feeling belongs to him and not to take it out on you." My *baba* presses his hand to his forehead. "But after speaking with Karim, I know that you have missed days of reading practice with Zohra and her grandmother."

"She did what?" my mother interjects. But my father ignores her.

"I had hoped that I was wrong, but I believe you have been

seeing that boy." My stomach drops. Zohra must have told her father. I don't blame her, but I don't know what to say now.

"Baba—" I get out before being interrupted by my mother.

"You whore!" She gets up and slaps me in the face. I feel my lips quivering, and my eyes begin to drown in tears. More blows come my way. "Stop your fake tears, you stupid girl! How could you do this to us?"

"Mossuma, stop it!" My *baba* holds her back.

"But, Mohammad, she keeps shaming us!" she says before turning back to me. "Whose daughter are you? Who do you belong to? I can't have given birth to such a disgusting whore!"

My tears flow fast and harder now. "I'm sorry! I swear nothing happened. We're just friends. We just talk. I swear on the Quran-e-sharif that we just talk. He is my friend! Like when we were kids!"

"Like when you were kids? Mohammad, are you listening to this? What kind of man are you? Beat this filthy girl! She deserves to pay for throwing our name, our family and our dignity in the dirt! She let a snake slither into our lives, and now it will swallow all of us!"

"Stop it! Both of you! You'll wake up the children. I'm not going to hit her. I haven't laid a finger on you your entire life," my *baba* says, looking at me with watery eyes. "I've treated you like a precious vase. My beautiful . . . precious—" His voice cracks. It sounds as though he is about to cry. He quickly clears his throat and takes a deep breath. My *baba*'s words are worse than any beating, because I know I have hurt him. I can't breathe I am crying so hard. I don't make noise, but I can feel the spit from my mouth fall into my lap. "Fatima, we have decided to marry you to Karim. Your mother and I talked about it, and I have convinced him to take you as his second wife. It is the only way."

"K-k-karim?" I manage to stammer out. "But . . . but . . . but, Baba Jaan . . . you . . . you . . . said Sami wants to marry me."

"Karim is your best option for a good future. For a family who will take care of you. He didn't want to take on a second wife but because of our friendship he said yes. Sami is not an option."

"But . . . but . . . why? You said that he cares for me. I care for him too. He is my best friend. He can take care of me."

"May the dirt fall on your head!" my mother hisses, wishing for my death. "*Khak da saret!*"

"He is not the right choice for you," my *baba* says. "I am your father, and I see things that you do not. I am making the right choice for you."

"But, Baba Jaan, you have known Sami all of his life. You know his family." My tears and sadness are replaced with confusion and despair. "You know they're good people. You know he'll do anything to make me happy and treat me with respect," I plead. Although I feel intimidated I find the courage to keep talking. "I don't understand . . . Is it because he's Pashtun? Didn't you say that we are all God's servants and no one is better than the other—that in the eyes of God, there are no differences between us? No matter our ethnicities? Baba Jaan?"

"You don't understand this world. You don't understand the hardships you'll face. This will be the easiest life for you. Karim will provide you a good home with food and family. He has agreed to take you in and care for you. This is for the best. That is my final decision. I don't want to hear any more—from either of you."

Lying on my toshak, I beg God to let me sleep, knowing that it is my only escape from the nightmare I am living. But my ghosts don't leave me alone, even in my dreams.

I dream of a future with Karim and without Sami. Living in a home with a family that once loved me but is now bitter to have a disgraced girl among them.

Zohra has changed from my dear sweet friend into an enemy who hates me for marrying her father. In the dream, she ignores me as I beg for her guidance. I need her, but my friend won't even talk to me.

My *khala* Zainab treats me worse. She is angry that her husband has taken on a new wife after decades of her being his only wife, bearing his children and taking care of his mother. Unlike Zohra, she does speak to me, but it's only to bark orders and slap me around. She uses me as a servant, one whom she hates. I endure the beatings and scolding from her.

Bibi is the only person who doesn't hate me. Instead she

feels sorrow for another future lost—especially after she put so much hope in us . . . in me. I am no longer a part of her reading lessons; she takes back the book she has given me. And I watch from afar as Zohra continues the lessons I loved and she hated. Bibi can barely look at me, let alone talk to me.

The person who feels the strongest toward me is Karim. But it's not love he feels; it's hatred and lust. Once my father's closest friend and a dear uncle, he is now the center of my universe. A universe that has gone black. He is angry at the deal he made with my father, marrying a girl he feels is a whore. And he treats me as such . . . I see his body on top of mine as I scream and cry . . . I feel his sweat on my skin and taste tears when I wake up.

My body still trembles in fear as I realize that this time my dream may come true.

fifteen

SAMIULLAH

I've been waiting all morning for her. After waiting all day yesterday. Hoping she will make her way out here. When I finally see her, I feel relieved.

"*Afo, bia . . . Afo, gak!* Little one, come here," I say to Fatima's little sister. Grabbing her attention.

I see her looking around. Looking for the sound of my voice.

"*Keeeeeeesht?*" she shouts, asking who it is. "*Jinn ashtee?*" She asks if I am a spirit.

"*Afo,* it's me." I poke my head and body out from behind the small tree that's barely concealing me. When she finally sees me, she smiles and toddles over.

"You're the sleepy man!" Afifa says, smiling. "My *madar* says I can't be friends with your family. Your *baba* wears a funny hat!" She starts to laugh again.

"You can be friends with me. But you're right, my *baba* does wear a funny hat." I smile at her and pinch her cheek. "How are you, my little one?"

"Good! I thought you were a *jinn,*" she says, looking down. "I got scared."

"Oh, Afo, don't be scared. Not all *jinn*s are scary. There are nice *jinn*s too."

"Really?" She looks up with excitement.

"Yes, of course. There are *jinn*s who want to help you and protect you from the bad ones. And since you're a good girl, the good *jinn*s are always near you, protecting you from the naughty ones."

She starts smiling at me before looking around, possibly for *jinn*s.

"Afo, I need you to do something for me," I say, getting her attention back. "But it has to be between you and me. It will be a secret. Are you old enough to keep a secret?"

"Yes!" she shouts with enthusiasm. "I *dokhtar kalon*!"

"Yes, you are a big girl," I say. "But no one can know, not your mother, not your father and not even your brothers."

"No one?" Her thrill turns to astonishment.

"Only one person can know—your sister, Fatima."

"Fato! Fato is my sister!" She smiles. "I love Fato!"

"I know you do. But you have to remember, you can only tell Fato. This is a secret."

She nods at me with fervor.

"Can you give your sister this letter? Remember, no one else can know. This is our big-person secret between me, you and Fato. Okay, *janem*?"

"*Kho!*" She grabs the letter. "Will the bad *jinns* come after me if I tell someone else?" She looks frightened again.

"Don't worry about the bad ones. The good ones will protect you even more when you keep your promises. Do you promise to give this to your sister and not tell anyone else?"

She nods at me and hides the letter in her *payron* before running back to their house. I hope this works. I have already caused Fatima so much torment. If this doesn't work . . . if her parents find the letter . . . I can't even imagine the danger that will come to us.

Sixteen

FATIMA

I pray to God that this is all a dream. I can feel pain in my chest, like a bandage stuck to my breasts, wrapped tightly, suffocating my heart. I guess that's appropriate, because right now my heart feels wounded and my body feels numb. It's as if I'm a spectator, viewing my life from the outside. All that I'm experiencing can't be real. I'll wake up at any moment now and realize it's just a bad dream and that none of this is true and that my father still loves me and that my life isn't over.

Last night, after my father made his decree, my mother said that I was lucky they weren't going to kill me because that was what I deserved. Her eyes ran through me like daggers and made me realize that if it were her choice, I would be dead. My father didn't disagree with her; he just turned his head and went to bed.

I felt her eyes burning through me when I woke from my nightmares, as if she was planning something. She knows she can't hurt me with my father around, but I'm afraid of being alone with her.

I decide to stay in our room when everyone leaves to go have breakfast. By now, my father must have gone out to the fields to meet Karim . . . my future husband. I still can't believe it. There has to be a way to change my father's mind. I'm piling all the sleeping mats on top of each other in the corner of the room when I hear footsteps marching toward me. My mother walks in with raging eyes, angry like a snake.

"*Salaam, Madar Ja*—" I try to get the words out before she makes her way to me and grabs me by the hair. I can feel the strands ripping off at the roots, and I start to scream. She drags me through the open doors and slams my head against the dirt walls, causing the world around me to spin.

"Shut up!" she yells at me as I desperately try not to fall to the ground, because I know it would rip my scalp even more. But she's moving too fast, and my feet keep tripping over each other. We make it to the room with the *tandoor,* and she throws me to the floor.

"Do you like being a whore?" she shouts. I notice the kettle is at full boil. I can hear the bubbles hitting the inside of the hot metal, and the steam is billowing from the spout. She lets go of my hair, and I instinctively reach for the kettle to take it off the fire. She stops me by kicking me in the gut. The jolt knocks me back and steals the air right out of my lungs.

"Don't touch that, you filthy slut," she screams as she picks up the kettle and places it on the dirt. "Do you know how much you have shamed yourself? How much you have shamed this family? How much you have shamed *me*?"

"I'm sorry," I manage to whisper but I know it doesn't matter. Nothing I can say will make my mother despise me any less.

"You're sorry?" she gets up and kicks my stomach again. This time her plastic sandal falls off her right foot.

"I had plans for you! For our family!" she yells as she begins to pace the room. "There was a good family. They were wealthy. But they won't marry their son to a whore!" I don't dare let out a sound. I know any noise from me will agitate her even more. The longer I leave her in her world, the longer she won't violate mine. "You didn't even think of your sister! We won't be able to marry her either now!"

Could I have ruined Afo's life too? In all likelihood, my mother may actually be right. Afo will always be attached to my disgrace. As I think about this I see that my mother has noticed my presence again.

"Pull your sleeves up and stick out your arms. Do it! Do it now!" she yells. I'm startled by her intensity and quickly push my sleeves up as I watch her walk to where she has placed the kettle. She picks it up. Her arms are shaking so much she is spilling some of the hot liquid on to the floor. She makes her way closer to me. Is she—this can't be happening. I don't believe it. No, she won't do it. She can't do it. I've heard stories of things like this happening to other girls in the villages, stories that made me cringe and count my blessings. But I never thought it would happen to me.

My eyes begin to blur with tears . . . I see her turning the kettle, preventing more water from spilling to the ground, but I still refuse to believe she'll do it.

"I said stick out your arms!" she spits. My body is shaking uncontrollably, but I know I have to do as she says. I hold out my arms.

"Pull your sleeves up higher!"

I obey.

She starts to tilt the kettle, and the scorching water falls onto my bare arms. The pain is searing, and I start screaming.

"This is what whores deserve!" my mother says with a look of delight on her face. "This is what *you* deserve for shaming us!"

I can stop screaming from the pain, but I can no longer see or hear anything. My vision blurs. The world goes silent. I feel the screams curdling in my throat, but I have no idea if they make a sound. The only thing I can sense is the excruciating pain. I know now what it feels like to be in hell.

Instinctively I try to pull my arms away, but my mother stops pouring only long enough to grab me by the hair again and spit in my face. A second of relief. The thick wet gob lands on my left cheek and eye, blurring my vision even more. The tugging pulls out more strands of hair that she throws to the ground, but I don't feel them being wrenched from my skull. The pain scorching my forearms drowns even that out.

"Put your arms out, or I will pour it on your face!" I hear her voice through my daze. The look of Shayton in her eyes shows that she means it. I have no doubt she wants to kill me right now. The only thing saving me is how my father would respond. But she knows she can get away with this.

I find myself paralyzed in terror, squatting on the floor, with my knees pulled in and my arms still out in front me. I am afraid to move them. The pain is too intense, and any movement will add to the throbbing that still sears through my skin, muscles and bones. All I can do is cry as I wait for her to finish. I try not to sob too loudly, fearing I will agitate her more. I swallow in as much as I can.

But instead of feeling more water on my skin, I hear a clamoring bang. I open my eyes and see that she has thrown the kettle to the wall. The water drips on the mud, darkening the areas it has touched. It leaves a scar on the wall like it has on my arms.

"Now pull down your sleeves. If you show this to your father, I swear the next time I will kill you. You stupid whore!" she says, picking up the kettle only to throw it again, this time in my direction. I miss getting hit only by ducking my head. I close my eyes and hear her sandals crunching on the dirt floor as she leaves the room.

That is when I realize that my mother doesn't love me

anymore. Her children aren't people to her. We are her accessories, like a new *payron* or bangle. She wanted me to marry the boy in the other village because it would have made her look good, not because she was looking out for my welfare. She sent Ali to Iran to make money for her, not so he could build a better life for himself.

If I am ever a mother, I will never be like her. Never! God protect my younger brothers and baby sister from her.

I wait awhile before I even attempt to move. I'm afraid that if I leave this room, my mother will attack me again.

An hour has passed by the time I finally stand and make my way out of the building. I see my mother from a distance washing the clothes in the stream. I quickly duck into the sleeping area to tend to my wounds. I find a bag of old medicine and slowly pour its contents to the ground. I see a cream my father received from the town clinic four years ago when the blisters on his hands were popping and oozing blood and pus. I don't know if the cream will help, but since my arms seem to have the same symptoms, I feel like I should use it.

I lift my arms and try to slather some cream on the tattered skin and exposed muscle. I can't keep myself from screaming and crying as I rub the lotion on as gently as possible. But still it feels like a rake scraping at my wounds. The coolness of the cream doesn't do much to stop the burning.

I don't know how long I have been at it when Afifa walks in. She takes one look at me and starts crying too.

My sweet baby sister doesn't know what else to do but cry with me. Her compassion helps my broken heart remember that at least *she* still loves me. She's too young to be ashamed, at least for now. She doesn't yet know what I may have done to her future. Her heart is still as sensitive as the fine-winged butterflies that roam our land in the summer—a trait she did not receive from our mother.

As our tears begin to taper off, she pulls out a letter and gives it to me. She says it's a secret letter from the sleeping boy with green eyes. I know she must mean Sami. My heart races, pulling my thoughts away from my throbbing arms.

"My *shadi gak*, you know I love you, right?" I say to her.

"Yes, I love you too!" she responds, her tears drying on her cheeks.

"I know it's hard to keep secrets from our parents, but this time we have to. If you tell anyone, these burns on my arms will get deeper, and I'll be in more pain. I'll be punished even more," I say, showing her my blistering skin. I hate doing this to her, but I can't have my parents know about Sami sending me a letter. Although I'm glad he has.

"No! I don't want you more hurt!" Afifa says, covering her eyes as she starts her sobbing again. "I'll ... keep ... the secret," she adds, taking deep breaths before each word. As much as it breaks my heart to see her cry, it makes me believe without any doubt that she won't let the secret slip.

I hide the exact details of what happened when Afifa

questions me on my injuries. And after a while, she falls asleep. Her head lies on my lap, and she drools on my legs as I open Sami's note. It takes some time before I can finish reading it. It's still tough for me to make out some of the letters when they're connected to each other. But Sami kept it simple:

> *Forgive me.*
> *As the sun sets, meet me at the well.*
> *We need to talk.*

I am far too scared to meet him. The excitement and joy I used to feel at the thought of seeing him has transformed into fear and despair. I don't know who knows what happened and who doesn't, but in a village like ours, word travels fast. If anyone sees me walking toward his family's house, I will quickly be known as the town whore, if I'm not already.

But to know that Sami is thinking of me provides some comfort. *Forgive me.* I don't even know what to forgive him for. This is my fault, too. I should never have gone to meet him. I knew what I was doing was wrong, but I did it anyway. The desire to see him outweighed the consequences, or so I thought. I never figured we'd get caught—or maybe I knew we would eventually by someone, but I thought that whoever found out might want to help us. If I am honest with myself, I secretly hoped that by meeting him, we could force my family and his family to let us marry—that it would mean we were no longer eligible to marry someone else.

I knew other girls had died because of what I was doing, but for some stupid reason, I'd thought I was different. Our families didn't really care that we played together when we were young. Our fathers interacted with each other often—and not as ethnic rivals, but as human beings. And my father was more open-minded than the rest. I'd thought that he would want me to be happy. But now I realize I was more naïve than I thought.

I want to see Sami, but I can't. How would I carry the water jugs with my arms the way they are? Besides, I can't do this again, not to my father and not to my family—they now bear the shame of my actions as well. But the more I think of not going, the more I think of Sami and his gentle smile and warm eyes. Eyes that see me for all I am. Eyes that make me feel protected and valued and loved.

I still hold on to the hope that this is all a bad dream, but the blisters on my arms and the stinging pain that shoots through the deadness every few seconds remind me that it is all very real.

Seventeen

FATIMA

Ironically, it's my mother this time who throws me in Sami's direction. She has ordered me to fetch water from the well. Even after the darkness of this morning, I can't help but be amused by the situation and see it as a sign that I must go. I want to say my last good-bye to Sami.

My mother breathes a pleased sigh as I go to pick up the two empty jugs and wince in pain. We both know the wincing will turn to groaning and heavy tears when I have to carry them weighed down with the water. On a normal day, my mother and I or Zohra and I would work together, carrying only one jug each.

There is still some time left before the sun begins to set when I make it to the entrance of the well. My face is wet with tears from the pain of carrying the empty containers. All that blocks Sami's home from my view are the pomegranate trees in bloom and an empty storeroom built of mud. The trees are dotted with crimson pomegranate flowers. In two more months, they will be fully transformed and ripened into my favorite fruit. It has always fascinated me how a little speck can blossom into a flower and then into a beautiful, juicy ball of fruit.

The decrepit storage hut next to the field isn't as pleasing to the eyes. Like many of the homes in our village, it is molded of mud. But this hut has not been used for as long as I can remember. It's just a neglected old building covered in cracks from the untended dried mud. Sami had told me it used to hold the feed for the horses. That's when his family owned horses. There aren't any more horses in our village. Now they seem like mythical creatures that exist only in pictures from the old days.

Zohra's grandmother told us that once horses were a sign of wealth, like cars are today. They were what the powerful and elite would use to make their way from village to village and what the tribal leaders would use to visit the cities. But as the wealthy bought cars, they sold their horses. The only animals we see now are donkeys and sometimes camels. This room hasn't been used since the day Kaka Ismail's father sold his last horse, before Sami was even born. So it stands there empty and forgotten, an existence I fear I will share.

I drag the jugs to the hand-dug well and set them at my feet, wincing in pain as I bend my arms. I unhook the plastic bucket that holds a rock inside of it to help it sink in the water. I release the rope and steadily let the bucket make its way down until I can feel it hit the surface. I let it fall a little lower and then begin yanking on the rope to bring it back to me. My arms burn, and the dried lacerations break open. My skin rips slowly and deeply. My body heats up as the blood and pus flow out. I feel the tears dripping down my face. I try to ignore the stinging and burning as much as I can and pour the water into one of the jugs, all the while looking up and around for any signs of Sami. But I see nothing. I repeat this process over and over again until I have successfully filled both containers. As I tightly fasten the plastic lids onto the jugs, I notice the pus and blood have soaked through the fabric of my dress. I flick some water onto my arms and pull the material away from my skin slowly, knowing it will be more painful to pull it off later after the cloth dries into my arms.

After this excruciating process, I take another look around for Sami, and I still don't see him. I peer through the trees, but all I see are the thin trunks spreading out their even skinnier branches. My stomach drops with disappointment; he's abandoned me too. Why would he ask me to meet him if he couldn't build up the courage to come himself? It's not like Sami to be scared, but maybe he has decided that it isn't worth the risk. That I'm not worth the risk . . .

The thought makes me feel even more hollow than I did before. I don't know if I will ever get used to this feeling of emptiness. And hopelessness.

I grab the jugs, letting out a groan as I begin my trek back.

But as I start to walk, I can't shake off the feeling that I'm being watched. I look around, peering between the trees.

"Fatima, quickly, over here." I hear Sami's voice coming from the empty hut. "Hurry, please." His voice has an edge, like he's agitated. Not angry, but desperate. No matter the tone, his voice still comforts me.

I bring the jugs with me and quickly drop them as soon as I get into the room, trying to hide my pain and praying that my tears will dry fast. The sun's setting rays pour into half of the abandoned space, providing light even to the shaded side—the side where Sami is waiting. There are dark circles under his eyes, as if he spent last night worrying instead of sleeping. The urge to reach out toward him is stronger than ever, but I stand still, keeping my blistered arms at my sides.

"I wasn't sure if you would come," he says, looking down. We are both silent before he looks back up, this time with eyes full of tears and a voice full of anguish. "Please forgive me, Fatima. I didn't mean for it to happen this way! Please believe me. I was forced to tell them. I had to because of Rashid!" His voice begins to shake. "They were thinking horrible things, and I wanted to fix it, but I couldn't. I don't know what to do. What do you want me to do? Please tell me how I can make this right."

Seeing his tears brings me to tears as well. I can no longer feel my scorched arms; I only feel that my heart is on fire, burning with the pain of losing him.

"It can't be fixed," I say through my whimpers. "Why would you tell Rashid? How could you do that? And why would he tell my father?"

"I swear to you, I didn't tell him anything," Sami says, pleading. "I swear on the Quran, I never said a word. He saw us in the woods. That day we heard a noise, it was him. And I don't know why he would tell. I honestly don't know what to think of him."

I feel dizzy now, thinking of what Rashid made of that meeting. What did he tell people? The truth alone is enough to ruin me—to ruin my family. I went to the woods alone to meet a boy. To the world, I have sinned against God and my family. My father has every right to kill me for this; it's the only way to regain our family's honor. My mother would have done it. She would have burned me to death. But my father has chosen to save me.

"Sami, I'm betrothed. My father says I must marry. He says it's the only way for me now."

Sami's eyes are fixed on mine. He looks confused and helpless. He walks to the corner of the room that is still bathed in the sun's rays and squats down with his head between his knees. All I see is his hunched back bouncing up and down as he sobs quietly. I want to go and comfort him, but I am paralyzed. We stay like this—not speaking, just crying. It pains me to see him so destroyed, to know that he's hurting too. This time I realize I'm crying for him, not myself.

I notice the sun's light fading and realize it is time to go.

"Sami, I have to leave now," I say softly as I wipe the tears from my face. "But I want you to know something. I want you to know that you are my best friend, and for the rest of my life, I will think of you just as I have always thought of you. There is goodness in you. Goodness I'm glad I had a chance to know. I've always felt happy when I've been with you. I've always felt special, and I've always felt important. Whenever I'm sad, I'll look back at our memories, and I'll smile. I'll thank God for giving me those days." I am unable to keep even the tiniest bit of composure and begin to stumble as I say my last good-bye. "But . . . pl-please kn-know, you will always be m-m-my dear, sweet, l-l-lov-loving Sami, and I will always hold you in my heart."

By the time I'm finished, I realize that my face is wet again. With all the crying I have done today, I'm amazed there are still tears left to shed. I use the bottom of my *payron* to wipe it clean. And walk back to my jugs.

"Wait!" he turns quickly facing me again. That's when I realize his face is swollen not just by tears, but by bruises as well. Those dark circles are not from exhaustion. He's been beaten.

"Sami, your face. Are you okay?" I want to run to him but clench my hands behind my back.

"I'm fine. My grandfather found out. It would have been much worse if the ladies of the house hadn't stepped in and begged him to stop," he says as he hesitantly makes his way toward me.

"I'm so sorry," I say.

"Forget about this. These bruises and cuts will heal. But I won't. *We* won't. Not unless we do something," he says with a look of determination. "I know this is going to sound crazy, but it is the only thing I can think of. And I know you will likely say no. But we do have one option. It's a dangerous option, and it will rip us away from our families and our lives here forever, but it's our only choice if we want to be together."

I'm afraid of what Sami will say. I'm scared of the unrealistic hope he will give me.

"We have no options, Sami. My father has decided to marry me off to save us from more shame. Before you know it, you'll be married too, and you'll move on and forget about your silly neighbor girl." The thought of it makes me nauseous. But I have to accept it.

Sami shakes his head in disagreement.

"I will never marry another woman. Never. Do you understand me? Fatima, I don't want to forget about you. I don't want to move on and pretend this never happened. I don't want to live a life that is based around pleasing others. We have done nothing wrong! At least not in the eyes of God."

He slowly makes his way closer to where I'm standing and reaches out for my fingers. But I can't bring myself to touch him, as much as I want to. I let him pick up my hand, but the stinging makes me cringe.

"What's wrong? Fatima, what's wrong?" He looks in my eyes, as if he's searching my soul. Without a word, I pull up my sleeves and show him my bloody pus-filled arms. "Fatima . . ." He stops talking and stands there openmouthed, examining my mutilation, his fingers gently holding up my elbows, avoiding the burns on my arms.

"My mother seems to share your grandfather's sentiments," I say, pulling my arms back and letting my sleeves down again.

"Fatima." He pauses, and I can tell he wants to choose his words carefully. "Fatima, you have to listen to me. Now more than ever, you have to hear me out. This marriage may save your family, but it doesn't mean you will be saving yourself. There will be people who won't forget and those who will want to keep punishing you . . ."

Like my mother.

"I deserve to be punished. I've hurt my father, and I can't hurt him more. I can deal with the pain. I'll learn to deal with it. No matter how much I'm tortured, it won't hurt as much as losing my father and losing you." I can no longer look him in the eyes. I've always been honest with Sami; he's always known my deepest secrets. But today is the first day I have shared my biggest secret, one that I even hid from myself for as long as I could: just how much I really care about him.

"Fatima, you don't seem to understand. There are people here who may want to do more than just hurt you."

I do understand, though. I look down at the blisters on my arms.

"Do you mean there are those who want to kill me? I already know this. My mother has made it very clear that she'd rather I were dead."

I see Sami wince at my words, but he doesn't refute them.

"There are people more dangerous than your mother who will want to punish us. Those are the ones I am afraid of. You are in the most danger."

The sun has almost set now, and the room we are in is dark.

"What do you mean?" I'm thinking of Rashid. I'm thinking of the familiar voice Sami and I heard when we were crouched behind the rock. Is Rashid more than just a village trouble-maker now?

"I just have a really bad feeling. And we need to get away from here." Sami looks at me with determined eyes. "What I'm about to say will sound insane, but just listen. Okay?"

I don't respond fast enough, so he asks again, "Okay?"

"Okay . . ." I wonder what he's thinking, what he's been planning all day.

"We can start a new life somewhere else, together. We can get married. I'll take care of you, and I'll be a good husband to you. I promise I won't let anyone harm you. I'll make you happy again, or I'll die trying. Please let me."

I'm at a loss for words, which is fine because he continues.

"There are so many people in Kabul, they'll never notice two more entering the city. They won't know who we are. We can get lost in the crowds and start our lives—together. We can be happy."

Listening to these words, it feels like my dreams have become nightmares. This is all I've ever wanted, for Sami to care for me, to live in Kabul, maybe even to attend the university there. Now, all those dreams are Sami's dreams too, but I still can't make them come true. I can't believe how cruel life truly is.

For the last week I've been imagining a life with Sami. In those dreams, we had children. Our parents supported us and were happy for us. My mother was still bitter because I married a Pashtun, but she softened at the sight of her grandchildren.

I now start to create a new fantasy. Sami and I are still together, alone without our families, but still happy. Raising children in a capital city I have never seen before but have always pictured as crowded and magical. We grow old together, me side by side with *my Sami*. But that's when I force myself to snap back to the present. This is an impossible dream. The words he says are based in desire, not reality. I can't leave my father, my little brothers and my Afifa. And he can't leave his parents, siblings and tribe.

"Sami, we both know we can't do that," is all I can finally say to him. I feel defeated.

"Yes, we can. Please, all I ask is that you think about it."

"No! Because if I think about it, I will make myself believe we can do this. Not because it is possible but because I want it to be!"

"You want it to be," he says, smiling. "And so do I." He gently touches the back of my hand. I feel a sudden sensation race through my body and into my heart. An electricity only he can generate inside of me. "Please, just think about it. That's all I'm asking. Give me a day to figure out plans, and Saturday night after my family is asleep, I'll wait for you behind the rock, our rock. I'll wait there every night for a week and head back to my house before my family wakes, if you don't come. But if you do, we'll go. You don't have to say anything now. Just tell me you'll think about it."

His eyes have regained the light that I've been so used to seeing there and are looking pleadingly into mine. His fingers are pressed against the back of my hand—his touch has warmed my whole body, but I still feel myself trembling. I hesitate before responding and look at his sweet, broken face. His small smile is filled with hope.

I don't want to see the light in his eyes dim; I want to always remember them as they are now: glowing. So I say, "I'll think about it." I slip my hand away from his as I walk away and wince as I pick up my jugs. I don't turn back for another look, because I know if I do, I will crumble. With my head down, staring at the dry fields and feeling the pain radiating up my arms, I make it home before the sun drops completely behind the mountains.

• • •

That night my father doesn't speak to me. My mother only barks orders. I am grateful that my siblings are too young to know what's going on, but I can tell by the way their doe eyes look at us during dinner that they know something's wrong. Still, by the time we get into the sleeping area, they are back into their world of marbles and giggles before being forced into bed.

I lay out my *toshak,* ready to sleep. I approach my parents. "*Shaw bakhair,*" I mutter softly as I look at the ground.

"Good night," my father responds, without looking up. My mother just lets out a *hmph.*

I make my way back to the *toshak* and get underneath the covers, keeping my arms on top of the fabric, but I don't sleep. Last night and today's events keep running through my head, and I try to make sense of it all. I hear my mother attempt to start a conversation with my father, one that begins with her cursing about me. But my father lets out a sigh and a prayer, which always indicates he wants to be left alone. My mother lets out another *hmph* before going to bed herself.

In the dark room, I run Sami's proposition over and over again in my head. I see flashes of my mother scalding my flesh. Then I see Sami's comforting green eyes. I try to feel his touch again and the sensation it caused, the one that made me shiver. I feel it again, that bolt, that tingle, so I keep reliving the moment in my mind—his skin against mine, over and over. I envision a future with him. I see us holding our babies and growing old together. But every time I get lost in that dream, I see my family, here, without me, shamed by my actions. How can I leave them with the shame of a daughter who ran away with a boy? Haven't I disgraced them enough?

I was born into this family, we share the same blood, the same ancestors, the same loyalties. But I know we will never be the same, not after all of this. My father won't be able to look at me after he has married me off to his friend. My mother will always hate me; forgiveness has never been a natural emotion for her. She will ban me from this house and from seeing my siblings. Likely tell them stories so they will hate me as they get older. But I can't blame her for what my life has become. My actions have set everything in motion. I am the one who is responsible for this. And I know what I need to do.

Eighteen

RASHID

I can't believe my uncle. He slapped me . . . me! He should be beating his son for the shame he brought on our family, but instead he hit me for shaming him in front of the peasants. He never laid a finger on his precious Sami. He did let my grandfather beat my snake of a cousin, but then he acted as if that's all that had to be done. He is wrong. So now it's up to me. Sami needs to be punished. His whore needs to be punished too. I know I'm right. If other boys and girls see them getting away with their actions, they'll think it's okay. Our society will change. God's laws will mean nothing.

I walk up to the lime-colored house, still annoyed that it has taken me three days to convince the morons I've been traveling around with to set up a time for me to speak with Mullah Latif directly. I've bounced from one imbecile to another, all picking their teeth and being as unhelpful as possible, wanting to know my issue before I speak with the mullah.

"I can't tell you first," I told them all, "but if you don't let me speak with the mullah *saib*, it will be you who burn with regret."

Some may have considered it smug, but I don't care what they think. Before long, they will be polishing my shoes. The lower-ranked thugs scrambled about, scared of the possible consequences, but the higher up the chain I went, the angrier they got with that answer. Everyone is trying to assert their power over me because they see me as a child. What they don't realize yet is that I understand God's word more than all of them combined, and I care more about spreading his message. I hope that Mullah Latif will see that too. I can't wait until I am rewarded and start spitting orders at them, whipping them into shape. They've done nothing to help our cause but lie around like cows. I'm the one going out and finding infidels. I'm the one who will even sacrifice my own family's sinners to follow the righteous path.

I make my way into the absurdly large home after being let through by the guards. And although the house already looks run-down, from its structure, I can tell it was built in recent years. This is the new Afghan architecture borrowed from the Afghans who lived for many years across the border in Pakistan. Some have labeled them the narcotic mansions because most have been built with drug money. But I call them Peshawari palaces, because I'm told that's the Pakistani city the design comes from.

When I make it through the entrance, I get a big whiff of

the scent of too many men. The smell is a combination of body odor, dirty socks and backed-up toilets. The interior of the home looks as dilapidated as the exterior. I'm escorted up a marble staircase with stained, chipped stones and am told to wait as my escort sends a text message.

These men are a disgrace to Pashtuns. But I will be the one who will restore our honor. I'll be promoted, clean up the ranks and bring back order. We'll take more towns under our wing, not by fear but by respect. Mullah Latif will see the potential in me, and he'll know that I'm the man to help him, not these half-wits. And slowly we'll expand our reach and lead our nation into Islamic supremacy and then, *inshallah,* the world. God willing, it will happen.

I'm awoken from my thoughts by a door slamming open. Another unkempt lackey walks out. This one is so much fatter than the rest, his vest won't even cover the balloon-sized belly drooping down over his waistband. His beige top and bottom were obviously once white; the stains are disgustingly visible. His hair is a mess, as if he crawled out of bed and started his day without even trying to clean himself up. His face is also desperate for a wash; I think I see lice jumping around in his beard.

"*Rasa!*" He yells in a brutishly garbled voice for me to come. Even his voice needs fixing. He eyes me with what seems like disdain as I get up.

"*Manana.*" I thank him and try to put on a smile as I cover my heart and bow in respect, even though by the looks of him, he doesn't deserve it.

I walk in and see Mullah Latif for the first time. He's sitting behind a large, dark wooden desk. I always pictured him to be an older man with a thick waist, bearing a stark white chest-level beard, and a perfectly wrapped *lungee* on his head. The turban a man wears tells so much about him—it expresses his dignity and honor. I was looking forward to seeing the mullah's *lungee* and interpreting what it meant.

But the man before me looks nothing like the one in my imagination. This man seems twenty years younger and forty kilograms lighter than I expected. And his dark hair is split down the middle, reaching his shoulders, no turban on top. The strands are so thick with grease I can't tell if the waves in his hair are natural or from the grime. But what I find the most disappointing is that his facial hair can barely be called a beard; a better term would be whiskers. He's sporting dark sunglasses with black plastic rims to match his traditional clothing, also in black. Although he doesn't resemble the Mullah Latif that was in my head, or any mullah I've ever seen, he still looks much more presentable than his lackey.

"*Asalaam aleykum.*" I greet him in the proper Islamic way. I hold my heart as I approach him to kiss his hand.

"And peace be upon you too, my brother," he responds, allowing me to kiss it. He then gestures to the chair at the opposite end of his desk and tells me to sit. *"Kena, kena.* Is green tea okay?"

"Yes, thank you. But there's no need for the trouble," I say out of respect, but in truth I'm completely parched.

"Omar, sheen chai rawra!" Mullah Latif has given a name to the disheveled lackey, ordering him to bring us tea. Omar nods and leaves the room. I'm a little disgusted that his hands may touch my tea glass.

"So you are Rashid." The mullah turns his face toward me. I can barely make out his eyes through his dark sunglasses. "Welcome to our group. I trust you are happy to be with us?" He leans back in his chair, slowly springing it to and fro while fiddling with prayer beads that seem to be made of lapis lazuli.

"I'm honored to be a part of a brotherhood that will restore humanity in our society and take it back from those who are leading us down the wrong path."

He starts nodding his head. "And you do see why we have to do this, right?"

"Absolutely. We have too many factions in our country right now that are trying to play us like puppets, when in reality, it's they who are the puppets. From the foreigners, to the faux government and even our Muslim neighbors who don't care about our people, they are all vying for power. And we also need to cleanse our society of the infidels who are trying to ruin our religion and culture—whether those infidels are outsiders or members of our own communities." At least that's what the mullah at our *madrassa* taught us. A mullah I respected even more after Sami decided he didn't like him. Sure, he was tough on us, but it was to make us stronger.

As I finish my sentence, a young boy walks in holding a tray with our tea. His head is down, and he's hunched over. He can't be more than nine, but his body already looks old. The sad sight makes me almost wish it were the soiled Omar bringing the tea now.

"Oh, there he is! My boy!" Mullah Latif's excitement doesn't bring the boy's head up. In fact, he looks quite frightened. Still staring at the floor, he quietly places the steaming glasses of tea in front of us along with a plateful of dried chickpeas. The boy turns to leave, but Latif stops him.

"*Rasa!*" he calls. The boy stops but keeps his back to Latif as he lifts his gaze toward the door.

"I said, come here, Abdullah . . ." Latif's voice is stern, and his smile disappears. Little Abdullah turns around, keeping his eyes to the ground, and walks to Latif, who grins and places the boy on his lap.

"You look so pretty today," Latif grabs the boy's emotionless face and kisses it. "We took Abdullah in after his family was accidentally killed during one of our operations. We found him crying in the corner of a room that had been rocketed. We felt sorry for him and brought him home with us, as good

Muslims should. He would be an orphan if it weren't for us. Now we take good care of him. He's my little angel."

Latif strokes the boy's face before placing him back down and tapping his butt, signaling that he may leave now. Little Abdullah looks more terrified than before as he scurries out of the room. "He's pretty, isn't he?"

"Uh . . . yes, he is a lovely child," I reply, though I'm confused. Why does Latif care about this child's attractiveness?

"So anyway, why is it that you need to talk to me so urgently?" Latif asks as he picks up his tea glass and begins to sip.

"Well, I have been a witness to dishonesty and improper relations between a boy and a girl, and I feel it needs to be dealt with through Islamic law." I straighten my back as I say this, trying to convey honesty and strength.

"This sounds quite interesting. So, do you know how Islamic law works?" he asks.

"I know more than others. I have studied in a *madrassa,* and I am a *qari,* able to recite the Holy Quran in its entirety by heart," I say, maybe with a hint of pride.

"Praise be to God for your accomplishment. What *madrassa* did you go to?"

"I went to the *madrassa* run by Mullah Rafi several villages to the southeast."

"Ah, yes. Mullah Rafi and I were educated in the same *madrassa* in Pakistan when we were young refugee boys," he says.

"I knew he had sent some students my way. It seems he has sent me his top scholar! So tell me more about this sin you have been a witness to."

"Well, we've had incidents in my district, and it has dishonored our village and my family. The wrong needs to be righted and our honor restored. As much as it pains me to say this, it involves one of my own family members." I look down and take a deep breath, hoping that I will look more sensitive about outing my own cousin, which is actually much easier than I thought. "A scandal has brewed between my uncle's oldest son and a Hazara girl. I myself saw them sneaking away and meeting in the woods. But I can no longer protect them, or else I will be contributing to the sin and God will never forgive me." My belief in what I'm saying makes me feel less guilty for what I'm doing.

Latif's mouth creases into a half smile as he starts tapping his fingers on his desk.

"You've done the right thing, Rashid, by coming to us. I know it's difficult to report family when they have done wrong, but to save our own souls from the devil . . . we must."

I turn my face away and nod, hoping I look somewhat desolate. Inside, I am happy he agrees with me and hopeful that Sami will get what he deserves.

"We can fix this together and restore your family's honor. But first, you must tell me everything, every detail of what you saw and the background to the story. I want to hear it all."

For the next hour, I tell him about our lives in the village. I don't leave any details out. I speak of Samiullah and Fatima, our families, and our history there. All the while, Latif nods his head and plays with the tiny tail of hair on his chin that I suppose passes as a beard. After I've finished explaining everything, I wait for Latif's reaction.

"Tak, tak, tak." He clucks his tongue. "This is an extremely bad situation. I see why you have come to me. How do you suppose we should handle this?"

I knew it! I had no doubt this would win me respect. "Well, according to my teachings, we need more witnesses to prove they have had indecent relations or have them admit to it. But we can find a loophole in which we can teach them a lesson and strike them with lashes—I'm not sure yet how many." One hundred sounds about right to me, but Latif might have a better understanding.

Latif just laughs. "Do you expect us to lash them like a father does his son for taking candy when he wasn't allowed?" He leans back in his chair.

"No, of course not." I feel blood rushing to my face in embarrassment. "That would just be the start."

"My dear boy, your cousin and this girl have committed sexual treachery!" He slams his hands on his desk. "If a girl is loose enough to leave her family's home alone, she is up to no good. And the fact that you saw her with your cousin proves that she is having sex with this boy before wedlock—and in their case without even the possibility of marriage. A Hazara with a Pashtun? A Shia with a Sunni? A peasant and a land-owner?" he asks sarcastically as he pretends to spit on the very idea. "This is all proof that they want Satan's pleasures without God's consent. We need to make an example of them in front of your whole village."

"Yes, I agree. They need to be made an example of. This is why I am here, Mullah Saib." I am thrilled that they will be punished in front of everyone so the public can learn and prevent further harm to our culture and society. But I am curious about what else we can do besides lashes. I also think he is too fast in his judgment about sexual relations. We don't know that or have witnesses who have seen them in the act. I can't see my cousin going that far into the abyss. But who knows?

The mullah starts tapping his finger on the desk, and that's when I notice a giant gold watch on his wrist. "Lashes will not be enough . . . Do you like my watch?" he asks, smiling, and begins twirling it around his wrist so he can look at the face. "I took it from the district governor who used to live in this house. He offered me his riches to spare his life, including his watch and this phone." He picks up a flat rectangular device. "Look, when you touch the screen you can move things with your fingers. It operates with your touch, not buttons. It's from overseas," he adds proudly. "He left me a lot of things, but I killed him anyway." He starts to chuckle. "Poor bastard, I kept him alive just long enough to let me know where everything was. I couldn't let him live, you know? He worked for the enemy, and we must help God in weeding out these bad people," Latif continues as he plays with his phone's screen. "Who's to say he wouldn't have gone back to Kabul and then to another province to terrorize the people there? I mean, look at this watch and this phone. Do you think a clean guy would own all of this?"

"No . . . ," I say in agreement. "A man of God would not sell himself for all of this." My eyes slide to Mullah Latif's watch again, and I wonder if this man I'm talking to is a real man of God.

Nineteen

FATIMA

I pull my body up off the mat in complete darkness. I know everyone is finally sleeping by the sound of their breathing. I've been awake, thinking of Sami and waiting for the darkest part of the evening before I go. I take the letter I wrote earlier out of my pillowcase and lay it on the place my head will never rest again. I start to crawl out of our sleeping area. Hands first, slowly feeling my way through to ensure I make no noise by hitting anything or anyone. I feel calmer than I have in days. I know I'm doing the right thing.

I slow my breathing, and I feel a pulsating drum in my temples as I try not to make a sound. My arms still throb, but I can tell they are healing.

I touch the rough carpet with my fingertips, feeling the stiffness from the years of sand and dirt that have seeped between its weaving, as I creep to the door. I finally take a deep breath as I make my way outside. I'm relieved to be out of the small room and in the open air, but I know I can still be caught.

The moon's gleam provides more light as I walk to our

storage room to retrieve the clothes I wrapped in an old sheet along with one of Afifa's undershirts so I don't forget the smell of my little sister, my father's old rag and a book of poems Bibi gave me when she saw my reading was stronger than Zohra's. I pause for a moment and think of my favorite poem in there. The one that says "This is love: to fly toward a secret sky." And that is what I'm doing. I'm flying, flying toward a secret sky to meet Samiullah, to meet my love.

I slowly unlatch the door and cringe at the squeaking sound as I pull it open. As I walk into the room, my vision weakens in the space covered by darkness and hidden from the moon's rays. I quickly look for the sack I hid under a bag of *quroot* from last year. When I finally feel the clumpy bag of *quroot,* I yank at it in order to reach my clothes, but it won't move. This can't be happening. Not now! My heart begins to race as I pull harder. But my newfound energy makes me drop the bag of solid yogurt balls on the dirt floor, setting off a rumbling noise. In the silence of the night, it sounds like I dropped dozens of bells in the still air. I'm frozen. Afraid to move. I stand there paralyzed for a minute, and when I don't hear anyone, I grab my bag and run. I'm running like I've never run before. Not even as a child racing my friends, racing Sami.

Perspiration makes my feet slip in my sandals, but I don't stop to take them off. Belatedly, I wonder if Sami will be there. What if he's not? I decide not to think about that. He said he would. And Sami has never broken a promise to me.

As I get closer to the rock, I turn around and see I am still alone. No one is chasing me. No one can see me. The only noise comes from the panting of my own mouth. My family is probably still sleeping, unaware that I'm gone.

My poor *baba,* he will be heartbroken. No matter how angry and disappointed he is with me, I know he loves me. But my mother will wish she had killed me when she had the chance. And my siblings, they will be confused. The boys will understand that I'm gone but not know why. I don't think little Afo will fully comprehend my absence and will probably expect me to come back before the sun sets—she'll sit waiting, like she always does.

I shake my head. I can't think of this now. Or else I won't go through with it. I chose to do this. I'd rather be afraid of a future of uncertainty than one of beatings and isolation. The last few days have been more miserable than I could have imagined, with my father ignoring me completely and my mother beating me and calling me a whore. When I saw my life unfolding like that before my eyes, I decided my survival was more important than my family's honor. I know it's selfish, but I'm hoping that once I'm gone, the villagers will forget. That my family will eventually be better off with me gone. Most villagers will likely feel sorry enough to leave them alone.

When I reach the rock, I find Sami leaning his head on the hard surface, sleeping with his hands wrapped around his body, keeping himself warm in the chilly morning hour. He looks so comfortable, as if he is in the confines of his home with nothing to worry about. Across from him sits a bicycle with a bag tied to the front and an extension added to the back.

The more I stare at him, the more real this is becoming. We are leaving this place forever. I feel a lump form in my throat.

"Fatima . . ." Sami's voice comes out softly. "Is that really you?"

"It's me." I look at him as he fumbles himself awake.

"So I'm not dreaming? This is real?" he says.

"I'm scared, Sami. I'm really scared" is all I can answer, feeling my eyes moisten.

"I know. Me too. But I'm glad you came." He smiles, revealing those twinkling eyes I was afraid of losing forever. "And I have a perfect plan. But we should start to go now. Before the sun comes up and our families notice we're gone." He looks at his wrist, now adorned with a watch I've never seen before.

"You have a watch?"

"I traded my cousin Daoud my fishing pole for it," he says, smiling, still with sleepy eyes. "Do you like it?" He lifts his hand up to show me.

"It looks like a plastic bangle," I respond, grinning, and Sami returns the smile.

He gets up and walks over to his bicycle, unzips the front of his blue bag, and pulls out a *chadari.* "For the first part of the plan, I brought my sister's *chadari.* You both are about the same height, and I figured you would trip less over this one than the other ones in my house."

I've always hated these coverings, but I know it's necessary for us to hide, and what better way than by covering myself in the blue fabric that most women in our villages wear, especially if they are traveling long distances. He then pulls out a *pakol,* the thick-rimmed, flat and ring-shaped hat most men wear if not wearing a turban.

"And here is my *chadari.*" He places the hat on his head and tilts it down so it covers his brow.

I pull the *chadari* on and cover my body.

I can barely breathe. It feels like I'm in a heavy bag that encloses me from head to toe. I gasp, searching for the air that will keep me from fainting.

We start to walk, Sami rolling the bicycle next to him. The farther we go, the harder it is for me to breathe, trapped in that sheet of fabric. The steaming heat makes it worse. It's as if there are coals surrounding my feet, raising the temperature around my body. Beads of sweat soak my clothes and slowly evaporate in the confined space, fusing with the air, making it even thicker. The only ventilation comes from the little holes pricked through the cloth. The holes are meant to help me see, but the truth is they don't help much. The dark fabric is blinding. But there's nothing I can do about it. I have to keep it on.

The troubles with the *chadari* are nothing compared to the troubles in my mind. I can't stop thinking of my family.

"How are you doing?" Sami asks after a while.

"I'm okay," I lie. If I talk about how I feel, I know I will break down and change my mind. "You?"

"I'm okay too," he says, holding on to his bicycle's handles. He's walking next to it, and I'm trailing behind. We go back to our silence with only the sounds of the wheels hitting rocks, our feet crushing the ground and the occasional desert critters scrambling, startled by our presence.

The pulsing sound of my heart is faint compared to the deafening noises it made this morning, but it still races when I think of all that happened and what may happen.

We haven't talked much since this morning, except for when we're going downhill and Sami tells me to sit on the bicycle extension, making it faster for us to get to our destination. We walk most of the time, since it's the easier option. It would be too difficult for him to pedal both of us. We've only stopped once so far, to drink some water from the bottle he had placed in the front basket and eat some old bread he kept in a plastic bag next to it.

He did explain that we were heading to a village to see a man he trusted who would help us. A man he said had saved him and made him believe again in God's true greatness. A man he said would marry us.

The more Sami speaks, the more I find it hard to. It's all happening so fast, and I haven't been able to come to terms with what is going on. I keep thinking of my family, which makes my eyes well up. I feel the sobs building in my chest and try to swallow as many of them as possible, hiding my crying from Sami. It makes me almost grateful for the repulsive *chadari*; it hides both my body and my heart.

We walk so much that my calves are numb and the heels of my feet crack and sting. With all my perspiration, the wounds on my arms begin to itch. I focus on the pain. The irrepressible itching, the prickling stings and the ripping skin. Thinking of this helps take my mind off all that has happened in the last few days and the unpredictable future that awaits us down this road.

We pass one rocky mountain after another, and it makes me wonder how Sami can tell where we're going. But we keep walking. We have yet to see another soul, and I'm grateful.

"We're almost there." Sami breaks our silence. "Maybe another thirty minutes. We should be passing a small village to our east before we get to his town. But don't worry, we likely won't see any of the villagers; they don't tend to come out to the main path unless they're heading to town."

"*Tashakur.*" I thank him and suddenly feel scared again. I'd almost forgotten about my fears when I started focusing on the physicality of the situation. But I don't want to pass strangers—I'm afraid of seeing my father in the crowds or Sami's family members or, worse, someone who will figure out we are unmarried and traveling together. I'm even scared to have a moment to sit and talk with Sami. I'm frightened of what I'll say, what I'll want to do once we're married. I feel confused, as if the world has turned upside down, and I don't know if I'll ever feel stable again.

As we get closer to town, we pass by some shops. Men are sitting outside of them, some sipping tea and others fiddling with prayer beads. But even through my fabric lens, I notice all eyes are on us.

"Sami. Sami, do you think they know?" I ask, trying to keep my voice down.

"No, they don't know," he whispers back. "They stare at everyone who rides into town. They mean no harm. But if you would feel more comfortable, why don't you sit on the back of the bicycle, and I can pedal. We're on flat land now. It'll be easy, and we'll get there faster."

I sit on the metal backing and hold on to the handles he has fitted for me. I tuck my *chadari* in to make sure it won't get caught in the wheels, and Sami starts to pedal. I can barely make out what the town looks like, but I'm amazed at the size and how close the homes and the shops are to one another. There are even black roads that are flat and smooth, making it simple to ride on. The town is so massive; I wonder how many people live in it. There must be hundreds!

We're winding through some back roads when Sami slows down. The area seems quieter than the one we rode through before. He eventually slows to a stop. "We're here."

I climb off the back and wait as he pushes the bicycle to a

building and leans it against the wall. He knocks on the door of the room before opening it. He looks around, then tells me to come in. I quickly step into the artificial safety of a room with walls and a ceiling protecting me from the outside world.

"You can take the *chadari* off and relax." Sami brings in the bag of the remaining bread and the water. "I'll be right back."

"Wait! Where are you going?" I don't want him to leave me in this strange place by myself.

"Don't worry. I'll be close by. You'll be fine, I promise," he says, and I believe him, but it doesn't stop the feeling of anxiety that is echoing through my body.

"Okay," I say. He looks at me and smiles before closing the door behind him. I promptly peel the sweat-ridden blue fabric off my body and throw it down next to me. I thought it would feel liberating to take it off, but I don't feel free, I just feel vulnerable. Although I can breathe again, I miss the protection. No one knows who I am when I'm wearing the *chadari,* but now people can see my face, my features and my ethnicity. Whoever Sami has brought us to will know he's a Pashtun boy and I'm a Hazara girl, and he won't approve. How can he if our families don't?

I suddenly want to drape that horrible blue *chadari* back over my face and body.

I want to feel safe again. I wonder if I ever will.

Twenty

RASHID

"I said, WHERE is she?" Mullah Latif yells at the old peasant again. His children call out, "Baba, Baba!" waiting for their protector to do something. But he can't. He's surrounded by all of us. He is helpless.

"Mossuma, take the children into the sleeping room," he says. The woman just stares at him like a frightened child herself. "Quickly!" he yells at her. She finally begins to move the crying children in the direction of one of their filthy rooms, but Latif stops them.

"No. They're not going anywhere," Latif yells as he taps Mohammad's nose with the muzzle of his pistol. The old man flinches as the steel hits his face. Latif is maniacal right now. You can tell he's enjoying every second. Psychopathic eyes that seem familiar to me somehow. "I want them to stay as I talk to their *baba*." Sarcasm fills Latif's voice. His gang of thugs gathers the crying children and wife, making them kneel on the dirt facing Mohammad as they continue to wail.

"Please don't do this in front of my children. I beg of you, please," Mohammad says faintly.

"What was that? I can't hear you. What is Baba saying?" Latif cups his ear. "Can you say it louder, Baba, so we can all hear?" He starts walking around, surveying the buildings, kicking the dried mud, letting bits of dirt fly in the air before turning again to Mohammad. "So no wall to protect your women from the eyes of strangers, huh? Could this be a reason why your daughter grew up craving the attention of men? It shouldn't be too much of a surprise the one she gave herself to is your neighbor."

"My daughter didn't give herself to anyone," Mohammad says through gritted teeth. I can tell his blood is boiling, but he is impotent and weak right now, outnumbered by Latif's men and weapons.

"Then *where* is she?" Latif strikes Mohammad's face so hard that spit flies out. The children start crying more.

"I told you, I don't know!" Mohammad answers. "I'm just relieved she's not with your disgusting men!"

Latif slaps him again. "Well, where could she have gone? If she's not with *my* filthy men! Are there other men she likes to meet on a regular basis?" he says with a smirk. Mohammad steps closer, the desire to hurt Latif written all over his face. Latif just laughs and waves his pistol, like a mother would raise her finger to a child. "No, no, no . . . Now, that wouldn't be a good idea. Would it?" he says, laughing.

"What do you want from us? We have nothing. This land doesn't even belong to us—"

"I know who your landlords are," Latif starts yelling again. "I know everything about you and your dirty family!"

"Then what do you want from us?"

"It's not what I WANT. It's what I NEED." He starts to bring his voice down. "What I need to do is make an example of your daughter, or else we will have more girls thinking it's okay to be with a boy out of wedlock. What I need to do is show the village what happens when you are scum. What I need to do is have a public execution of your dirty little girl so everyone can see and enjoy justice being served. You see, it's not that I want to do it, but I need to," he says with a sneer, exposing his crooked yellow teeth. It repulses even me. He seems to enjoy the idea of death more than justice—I am a bit thrown. I didn't think he would really want to kill her. Maybe it's better that she's not here right now.

"Please leave my daughter alone," Mohammad begins to plead. "She's not a bad girl, no matter what you have heard. She is to marry soon. She is of no harm to anyone. Please . . . please . . . leave her alone."

"She's not a bad girl? That's not what I heard." Latif turns and stares at me. Although my face is masked with my scarf, I suddenly feel exposed. "*Rashid, rasa!* Come here, my boy!" I cautiously walk to Latif, avoiding Mohammad's eyes. "Take off that stupid scarf," Latif demands. I shake my head. I don't want Mohammad and his family to see me. "Don't be a *qussy!*" Latif curses as he rips off my scarf, exposing me.

"Rashid?" Mohammad says with disbelief. I feel a pang of shame.

"Rashid here has told us everything." Latif starts to speak again. "He was obviously worried about his village and the women in his family. The example your daughter is setting is dangerous for everyone, and we have to fix it. Isn't that right, Rashid?"

I nod, but I'm unable to look up.

"Rashid, my boy, please tell them this is wrong. Tell them the truth about my daughter. You've known her since you were children. Please!" Mohammad starts to plead with me now. I avert my gaze even more. "Rashid, you know this isn't right. You know it's not. This is not what God wants."

"What God wants?" His words fill me with rage. "What do you know of what God wants?" How dare he tell *me* what God wants! A man who shares the blood of the monsters that killed my family! "What your daughter and my cousin did was wrong. What they have done is an insult to our religion and our culture, and they deserve to be punished!"

"They don't deserve death," he continues to plead. I turn my eyes away. "You are sentencing both my daughter and your cousin to death. Can you tell me that is what God wants?"

The truth is, I don't know if God would want them to die.

But I know I don't want to spend another second arguing it with the old man. "She's obviously not here. Can we go?" I ask Latif.

"We're not going anywhere yet," Latif responds. "Not until we get what we came here for."

"But she's not here. What else can we do?" I am now turning my frustrations on Latif.

"Well . . . if we can't have one daughter, we can always take the other." Latif turns his attention to Fatima's little sister, who can't be more than three years old. She is cute for a little Hazara baby. The little girl is grasping her mother, wide-eyed and afraid. Her gaze is set on a gunman not far from them, leaning against a mud wall picking his teeth with dirty fingernails.

"No! Please don't do this!" Mohammad drops to his knees, no longer able to hold himself up. The same way I remember my father dropping to his knees, trying to save us. I suddenly see flashes of that horrible day. My mother's screams, my father's pleas, me lying on the floor in my sister's blood, pretending to be dead.

"Please, she is an innocent child!" Mohammad yells, bringing me back to today.

"Then maybe we should keep her innocent." Latif walks over to the little girl, who immediately starts crying as she sees him approaching. "It's okay, my darling. Come here to your *kaka*. I want to talk to you with your *baba*." She digs her face into her mother's thigh. Latif sticks his gun to the mother's temple before he begins speaking again. "It's okay, little angel. Even your mother wants you to come with me, right, Madar Jaan? Right?" He jabs the woman's head with more force. She looks at her husband for guidance, but all he can do is sit there, paralyzed and afraid.

I have no idea what Latif's plan is right now. But maybe he is using her to get Mohammad to tell the truth about where his filthy other daughter is.

"Yes," the woman finally says. "It's okay, my *azizam*. Go with Kaka so he can take you to your *baba*." The child wipes her face on her mother's skirt before she takes Latif's hand. This doesn't feel right. He shouldn't be touching this baby who wobbles with every step as she comes near. Her eyes are swollen from crying, and her face is still moist with tears.

She tries to run to her father, but Latif yanks on her arm, and she winces in pain without making noise. "No, no, my dear. Not yet." He kneels down to face her. She looks frightened and confused. "You see, your *baba* has to make a decision right now. It's a hard decision, but he needs to do it."

Latif shifts his attention back to Mohammad and begins to speak in Pashto instead of Dari. "*Pakhto ghagaygay?*" He asks the old man if he speaks the language. Mohammad nods his head. "What about the rest of them?"

"No, I'm the only one in our family who understands Pashto," he says, keeping his focus on the little girl, whose eyes dart back and forth from her father to Latif and to her mother, who is quietly sobbing.

"Good," Latif says. "Then we can make this your sole decision. I will give you three options. Option number one, tell me where your whore of a daughter is."

"I told you, she is not a whore, and I don't know where Fatima went!" Mohammad yells out in exhaustion and defeat.

"Okay, then that leaves you options two and three. Option two, we take this little one with us until you can present your other daughter. And don't worry, we will take good care of her." He strokes her damp cheek and then kisses it. "Oh, salty! Her tears taste so salty." Latif smirks at his men, who begin to laugh. It seems as though I'm the only one who doesn't find this funny. This disgusting creature calls himself a mullah?

He turns his attention back to the little girl and speaks in Dari again, "Don't be scared, my little sugar cube. Kaka Latif and your *baba* will work this out soon. Don't cry anymore. Okay?" She nods her little head, bouncing her short red hair.

Latif looks back at Mohammad, speaking in Pashto again. "Are you ready for option number three?" He waits for a response. There is none. "Okay, I'll tell you whether you're ready or not. Option number three is that we kill this little one in the place of your other whore. It's only fair, don't you think?"

"Please stop! Please!" Mohammad begs, covering his face with his hands. It looks like he is trying to prevent his child from seeing his tears. His wife is frantic and keeps yelling and asking what is going on. But he holds his hands in front of his face and continues his quiet sobbing.

Latif can't be serious about this. He won't kill an innocent baby. He can't. There is nothing justifiable in the eyes of God about that.

"What's the matter? Like you said, she is innocent. We would be doing her a favor. Letting her die innocent, before she follows your other daughter's footsteps. We should all be lucky enough to go to our graves so innocent and pure."

"Please. Please!" Mohammad starts screaming. This causes more tears from his family and more laughter among Latif's men, who are now holding their guns to everyone's heads. I can't believe what I am witnessing. These guys are worse than thugs—they're animals. But I'm too afraid to say anything. The baby is huffing and swallowing her tears in fright, still holding the Latif's filthy hand, unaware of what is going on.

"Rashid, my boy. Come here." Latif yells out to me. I don't want to go to him, but I'm frightened about what he'll do if I don't. So I hesitantly go closer.

"Please, Rashid, please help us! Please, Rashid!" Mohammad starts yelling. His eyes spark with hope at the sight of me.

"Rashid, it doesn't look like your neighbor wants us to take his little girl. I don't think he trusts us," Latif says, looking at me. "And since you were the righteous one to bring this to our attention, I want to give you the honor of performing God's glory and helping us serve justice."

What! No. I can't. I won't. "But . . . but . . . she's a baby. She wasn't the one who committed the crime." I turn my eyes to Mohammad, who is still looking at me through his tears.

"Are you questioning me?" Latif says. I turn and see the anger on his face.

"No . . . no . . . no, that's not what I am trying to do." I'm afraid now of what he'll do to me if I don't do what he asks. I look around and see all the men holding their weapons with their eyes on me as well.

"Good. Then take this and do it." He hands me the pistol. My hands are trembling, and I can barely hold the cold metal. "Now place it on her forehead and shoot!"

"Please . . . please . . . God, please . . . ," I hear Mohammad mutter. "This can't be real . . . this can't be real."

I try to walk toward the little girl. My feet stagger forward and then back. I notice her brown eyes, full of fear and confusion. They're big and round, like my sister's used to be. My hand starts to quiver uncontrollably, and I think I'm about to drop the pistol.

"Give me that." Latif snatches the gun back. "With the way you're holding it, you'll kill all of us." He puts the gun away and into his holster. "Besides, I've changed my mind."

Oh, thank God. I start breathing normally again. I look at Mohammad who is smiling and starts saying, "Thank you. Thank you!"

Latif then squats back down behind the baby. He strokes

her bright red hair and looks as though he is about to hug her from behind. But that's when those demented eyes return. The eyes of Satan. And before I can make out what is about to happen, he twists her neck and her lifeless little body drops to the ground. "Can't waste precious bullets on her, now, can we?" He turns to his men, laughing. But all I can see is the little girl lying there as if she's sleeping.

Twenty-one

RASHID

As we board the motorbikes, I hear their screams. The wailing burns through my ears and into my stomach. I'm about to get on behind Azizullah, one of Latif's gangsters who I noticed enjoyed the show, when I have to jump off. I hunch over and feel bile burning through my throat. The vomit tastes of the bread I had this morning. I continue to heave, gasping for air, my hands pressing against my knees. Something wants to escape from my body, but it's stuck.

Azizullah sits on the bike and laughs at me. "The first time is always the hardest. But you'll get used to it."

I ignore him as my body contracts, trying to push it out. But all I get is burning bile.

"Come on, we have to go. Stop upsetting yourself over it. Besides, it was just a little Shia Hazara baby. She would have gone to hell anyway, with parents who can't teach her real Islam. No one will miss her."

I glance up and see Mohammad cradling his baby in his

arms. He's kneeling on the dirt floor holding her small corpse, swaying back and forth.

"Wake up, Afo. My Afo, wake up!" He's yelling at her and then looking to the sky. "Why, God? Why? She's innocent! Why?"

The mother is leaning against one of the mud walls, staring with vacant eyes, unblinking, her mouth open in shock. The two young boys are sitting behind their father, hugging each other and crying. The more their dad screams, the stronger their tears flow. The sight makes me cough up more bile before I force myself onto the bike. I straddle the back end of the seat and hold on to the sides as we speed off to my uncle's house. The cold wind blowing on my face helps settle my stomach, but the bouncing on the gravelly fields knocks my brain around, making it harder to make sense of what just happened. Before I can figure it out, we're at my family's home.

"Get over here, Rashid," Latif calls out before spitting on the ground. "Bring the men in your family out so we can talk. Tell them to bring Samiullah with them." I nod to let him know I understand.

I approach our door and knock lightly on the cool metal surface. By afternoon, the sun will be heading east and will scorch the exterior, making it almost impossible to touch, but for now, the metal is almost soothing as I press my hand against it. I futilely hope that if my family can't hear the tapping, no one will answer, and we can leave.

After what happened at Mohammad's place, I don't want to see any more, at least not for today. I didn't expect anyone to be killed, let alone someone innocent. I keep searching for justification. Maybe Latif is right. Maybe the child had to die so she wouldn't grow up like her sister. They already raised one sinner—who is to say their next daughter wouldn't turn out the same or maybe worse? Maybe we did do her a favor by letting her die as an innocent. But if that's the case, why do I feel sick again?

"Rashid!" Latif calls out, snapping me out of my thoughts.

"No answer. I'll try again," I say as I thump on the door with my knuckles a slight bit louder this time, loud enough for Latif to hear. I listen as a pair of feet crunch the dirt and rapidly make their way to the door. Not long ago, this noise lifted my heart, but today it makes it sink. I hear the peephole slide open and see my aunt Gul Babo's eyes.

"Rashid! My son, it's you!" Her eyes brighten at the sight of me, which fills me with shame.

"*Salaam*, my dear aunt—" She closes the peephole and un-latches the lock to let me in. She embraces me before I can even attempt to kiss her hand.

"I'm so glad you're home. We need you to help us." Her eyes are filled with tears.

"What's the matter? Are you okay? Is anyone hurt?" I feel a chill run through my body.

"No one is hurt, but Samiullah is missing." She starts to

sob. "We don't know where he is." She falls into my arms, and I hold her. I'm craving her embrace just as much as she's craving mine right now. I cling to her for as long as I can before I peel myself away.

"Gul Babo, I have to go now."

"But you just got here. You have to help us find him!" She's clutching my arm, pulling me toward her, but I stay outside the house.

"The best way I can help you is by going right now."

"Rashid—"

I yank my arm away. "Quickly lock the door," I tell her. "You have to listen to me. Lock it now."

"Rashid, you're scaring me." Her eyes are beginning to overflow again.

"Please just do it now," I say, turning around. When I hear the door close and the lock latch back into place, I breathe out the air trapped inside me.

I walk to where Latif and the other men are waiting. Latif looks at me and shrugs his shoulders. "So where are they?"

"Samiullah's not there. It seems as though he's run off as well. Likely with the girl." I look around. "I say we don't waste our time here and we head out to look for them. They couldn't have gone too far."

Latif starts to chuckle and walks over to me. "So is that what you think we should do?"

"I think we should go now so we don't lose their tracks and—"

Latif grabs my shirt and pulls me toward him. He shoves his face into mine. "I don't care what YOU think we should do," he says. I feel his spit fly onto my skin, and I can taste his sour breath. "You are not in charge here. I am!"

He throws me hard onto the ground before he kicks me in the gut, knocking all the air out of my body. "We're going in. You can come with us, or you can lie here. What's your choice?"

I gather enough strength and push myself up.

"Good boy." He pats my back. "Come on."

Before we make it back to the door, it creaks open. Then I hear my uncle Ismail's voice. "Rashid? Rashid, it *is* you!" he says and then takes a look around. *"Asalaam aleykum . . . ,"* he greets Latif and the other men. His eyes search the group.

"And peace be with you!" Latif replies. "We're so sorry to be intruding. I am Latif—"

"I know who you are," my uncle says with an edge of contempt in his voice. I don't think he's ever met Latif, but he definitely knows of him and despises him. Latif's men have come to take illegal taxes from my uncle's shop in town on many occasions, and my uncle has never agreed to it lightly.

"Oh, good, then. You must be Ismail Khan. Yes?" My uncle nods. "Well, we are looking for your son, Samiullah."

My uncle's eyes widen, and he shifts his gaze to me. I quickly avert my eyes; I can't bear to look at him right now.

"What do you want with my son?" My uncle has closed the door behind him.

"Well, we have heard that he has shamed his family . . . your family. And we just want to help fix the situation."

"This is a family matter, and we are taking care of it ourselves. You can leave." My uncle waves his hand, gesturing for them to go.

"You see, Ismail Khan, we can't do that. It's not that easy."

"It's very easy. Get on your bikes and leave. This is our family and our tribe; we will handle this from within." I don't believe for one second that my uncle will punish his son. But after what happened earlier, I don't blame him for not wanting Latif to be involved.

"That wouldn't be fair to everyone else. Your son and your neighbor's daughter have shamed the village. And as much as I respect that you want to handle this within the family and tribe, you can't," Latif says with mock sincerity. "It's in our hands now, and it's our job to take care of the situation."

My uncle raises his right eyebrow, a gesture I've become familiar with, growing up in his house. He knows that his black beard, dark eyes and massive charcoal-gray turban can be intimidating, so he always works extrahard to put people at ease, primarily with his eyes. But every now and then, there is someone who causes his kind eyes to harden. And Latif has done just that.

"How, exactly, do you plan on taking care of the situation?" my uncle asks Latif.

"The proper way. As we both know, the Kabul government is useless here. We will take it to the shadow governor and let him decide the punishment. And if we can't reach him, *we'll* decide the punishment ourselves, and we'll execute it in the village so everyone can learn from your son's mistakes." Latif adjusts the gun that is slung over his shoulder.

"So you are telling me you want to *kill* my son?"

Latif lets out a snort. "Look, since your son is one of ours, we'll try to be more lenient. Maybe we can work out a way to save his life. There have been times where the punishment given was death, but it was reduced with a cash fine or land donations to lashes so the public could see some sort of chastisement. The girl, of course, will die. As you know, it's necessary to save your honor and our people's honor. A family that raises such filth can't be forgiven."

My uncle's eyebrows have not shifted at all. He stares at Latif. "Get off my land." He then looks at me. "All of you! And never come back!"

"I'm sorry it had to come to this. I didn't mean to upset you, and I'm sure you don't mean to insult me." Latif looks at my uncle but receives no reaction. "But, you see, we can't leave. I have a funny feeling you are hiding your son inside your home. Meaning we need to take a look around."

Latif snaps his finger at one of his men. The man rifles

through a bag before running to Latif and handing him a pair of handcuffs. Two other thugs grab my uncle throw him against the wooden donkey pole. They wrap his arms around the wood, and Latif cuffs him.

"Rashid, don't you let them dishonor us and our women!" my uncle yells at me. Although clearly they have already dishonored my uncle and our entire tribe for how they have just treated him. But even my uncle knows what matters right now is the women.

I run up to Latif. "Please don't do this. Our women are in there. It's clear Samiullah isn't here. Please!"

"How do I know he's not in there? It sounds like this *khan* here is protecting his son. We are forced to go in there now," Latif says. There is something in his eyes that unnerves me. I don't want him near my aunts and cousins.

"Let me do it. I'll search for him in there. We can't have strange men in our home. Our women are in there."

"You think I'm going to trust you?" he snorts. "I barely know you. And you proved your weakness when you couldn't kill that stupid little *kafir* baby. I'll allow you to come with us, but that's all I'm giving you. Or you can stay here with your dear uncle." He kicks dirt in my uncle's direction.

I'm ashamed even to look at him. I keep my eyes on Latif and agree to his offer.

"Rashid!" my uncle screams in vain as I lead the men into our home. I've never felt this low in my life. I never thought

I would be leading a group of strange men into my family's home, where our women are sitting not properly draped.

The thought of these men looking at my women makes me feel dirty. It will pollute them to be seen by strange men. As we walk through the main gate and into the courtyard, I see two of my aunts and three of my female cousins standing, as if they've been trying to figure out what's going on. As soon as they see us, they start to panic and quickly cover their faces. They run into the closest room, the room with the *tandoor*. Latif giggles, a high-pitched noise that sets my teeth on edge.

Soon my Gul Bashro's voice comes from inside the mud room they ran to. "Rashid! Who are these people?" she is yelling. Then my male cousins and uncles come out of various rooms with looks of murder in their eyes, but they stop in their tracks as Latif's men raise their weapons.

"Please don't be afraid. I am the one they call Mullah Latif, and I'm here in search of your nephew and son Samiullah." Latif looks around the grassy courtyard, empty of people but full of our roosters and chickens. He looks at the men standing to the side, still in attack-ready positions but frozen because of the weapons pointed in their direction. Latif holds his heart and bows to them in greeting. The men don't return the greeting; they are waiting for their moment to pounce. "We apologize for coming in like this, but it's necessary. We ask that you all come out to the grass so we can search the home."

We wait in silence, and right when I think no one is ever going to move, Samiullah's mother, my dear Gul Bibi, steps out of the room the other ladies ran into. Her face is partly covered by a white head scarf bordered with lace. The white makes the purple in her top pop out. It's the first thing I see until I notice the rage in her eyes. "What do you want with my *zoy*?" She comes closer until she is face-to-face with both of us.

"Asalaam aleykum," Latif says to my aunt, but his greeting is not reciprocated. Gul Bibi makes it clear she wants nothing to do with him . . . or us. "We just need to talk to your son, dear auntie."

"I'm not your aunt. You!" She directs her attention to me now. "What kind of man are you, bringing strangers into our home, exposing your cousins and aunts? What is wrong with you?" She slaps the side of my head. The impact stings my ear. I can hear the blood rushing on the inside of my skin. "Have we not raised you to be a man? It seems as though we raised a donkey!" She continues to slap me. This makes Latif chuckle. "Is this funny to you? Do you have no honor? No honorable Pashtun man would walk into a stranger's home like this." It looks as though my aunt is about to slap him as well, but she holds back. This doesn't stop Latif from putting his arms up in preparation to block any incoming assault. I have no doubt this isn't the first time he has invaded someone's home, but I think this is the first time he has been confronted by a woman in the home. He looks shaken.

"Our intention is to find your son so we can talk to him. We are here to help him . . . to help you," he says as tries to regain his composure.

"We don't want your help. Leave us alone and leave my son alone. Go!" She says turning around and throwing her hand up in the air. "Go now!"

Latif just looks at me as if I can fix this. And that's when I realize this is my chance to make myself look strong in front of Latif and his men again. I can't fix the way I've dishonored my family, but I can fix how I appear to Latif's men. Besides, I am Qadir's son, my aunt's dear brother's child. She will forgive me later.

"My dear auntie, let's not drag this out. Let them quickly search the house and then they'll leave." My aunt turns around with bulging eyes and makes her way back to me. I hold my head high and try not to show fear. Preparing for more slaps, I tense every muscle in my body. She may be a little old lady, but her bony hands are like sharp knives when they strike.

"You are a shame to your dead parents!" she says with her deep green eyes flashing—eyes like Sami's, like my father's. I take a step back. It feels as though I've been hit, but she hasn't laid a finger on me. "If your father knew what you would become—selling out your own family, spending time with thugs, giving your cousin to these dogs—he would have asked his murderers to kill you along with him!" All I can do is stare at her in silence as I try to catch my breath. She has never said a harsh word to me in my life. And now this. I want to respond, but I can't. How can I speak if I've forgotten how to breathe?

I hear her call the families to come out of their rooms and into the courtyard. There is a steady stream of children and men who come out first. The women, in their colorful clothes, follow. Some are holding their scarves to their faces using both hands; others are holding their infants in one while covering themselves with the other. As they all make their way out, I can feel the stares, but I can't focus. Their faces are blocked by flashes of my family's murder. I hear my father's screams, I see my mother lying on the ground, I see my baby sister's lifeless body in my mother's dead arms, and suddenly the scenery changes, and I see Mohammad with his baby Afifa.

I feel myself fall back onto the dirt floor. The world around me has turned hazy. I see bodies moving. I see men throwing pillows and sheets through windows and doors. I see plastic jugs falling from the roof as Latif's men run up to the top of the house. I hear the children and the women crying. I hear the men in my family screaming. But I can't move. The voices are all muffled; nothing is comprehensible. The only thing that's as clear as freshly wiped glass is my father's desperate voice screaming for his murderers to spare us, his son, his daughter, his wife.

"Rashid! Rashid!" I think it's my father calling me, until I feel a slap on my face and I see Azizullah. "Come on, Rashid, we're done here. Let's go." I'm unaware of how much time has passed and what has happened, but I've regained my vision and see what we have left behind. The house looks like it has been looted, with clothes and furniture scattered throughout the courtyard. Some of the window screens have been ripped from their frames to make way for everything Latif's men were flinging out.

"I hope you don't mind that we took some items for the cause." Azizullah smirks as he shows me a bag full of batteries, a flashlight and a small radio—my family's only radio. I don't even look at them as I turn to leave, but I can hear my great-uncle Jaan Baba's weak voice trying to yell.

"You are dead to us, dead!" His screams are shrill. "You have brought more shame to us than your cousin. Don't ever come back."

I hear women wailing in the background, and I turn to see their faces. And that's when I find her. My beautiful cousin Nur, dressed in a ruby-red dress with a green head scarf to match her eyes, holding on to one of the children. She is stunning, even when her eyes are downcast, dripping tears.

I notice that tears are also streaming down my face. I wipe them away, turning my back on my family, and walk out of my home.

Sami will pay for ripping me away from my loved ones.

Twenty-two

RASHID

I splash the river water on my face, feeling the icy burn on my parched skin. The day is hot, but my body cannot stop shivering. Just days ago, I was at the same river with one of Latif's men, strapping my village's water to the motorbike as we rode by, and today I'm wondering if I can ever show my face in this village again. My head races with thoughts of this morning's events. First at the farmer's house and then at my own. I hear my aunt's words, and I hear Mohammad's screams. Flashes of my own parents' voices echo through my brain. I hold my hands to my ears, turning my head so the other men don't see the struggle I'm having with myself, hoping if I squeeze my head hard enough, the sounds will stop.

I feel a push on my back and instinctively swing my hand around in order to hit whoever it is. But I miss.

"Calm down!" Zaman says, catching my hand. "Are you okay?" I barely know Zaman, but he seems different from the louder men in Latif's gang. I noticed he was one of the few who wasn't laughing when Latif killed Fatima's sister.

"I'm fine," I say, looking away, not wanting to make eye contact with any of them. Partly out of anger and partly out of embarrassment.

"You're not okay. But you need to act stronger, or they will bother you too," Zaman says.

"What's it to you?" I snap. I don't know this guy, and I don't like that he is poking his nose in my business.

"I don't care what happens to you!" Zaman says through gritted teeth. "I just don't want to deal with any more crazy nonsense today. So get up and act like a man so they don't find a reason to treat you like a boy!"

I get up from my squatting position and look over to the men farther down the river. Some are lounging on the rocks, soaking in the sun's rays, others are drinking and bathing their feet in the ice-cold water. Latif is one of the men lying on the rocks and laughing. I can feel my hands start to clench into tight fists, and I dig my nails into my skin. He violated my family!

"Let it go," Zaman says as if he had just read my mind. "There is nothing you can do to fix it now. Just let it go."

I look at Zaman puzzled. "What do you mean, 'let it go'? I have nothing now!"

"Going after him isn't going to change anything." Zaman glances at Latif.

"I suppose you would kill me if I went after him?" I now have the strongest urge to tackle Zaman but I just stare at him.

"I couldn't care less if he were killed," Zaman says.

I am stunned.

"Stick your eyes back into your head." Zaman shakes his head at me. "You can't be surprised that not everyone is impressed by that fraud."

"But . . . then . . . why . . ." I try to get a sentence out, but I'm too confused by Zaman's words to complete it.

"Look, the scoundrel helps me earn some money that I can give back to my family," he says before I can finish my sentence. "I don't like what I do, but at least I can give my parents and siblings enough money to keep them fed. I have no choice."

"And you're okay with destroying families and killing children?" I feel the bile come up in my throat as I remember the death of that little baby girl today.

"No, I'm not. But I would rather have someone else's family destroyed than my own. It's survival," Zaman says without any shame. "What did you think would happen when you complained about your family to a thug like that?" His words make my insides sink. We both look at Latif, who is now laughing at one of the men who can't last ten seconds with his feet in the water because of the cold.

"But . . . I thought it would be . . . I thought . . ." I struggle to get my words out as Zaman grabs a cigarette and sticks it in his mouth. "I thought it would be done according to proper Islamic law." My words send him into grunts of laughter.

"Do you really think that man knows anything about Islamic law?" Latif has grown bored of the jackass in the water and is now fixing his hair in the reflection of his sunglasses. Zaman pulls out a match and lights his cigarette. "The only reason he has authority in our villages is because his uncle is a big-time warlord in the capital of our province. He has ties with some crooks in Kabul and some Afghans hiding across the border in Pakistan. They're all scum, but they're the scum that keeps me fed—even if they are stealing it from someone else's plate." Zaman blows out smoke and looks down again. "They talk about Pashtun *this* and Pashtun *that*—did you know we have Tajiks and Uzbeks in this group? Rumor has it Latif's mother was from Panjshir. Anyone who is hungry for money or blood, or both. *This* is our Afghanistan," he says, shaking his head. "How did you get stuck with us, anyway? It didn't look like your family needed the money."

I wonder why Zaman is telling me all of this. It doesn't seem like he's the slightest bit scared of Latif. "The mullah at my *madrassa* told me that it would be good for me to meet with Latif and join his men. He said they were Taliban fighters who will help rid our country of the infidels and bring back an Islamic state. So I started spending time with them in the last few months with permission of our mullah."

"It wasn't Mullah Rafi, was it?" Zaman snorts again, this time letting out smoke from his nose and mouth.

"Yes, do you know him?" I ask.

"That's Latif's brother. They're both jackasses," Zaman says, coughing out a chuckle. "They're all donkeys with power—I don't think the real Taliban would even accept them."

"But Mullah Rafi was a wise man who taught us so much about what's ailing our country!" I feel heated by the fact that he would call a religious scholar a donkey.

"He is a hypocrite, and so are you if you believe in Islam and believe in him at the same time." Zaman blows smoke in my direction.

"How dare you—" I start, but he interrupts me.

"I dare to say this because he rapes children, sends them off on suicide missions and tells them they will survive all because they are wearing a talisman," Zaman says with fierce eyes. "And if you think they are great men, you should be prepared to be their next mule." Zaman takes a drag from his cigarette. "Looks like he didn't play with you. You should be thanking God for that every day. Maybe he thought you were too ugly." Zaman snorts before taking another drag.

Could he be telling the truth? Did Mullah Rafi violate his power with children? No, it can't be true. But why would Zaman lie to me?

"Hey! You two! Come here!" Our conversation is interrupted by a goon waving us over to Latif. Zaman throws his cigarette to the ground and steps on it before walking over.

"What were you guys doing over there? Giving each other

some ass?" Latif says. His followers laugh. That sick son of a bitch! I'm about to give him a piece of my mind, but Zaman answers first.

"We were taking a leak. We wanted to piss upstream so it went in all of your mouths."

The men stop laughing and start wiping their mouths and smelling their hands. Latif laughs at the retort and looks back at me. "So, where are they?" he asks.

"Sami and the girl?" I look at him. "I don't know. They must have run away together." I feel my anger boiling again at the thought of my snake of a cousin, whom my family has chosen over me.

"Yes, I know that," Latif says, "but we need to figure out where they are. Who would they go to for help? Where do they have more family? What members of your tribe would take them in? Do they have friends who would shelter them?"

Family. Tribe. Friends. Is this animal serious? Does he think I would give him the locations of more of the people I know so I can be shamed even further than I already have been?

"I don't think he would be able to take a girl to any family members or tribesmen. They wouldn't allow it," I say quickly.

"Then where else?" Latif's voice sounds agitated. "Has he lived anywhere else besides this village and the *madrassa*? Does he know other places?"

"He traveled a lot with his father before we became students at the *madrassa*, but the people he saw were all people who knew his father. They would never help him," I say. They would turn him away, if not shoot him on the spot for disgracing our people. I consider our friends at the *madrassa*, wondering if any of them would help him, but I can't think of one person who would even dare. Then I remember that when Sami left the school, he didn't come straight home. He spent a month with that old mullah a few villages over before making his way back to our tribe. Mullah Sarwar! That's his name!

I look at Latif, who is still staring at me. And I wonder if I should share this information with the animal who is intent on killing my cousin and his whore or if I should keep it to myself and figure out my own punishment for them.

Oh, Samiullah, your life is not in God's hands now. It's in mine.

Twenty-three

FATIMA

"Are you sure this is what you want?" Mullah Sarwar asks.

"Yes," Sami responds immediately.

"I was actually asking Fatima." Mullah Sarwar looks at him and then back at me. "My child, I want to make sure that this is what you want. I don't want you to feel forced into doing anything. I know you think there's no turning back, and you might be right. But there are different options moving forward, and this is just one of them. No matter what you choose, I'll help you."

I look at Sami, who is staring at me with the eyes of a worried cat, waiting for my response. We just spent the last hour explaining to Mullah Sarwar why we felt justified in running away together. He listened with kind eyes and patient ears. Without judgment. I first avoided the mullah's eyes, afraid of disapproving stares, but not once did this gentle old man make me feel like the whore my mother must be calling me right now. Instead, the mullah has been trying to hear my intent through my quiet, short answers. When he found out about my burns, he left the room, only to come back with medication. I find myself avoiding his eyes again, now afraid to see the sympathy in them because I know it will bring me to tears.

"Don't listen to what people may have told you growing up," Mullah Sarwar continues. "Our culture and tradition is not our religion. As a Muslim woman, you have the right not to be forced into marriage. And I can't marry two people without knowing they have both come to me of their own free will. Do you understand? I wish your families were here to accept this union, but I understand that in this case, they will not. Still, this is your choice—not mine and not theirs."

I nod and look at Sami, who seems nervous. His gaze has fallen to the carpet. The man I ran away with now looks like the little boy I once knew. The boy who has always taken care of me. The boy who always made me happy. And the man I can't imagine a life without. I am more sure than I have ever been.

"I want this," I finally whisper.

Sami's head pops up, and he looks at me, a smile on his face. I can't help but return it as I turn my face away in embarrassment.

"There is nothing to be ashamed of, my dear," Mullah Sarwar says to me. "Love is a gift. And this gift will give you the strength for what lies ahead. It won't be easy. There won't be a day that you won't miss your family." I feel my eyes begin to fill with tears again, thinking of my parents, my brothers and my baby sister. "But you have both made your choice. And until we can make sure you are both safe, you will stay with us."

"Thank you, Mullah Saib." Sami goes to kiss his hand. Mullah Sarwar pulls his hand away and taps Sami's head.

"My son, you don't have to thank me." He looks at Sami with a smile so powerful that it lifts my heart. "The family will get you both situated."

"I'm sorry," I find myself saying. "I'm sorry for the trouble we're causing you."

The mullah looks at me with his sympathetic eyes again. I feel my emotions swell as a teardrop falls from each of my eyes. "I'm not here to judge you. I'm here to help. I know Sami is a good boy. And I can see the love that you both share." I am embarrassed at hearing the word *love*. Sami and I have never used that word or words like it, even though I feel it in my heart. "But you both must know that even when we make this right in the way of Islam, there will be those in our society who will never approve. And you have to be ready for that."

I look at Sami, and I know that I am.

Mullah Sarwar asks his grandson Walid and an older son named Ahmad to be our two witnesses. Usually the bride's and groom's family members perform that role, but in our case, he says Sami is already like his own son and now I am like his daughter, making us family. I'm still in disbelief that this is really happening. I'm about to marry Sami. This is not how I imagined it. I had dreamed that our families would be with us. At least showing us their support, if not happiness. But today we are with three men I have just met, only the five of us. Despite the circumstances, I don't feel sad or alone like I did so many nights in my own home.

"This *nikah* will join your lives together. After the agreement of marriage, no longer will you have two separate lives, you will become one," Mullah Sarwar says. I can't stop a smile from spreading across my face. I'm going to marry Sami, and we will start our new life together. I'll never feel alone again.

"I know you do not have something to offer Fatima for her *mahr*, but as my son, you may have this." The Mullah pulls off his own wedding band and then reaches into a small leather pouch and brings out a ring decorated with small beads of emeralds and rubies. I can't believe my eyes. I have never owned jewelry before, except for the bangles I had around my wrists when I was Afifa's age—as my arms grew, the bangles popped off one by one.

"Mullah Saib, I can't . . . we . . ." Sami starts to talk but can't finish his sentence.

"Please accept this, my children. My wife and I wore our rings every moment of our lives together." Mullah Sarwar examines the sparkling band and takes a deep breath. "I hope that the bond you feel with each other is even stronger than the bond Aziza and I shared. May God bless you both a thousand times over." He puts the rings down on the carpet and pushes them over to Sami.

"Thank you, Mullah Saib, but we can't take those from you," Sami says. "They hold your memories."

"Don't be silly, my boy. The memories are here," the mullah says as he taps his heart. "These will now be tokens of our love passed down to you. And maybe one day you will pass them down to your children. Besides, there needs to be a *mahr*; this can't happen without a marriage settlement from the groom to the bride. And since you are my son, this is our gift to Fatima." Mullah Sarwar smiles at me.

"But Mullah Saib—" I finally have the courage to say, but the mullah holds up his hand to stop me.

"Fatima, my dear, please don't refuse. You will hurt me if you do." His eyes look so sincere that I no longer resist and instead thank him.

"Okay, let's get started," he says, smiling at the both of us.

I brace myself to feel anxious, but the nerves don't come. I am relaxed and confident—feelings that have felt so foreign to me in the last several days.

"*Bismillah Rahman al Rahim*," he says.

"In the name of God, most Gracious, and most Merciful," Sami and I repeat.

"Do you both come here willingly wanting to marry each other?" he asks.

"We do," Sami and I say together. I smile and notice he is smiling as well.

"No one has forced your hand into this marriage?" Mullah Sarwar looks at us for our response.

"No," we say in unison again.

"Fatima, do you accept Samiullah as your husband?" he asks me.

Before answering I look over to Sami, who suddenly seems nervous.

"I accept," I answer, watching the relief on Sami's face.

"Samiullah, do you accept Fatima as your wife?"

"I accept," Sami says without flinching. I can feel his love for me in this moment even more than before.

This question and our acceptance is repeated two more times.

Mullah Sarwar then pulls out a piece of paper and a pen.

"This is your *nikah khat*. Fatima, sign here," he says, handing me the pen and marriage contract. I sign above my name before handing the pen to a grinning Sami. My grin matches his.

"In the name of God, the Beneficent, the most Merciful, please bestow on Samiullah and Fatima's marriage your greatest blessings of love, happiness and piety. We trust in only you and believe in only you." Mullah Sarwar finishes this prayer by covering his face with his hands.

"Congratulations," he says, smiling. "May God bless you

and may His blessing descend upon you and unite you in goodness."

"That's it?" Sami asks.

"Yes, that is it." Mullah Sarwar, his son and grandson all grin at us. "You are married now."

"But I thought there was more to it?" Sami says the words that I'm thinking.

"Like what? Is there something more you would like us to do?" Mullah Sarwar asks, laughing.

"No, I just…" Sami looks at me. "I mean, we're … married?"

"Yes, my son and daughter, you are married," the mullah says while Walid and Ahmad throw sugar-covered almonds over our heads.

Like Sami, I am in disbelief. And just like him, I can feel my cheeks flushing. We did it. He's my husband. I'm his wife. And now God will bless whatever comes next.

Twenty-four
RASHID

We zigzag along the dirt road and make it to town. The sight of our motorbikes scares the shopkeepers; some shut their doors, and fathers pull their children in closer. The fear in their eyes is empowering. I know I shouldn't enjoy it, but I do. As much as I can't stand Latif, I realize being next to him gives me the authority I have always known I was destined for. Which is why I told him. Why I decided that he should be the one to punish Samiullah.

The late-afternoon sun is beginning to paint the sky orange. We pull into the street where Mullah Sarwar's *masjid* stands and park our bikes outside. I've never seen men put on their sandals so fast to leave an area. Over by the wall, the old mullah is whispering something to a boy. The teenager gets on his bicycle and leaves. The mullah looks at us and walks into the *masjid,* making us follow him.

We have reached the door of the building when he finally speaks.

"*Asalaam aleykum,*" he greets us. "Please take your shoes

off before entering." Mullah Sarwar smiles as he lifts his hand to stop the men from entering with their dirty sandals and boots. "Thank you."

Latif and his men just stare at each other. Stupid fools think they have authority even in a *masjid*.

"Why don't you guys wait out here?" I say to Latif. "I'll talk to the old man and see if he knows anything." I don't want these morons in here. It makes me feel dirty to see them even in the vicinity of the *masjid*.

"Fine. I need a cigarette anyway," Latif says before they walk back to their bikes.

"*Walaykum asalaam*," I respond to the mullah's greeting as I take my sandals off.

"Would you like to pray with me?" the mullah asks. And I suddenly remember I haven't prayed since morning.

"Umm . . . yes, please." I walk out of the *masjid* and make my way to the fountain in the courtyard to perform my ablution. As I walk out, I can see the men at their bikes, and most of them start rolling their eyes. Those infidels! They should be joining me! They're the worst excuses for Muslims I have ever seen. I can't believe they are all that I have left in this world.

After my ritual cleaning, I head back into the *masjid* and pray side by side with the mullah. After my recitations, I ask God to take care of my parents and sister and grant them heaven as I always have. I then find myself begging God for forgiveness for how I treated my family today. And for causing the Hazara family the same pain that I lived through. I feel uncomfortable praying for them, but I can't shake off the feeling of horror when I think of that little body falling to the ground. She was a child, like my sister.

By the time I spread my hands on my face to end my prayers, I notice my face is wet. I quickly wipe the tears before the mullah can see my weakness.

"May God grant you your prayers," I hear the mullah say.

"Thank you, and yours too," I mumble, still wiping my face.

"Are you okay, my son?" The mullah's eyes glimmer with sincerity.

"Yes, I just have some dirt in my eyes from the trip," I say as I rub my eyes to play along with my lie. I turn to him. "I'm here looking for my cousin. And I think that you know him."

"Oh? What's his name?" the mullah asks with his eyebrows raised.

"Samiullah Ismailzai," I say. I look at the mullah's eyes for recognition, but his eyes are still soft. "I believe he stayed with you after disgracefully leaving the *madrassa* we were attending."

"Yes, I know Sami Jaan very well. You must be Rashid Jaana," he says. God knows what Sami has said about me to this old man. "Sami spoke very highly of you. He cares for you a lot." I don't believe him for a second. It looks like I have found another lying mullah!

"Well, we are here to arrest him for breaking the laws of God," I say, ignoring his words.

"What kind of law did he break?" The old man looks at me with curiosity.

"He has fornicated with a girl he is not married to, and she is a Hazara at that." I now agree with Latif's logic that they must have done more. They had to have, or else why have we been going through all of this?

"Are there witnesses to this supposed crime?" he asks, pulling out his wooden prayer beads and flicking them one by one.

"Yes, I saw them together in the woods talking, and they ran off like criminals," I say with authority.

"But they were talking?" He continues to flick his beads calmly.

"Yes. Alone." Is this guy listening to me? They were alone in the woods! That should have set him off immediately. But still it's *flick, flick, flick*!

"I'm sorry, my son, but that doesn't prove anything."

"Are you defending such lewd acts?" I hit my hand on the floor that we just prayed on. What kind of religious man is this? What kind of *Afghan* man?

"I'm just saying that there could be more to their meeting," he says to me. "Maybe they were having a friendly conversation. And I don't want innocence falsely punished. God would not want that. God is the judge, not us."

I know God is the only judge, but as a religious scholar, he should understand. He should be enforcing God's law! We are here to help God!

"I am worried about what may happen to this young man and woman for something as innocent at talking," he continues. "Do you trust those men out there?" His eyes glance up to the entrance. "Do you want them to hurt your cousin?"

"He is a disgrace! He is not my family anymore," I snap. "And she is a whore for meeting with him! Whether they were talking or doing more, they have violated Islam!"

"Be careful, my son," he says to me. "There is only one God. And it is God who knows best. Not us." He looks at me. His eyes aren't condescending. They actually look concerned. "And there doesn't seem to be enough evidence to accuse these two for violating Islam."

"Who are you to tell me about Islam?" I retort. I don't care if he is a mullah and can play tricks with his eyes. I won't be a fooled by another fake *holy* man! "Sami deserves to die for what he has done to me and my family! I don't even have them anymore because of his sins!" I can hear my voice crack with the sadness of my loss. This enrages me even more. "I have to make sure Sami receives his punishment!" I feel my eyes filling with tears, and I look up in hopes that they'll dry before anything falls.

"Rashid Jaana, no matter how far you go in this world, you leave your heart with your loved ones," the old man says to me. "But when you take those you love out of your heart, you fall into a dangerous insanity that you may not be able to come out of."

His words ring in my head, but I try to silence them.

"But what if you are torn from your loved ones? Or what if they are torn from you?" I ask, still avoiding his eyes.

"My son, even if you never see your family again, they have filled you with enough love to survive. But you have to hold on to it. When we receive this kind of love, we have to make sure that we keep it locked safe inside our hearts, where no one can touch it, because it is the one thing that belongs to us and us alone."

I try to understand what the old man is saying. Does this mean I haven't lost my family's love? "But what if we have done horrible things and have pushed them away? Or hurt them?" I ask, wanting to hear more.

"Sometimes in life," he continues, "whether with good or bad intentions, we commit acts that we later regret. They are actions that will require forgiveness from others, from ourselves and, most importantly, God. If you are truly remorseful, God will forgive you. God is most merciful and most compassionate. To know that God can forgive us makes it easier to forgive ourselves. And if we are lucky, our loved ones will forgive us too. But we have to mean it, and we have to prove our sincerity."

"But what if they are already dead?" I feel a lump in my throat as I think about the day that I lay on the floor faking death, unable to help my family as they were massacred around me. All I could think about was my own survival. A trait I can't seem to let go of.

"You can still talk to them in your prayers," the mullah says, without hesitation. "It helps to cleanse your soul."

I have tried talking to them in my dreams, but the words always get stuck in my throat. I feel more and more unworthy as the days and years pass.

I clear my throat and shake these thoughts out of my head. I look at him and realize this man is tricking me. He's fooling me into forgetting about my cousin and his sins. It won't work. I won't be tricked!

"I need to find Sami. Do you know where he is?" I look at Mullah Sarwar as sternly as I can.

"Do you really want to find him with men like that by your side?" he asks, motioning his head in the direction of the motorbikes.

"I need to make sure he is punished and that other people learn from his sins!" I raise my voice. And I need to show my family that I am the good one. They will see. I know they will.

"What you want to do to your cousin and that poor girl will not make you a hero," the mullah says. "It will send you deeper into the darkness. It will make this another tragic story in our desolate country."

"You're wrong," I correct the old man. "It will make our country stronger and our people wiser. I'm helping them learn what's wrong and what's right." If my family doesn't see it now, one day they will, and they'll be proud of me again. "If you don't tell us where they are, I can't guarantee your safety or your family's." I feel powerful with my words, and a little dirty. At least it will make the old man respect me more. But his eyes don't show fear; they show pity.

"It is getting late," he responds. "Why don't you and your men stay at the *masjid* tonight? We can talk more in the morning and see if anything has changed." He looks away and lets out a breath.

"What? I said if you don't tell us where he is, these men may . . . they will . . . kill you," I say. This time it feels less powerful, more shameful. And I am scared that my words are not a threat but a reality.

"I heard what you said, my son." Mullah Sarwar doesn't even blink an eye. He seems as calm and gentle as before. And for once, he stops flicking his beads and looks at me. "I understand you are very angry. But you should know that your rage is not because of Sami or that poor girl. The anger is a part of the darkness you are holding inside yourself. It's a darkness you must let go. No one can fix your heart but you. Not the men out there and not even your family. If you don't fix it, your suffering will only increase as your sins grow in number." I find myself staring at him, taking in all he has just said.

"I . . ." I try to speak, but I don't know what to say. I continue to stare at him, but thoughts of the little girl dying this morning fill my head. Her family's wails fill my ears again. My anger toward my cousin led to that. Even if it wasn't these hands that twisted her neck, I am still responsible for her death. Her murder. It was me. I am the killer. I am the sinner.

"What's going on?" Latif's voice breaks through my thoughts. "We've been waiting so long the sky has turned black!" He walks in with his dusty boots, leaving prints on the lime-colored carpet. He points his finger at Mullah Sarwar. "Does he know where they are?"

"I . . . uh . . . no. He doesn't know," I finally say, trying to protect the mullah from any more trouble. I've done enough harm to him by bringing these men here.

"Then what has taken so long?" Latif sputters out with increased agitation. He turns to the mullah. "Old man, do you know where the two lovers are?"

"Even if I did, I wouldn't tell you," Mullah Sarwar says. I turn my head and stare at him in shock. What is he doing? Latif is crazy. He doesn't take well to being spoken to like that.

"Oh . . . really? Is that true?" Latif comes closer. "So you do know, or you don't know? It's better for you to tell me." He pulls out his handgun and starts to wave it around near his waist.

"He doesn't know." I get up and turn to Latif. "Let's just go. I have another idea of where they may be." I attempt to walk out, in hopes that he will follow me.

"I want to talk to this old man a little bit longer," Latif says and swings his gun, slapping me in the face. The pressure throws me to the ground again.

"What are you doing?" Mullah Sarwar yells at Latif as he rushes to me. "Are you okay, my son?" he asks. I nod.

"This is so cute! The old man cares about you," Latif says mockingly. "But does he care about his own life?" The look of the devil is back on Latif's face. The same demented eyes from this morning. He takes his gun and hits Mullah Sarwar in the face, making him fall to the ground. I can see blood dripping from the mullah's mouth. In the gush of red, there is a white chip that looks like a tooth. Latif grabs Mullah Sarwar by his long white hair, exposing his blood-soaked beard. The crimson color looks almost electric against the white hairs. "Tell me where they are!" Latif spits those words in the mullah's face, but he doesn't answer. Instead, he starts reciting a prayer from the Quran-e-sharif:

> In the name of God, the most Gracious and most Merciful.
> Praise be to God, Lord of all the worlds.
> The Compassionate, the Merciful. Ruler on the Day of Reckoning.
> You alone do we worship, and You alone do we ask for help.
> Guide us on the straight path, the path of those who have received your grace;
> not the path of those who have brought down wrath, nor of those who wander astray.
> Amen.

Latif stares at the mullah, who recites more prayers. "Answer me!" he yells over the mullah's words. "I said answer me!" He looks more enraged as he pulls on the mullah's hair. Mullah Sarwar does not flinch. He seems to be in a trance with his recitation.

There isn't a trace of fear on his bloodied face. I swear I can see him smiling as he continues to recite and Latif continues to yell and pull on his hair. Latif looks confused and unsettled by the praying. Probably because he is seeing a real mullah pray, not a fake like himself. And then it happens. Latif points his gun at the mullah's chest and fires. Blood and flesh splatter on my face, but I can't close my eyes. Mullah Sarwar's body falls onto the floor. I look up, and Latif is staring at the twitching body, his gun still pointing in the direction the shot was fired. Even he seems startled by what has just happened.

My ears are ringing, but I can still hear thumping noises rolling their way into the *masjid*. Latif's men all make their way in. Many stop as soon as they see the body on the floor. Latif regains his composure in their presence.

"Hang his body outside." I can barely make out the words coming from Latif's mouth. "And place a paper in his pocket with the word *traitor*."

But it feels like I have been the traitor, not Sarwar.

Twenty-five

SAMIULLAH

We've been sitting here in silence for hours, except for occasional questions: How are you? Are you cold? Are you hungry? Mullah Sarwar's grandson Walid rushed us away from their home after the thugs approached the *masjid*. He brought us with supplies and dropped us off in a cave far from town.

"I'll come for you when my grandfather thinks it is safe," Walid said before leaving.

I wanted to be honest with Fatima, so I told her about the men on motorbikes that Walid saw. But my candor may have just frightened her into silence. I am sure she is regretting it all. Leaving with me. Marrying me. Risking her life with me. I can't believe how stupid I was to put her in this position. She may die now, and it will all be my fault!

"I'm sorry." I have finally mustered the courage to say it out loud instead of repeating it over and over inside my head.

"What?" She looks up from where she is crouched against the dingy stone wall.

"I said, I'm sorry..." I can't even look her in the eyes. She's my wife now, and I can't even look at her. I'm afraid of seeing the trust in her eyes. I feel I have betrayed her already. "I shouldn't have . . . I shouldn't have asked you to meet me that day in the woods. Or to spend the afternoon with me at the river. I was wrong. And now we're here, in a dark cold cave, away from your loved ones. I'm sorry."

Fatima doesn't answer me. But I can hear her whimpers. I finally look up again and see her in tears. I want to console her, but I hesitate. I am afraid to touch her. I know the wounds on her arms haven't healed yet, and I don't know if she would want my hands on her.

"Sami, you saved me," she says through her tears. "My family wanted to give me away to get rid of their problem. They didn't want me anymore." She drops her head and starts her quiet sobs again.

"But I put you in that position." I feel as defeated as ever. I hate that I've brought her to this. I've brought on this sorrow. "If I hadn't asked your father in town . . . If I hadn't embarrassed him . . . If . . ."

"Why did you ask him?" Fatima looks up at me with her tear-streaked face. She looks curious, not angry. "What made you ask then and there?" Her voice trembles, and it breaks my heart over again.

"I didn't want to do it like that. I wanted to wait and make it proper. I'm so sorry. But that's when Rashid exposed our meetings and gave me no choice."

She nods, and then looks as if she's thinking about something. "Do you remember the day we ran from Latif's men?" she asks as she rubs her forehead. I let her continue. "I thought one of the voices sounded familiar." She stops. She looks up and then back at me. "You don't think that . . . No, I must be wrong. Rashid wouldn't associate himself with those thugs." Fatima shakes her head, finding the idea unimaginable. But I know it's possible.

Rashid changed so much because of that horrible *madrassa*. Could he have sent Latif's men to Mullah Sarwar in order to find us? Could those be the men who approached the *masjid,* forcing Fatima and me to hide in a cave?

"Sami?" Fatima breaks my train of thought. "It wasn't his voice that I heard, right?"

I pause before I answer. Even though he has betrayed us, he's still my cousin, and I need Fatima to understand.

I can't hide this from her. She needs to know. We are in this together.

"Fatima, a lot has changed because of that godforsaken *madrassa*. It wasn't what we were expecting. It wasn't the same type of school my father went to," I say.

She stares at me, confused. "But what do you mean? I thought you were learning more about the Quran-e-sharif and Islam?"

"That's what my father thought too, when he sent Rashid and me there," I answer. "But what they tried to teach us is nothing like what we were taught growing up." I pick up a rock, examining it before rolling it on the ground to the opening of the cave. I've known since our conversation in the woods that I would have to explain the darkness of that school to her eventually. "At first it was all so new and fascinating. Although I was sad and scared to be away from my family, I thought that it would be fun to live with Rashid and a bunch of other boys. We'd bathe in the nearby river, run around the fields and be like brothers. And most important, I'd learn more about Islam, and I'd come back home, and everyone would respect me. They would call me Qari Saib because I'd be one of the only people in the village who knew how to recite the holy book and knew the meaning behind the words. Even though Rashid was there too, I was arrogant enough to think that I would do better than he would because I was always the more obedient one." I feel ashamed to admit this, but I continue. "People would come to me to help them solve their problems. They'd come to our home. I imagined how proud my parents would be. I know it was their dream too. And I thought I could impress people, including you." I want to look up at her, but I am afraid to see her reaction. "To be honest, I'm embarrassed by the fact that I fell for it."

"Fell for what?" she asks. The only other person I've shared the true story with is Mullah Sarwar. It's hard for me to talk about. It makes me feel like a lesser person every time I think of those days.

"I thought they were right," I finally say. "I thought what they were teaching me was real Islam. They made everything and everyone I ever knew seem so simple and stupid. 'We are right—they are wrong.' That's what we were told, and that's how I felt. When I was there, I was brainwashed. I was taught to hate more than I was taught to love. I had the fear of God flowing through my veins. But I also had the arrogance of the devil overtake my soul."

I pick up a ball of dirt, breaking it into little pieces and turning it to dust before I speak again.

"I believed them. I would pray and I would recite the Holy Quran every day. We were forbidden to bathe in the river; we were forbidden to play in the fields. We were told not to communicate with any other children in town who weren't students at the *madrassa* because they were going to tempt us with their devilish behavior and sinful ways. I obeyed all their rules, and I was still lashed if I mispronounced even one word in a recitation. So I tried even harder. But the lashes kept coming."

"Lashes?" Fatima whispers.

I turn my back to her and pull up my *payron,* exposing my skin and scars.

"Sami . . . ," she says, looking at the same scars I sometimes spend hours staring at with mirrors. Protruding flesh I can't help but touch at night; they feel like swollen snakes curling up, down and around my back—some are still red, the freshest wounds. Others are white lines, older wounds that mark my first days at the school—scars that have healed but will never go away. If I am so disgusted by them, I can only imagine what Fatima is thinking right now.

I hear her sandals crunching on the ground, coming toward me, and I drop my *payron* back down. I turn around, and she is next to me with watery eyes.

"I'm sorry," I say, averting my gaze, "I shouldn't have pulled up my shirt. That was disrespectful, and I apologize."

"Sami, I'm the one who's sorry," she says. "I had no idea. What they did to you is awful!"

"But I deserved it. And I deserved more," I say, feeling angry again. I am not worthy of her sympathy, or anyone's sympathy.

"Why would you say you deserve that?" She points at my now-covered body. "Nobody deserves that!"

"I can say that because I did worse," I say, walking away from her. I can't believe I'm telling her about the most despicable part of me but I can't keep it a secret from her. Not anymore. I take a deep breath and continue. "A few of us would head to town in the morning to buy bread from the bakery. There was a boy from town named Sardar. He would always say hi to us and try to start a conversation. He had to have been my age, maybe a little younger. Sardar would follow us to town and ask us to play, and we would just ignore him. I still don't know if we were all being obedient, or if we were afraid that someone else in the group would tell the headmaster on us. We all knew the consequences of playing with him, and it wasn't worth it. But every morning he tried. He had bright red cheeks, covered with a layer of dirt and cracked by the sun. His smile was so kind." I catch myself smiling and quickly wipe it away.

I notice Fatima try to take a step forward, but she stops herself. I wonder if she is regretting that she married me. But I continue. I must tell her everything.

"Sometimes he'd bring a toy and try to persuade us to play with him. I remember the temptation on the days he'd bring his soccer ball, kicking it in our direction. I eventually got fed up and yelled at him. I was full of rage, thinking he was one of the devil's tempters, just like the teachers said, trying to distract us from the way of the righteous. I remember screaming at him, 'Leave us alone! We will never play with you. We are students of God, and we don't play with stupid village boys!' I told him he wasn't worthy of our time. The worst part is that I actually believed what I was saying. Those words made me feel such pride."

I hang my head, hoping to hide my face from Fatima. I can't bear to have her see the shame I know is there.

"The next day, we didn't see Sardar on the way to get bread. I felt guilty, but ignored it. We bought the bread, brought it back, had breakfast and began our lessons—like any other day. Later that morning, as we were preparing for lunch, I noticed a group of boys huddled and spying on something. Some were giggling, and others were silent. My curiosity got the best of me, and I went over to join them. That's when I saw him. Through the dried brush field, between the shrub the boys were hiding behind and the headmaster's office window, I saw Sardar. He was bent over crying with his pants around his ankles and the headmaster behind him."

"What do you mean?" Fatima asks. I look up and meet her eyes. She covers her mouth with her hands and takes a step back. And I know she knows.

"I found out later that Sardar came by the *madrassa* to ask the headmaster if he could join us," I say, my vision blurring from the tears that have filled my eyes. "It's because of me that he came, and because of me, he left no longer that boy with a kind smile."

Fatima comes closer and sits next to me. She takes hold of my hand without saying a word. I squeeze it gently, grateful to have her here. It's comforting to feel her so close to me. I touch her hand against my cheek. When I look at her, I find her staring back at me. My heart races, and my body stiffens. Her pink lips look so perfect, and her eyes are so comforting. I take a deep breath. I've never done this before, though I have dreamed of it many times. But now she's my wife. Now it's okay. I lean my face slowly toward hers. When I see she's not pulling away, I get closer. Gently pressing my lips against hers, I taste her sweetness. The sensation sends ripples through my body. It is even more wonderful than I'd imagined it would be. I don't want to stop kissing her, but I know I have to, or I might lose all control. As I slowly pull away, I notice Fatima's deep breaths. I wonder if she's feeling what I'm feeling.

"I really love you," I say to her.

"I love you too," she says her face flushing as she smiles that shy smile I can't live without.

I wrap my arms around her and bring her toward me. She lies nestled against my chest, and we stay like that, silent, for some time.

Fatima finally looks up at me and breaks our silence. "Why didn't Rashid leave when you did?"

"I asked him to, but he refused," I answer. "He changed at that school. He let pride take over. He was no longer the Rashid we grew up with."

I hesitate for a moment before telling Fatima that I think Rashid is after us with Latif's men.

"You think he's changed that much?" she asks. All I can do is stare into her frightened brown eyes. "If they find us, they'll kill us! How can Rashid do this? We were all friends. Why is everyone changing! Why is everyone so horrible!" She starts sobbing again.

I hold her tight before getting up and making my way to the supplies Walid left for us. I find a box of dates, some water and a blanket. I put the water under my arms and open the paper box holding the dates and bring it to Fatima. "Here, have some."

"No, thank you. I'm not hungry." She sniffles, trying to stop her tears.

I place the bottle on the ground and sit back down next to her. I open the blanket and cover both of our bodies with it. She stops crying and just looks at me.

"You should eat something," I tell her. "We need our strength." I grab the biggest date in the container and bring it up to her lips. Fatima opens her mouth and takes a bite. I take a bite from the same date and pull out the seed before letting her finish it. "Good job. Tastes delicious, doesn't it?" She nods. "See? You are already a good wife listening to your husband," I say with a light laugh. Fatima gently slaps my shoulder, smiling. And that's when I see her again. My Fatima. My playful, happy Fatima.

We eat more dates and drink some of the water. But the dates don't help warm us up in the cold night in the grim stone cave that seems to trap icy air. I would give anything for a hot glass of green tea to help keep us comfortable. I wrap the blanket around our bodies and put an arm around Fatima's shoulder to bring her closer. We can be each other's glass of warm tea. She puts her head on my chest, sending my pulse racing again. The pounding of my heart warms my body in seconds. And after a few minutes, her shivering stops and she falls asleep. I lean my cheek on top of her head. I still can't believe I am here with her as my wife. No matter what is out there, in this moment, I feel like I am in heaven.

Twenty-six

FATIMA

The morning sun rises over the mountains shooting its light into the cave. The brightness hits my eyes, waking me. My head is still on Sami's chest; it feels so hard and warm. I look up and see that he's still sleeping. His perfect lips are slightly parted, letting out small breaths that create a cloudy mist when they mix with the cold air inside the cave. I can hear the thumping of his heart. I close my eyes and take in the perfect rhythm.

Dum-dum ... dum-dum ... dum-dum ...

It's one of the most beautiful sounds I have ever heard. I can't believe I am here in Sami's arms as his wife. For a moment, I allow myself to forget that we are in a cave, in the middle of nowhere and on the run. For now the fears and doubts from yesterday have disappeared, and I thank God for letting me be here, listening to the drumming of his heart. I feel comfortable knowing that Mullah Sarwar married us by the hands of God. I'm grateful to him for confirming that our feelings are not wrong, for making me cherish the memory of last night's kiss. I feel my heart flutter, recalling Sami's lips on mine. I'm happy, so happy right now, knowing that he is my husband and not Karim.

"Fatima, are you awake?" Sami whispers.

I look up at him and realize I have been grinning this entire time. But I am no longer shy about my joy in having him near. So I keep smiling. "Yes, I'm awake." Sami beams back at me and brings me in even closer with a gentle hug.

"Good morning, *azizam,*" he says and kisses the top of my head. We sit in silence for a while longer, enjoying the moment. "Are you hungry?"

"Yes," I say, feeling the emptiness in my stomach. I would have said no to keep us in this position just a bit longer, if it weren't for the fear that my stomach would start making noises soon, mortifying me in front of him.

Sami gets up and tucks the blanket completely around me before walking toward the supplies Walid left for us, rubbing his hands to keep warm. He unwraps a sheet and pulls out some bread and two oranges.

We feast on the fruit, bread and some dates. The temperature in the cave is still chilly but becomes bearable as the sun continues to rise.

"Looks like we need more water," Sami says, turning over the empty plastic bottle. "I can go out and search for some."

"No, don't go. It's too dangerous. What if someone sees you?" I'm frightened at the thought of being alone in this desolate cave.

"I won't be long, I promise," he says. "I think I saw a small spring not too far from here when we came. And I need to get us some branches or dried grass to burn if we are here another night. I don't want you freezing to death. We have a new life to begin together." He smiles and grazes my face with his warm hand, making it tingle.

"But I thought Walid would come get us today," I say.

"Hopefully he will. But we can't be sure. If they're being watched, they'll wait," he says. Yesterday's worries begin creeping back. "Don't worry. We'll be fine. I'll take care of you." His smile makes me feel at ease again. "Try to rest some more. I'll be quick." Sami picks up my hand and kisses it before looking back at me with his crooked smile. My heart races. I can't believe he is truly my husband. He reaches the opening of the cave and turns to look at me again. "*Dostit darom*," he says, before running off.

"I love you too," I say, knowing he is already gone. "I love you too!" I scream it this time, and I cannot stop grinning.

I'm not able to get back to sleep after hearing Sami's words again. I knew he cared for me. And deep down, I knew he loved me. But now that he's said it, it feels like so much more. I've smiled so much with memories of last night and this morning that my face is beginning to feel sore. But I don't care. After all the pain of the last few days, it's so good to feel joy again. The dark clouds have parted, and hope is shining through. Even though I'll miss my family, I know I have Sami, and that makes everything okay.

To pass time, I get up and shake the blanket, trying to get the dirt from the cave floor off of it before folding it up and taking it to the box Walid left for us. He tied as much as he could to the back of our bicycle before walking us here. A walk that took us at least two hours in the early evening; the only glow lighting our way was the star-sprinkled sky.

I look in the sheet Sami opened earlier and find more bread and fruit—apples, oranges and some bananas. I tie the embroidered white fabric tight, protecting the food from the dirt. I open the box and find matches, a knife and some papers. I put the food into the plastic box and close the lid, placing the blanket on the seat of the bicycle.

I walk to the opening of the cave to see if Sami is nearby. I step out and look at the beautiful landscape of mountains. From here, it looks like there is no end to the stunning hills painted by God in the most striking colors. Some are light brown, dried from the sun's rays. Others are green with the grass that grows from rich black soil. And some are a rustic red, like the feather of a rooster. Seeing the rocky peaks reminds me of a joke my father once told me: "While God was making the world, he carefully placed his rocks in different countries. Giving everyone the perfect amount. Then he dropped what was left over in Afghanistan." I always smiled when he told us that joke, but now it makes my heart sink, reminding me of how much I miss him. The sadness that overcomes me makes it difficult to enjoy the beauty anymore. I take one last look around for Sami, but I don't see him.

I walk back into the cave and try to make myself think of something, anything else to get my mind off of my family. The family I shamed. The family I left behind. I see a small stone and pick it up. I scratch it on the surface of the cave wall and see that it leaves a white mark. So I decide to write out the alphabet and practice my schooling. If Sami and I can get to Kabul, perhaps I can go to the schools there after all.

I scrape the stone on the hard wall and write the letters one by one.

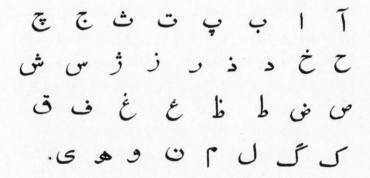

I make it through the entire alphabet, and I am very pleased with what I have done. I take the plastic box and put the blanket on top, making myself a cushioned seat. I decide to read the letters over and over, and configure them into words.

As I keep reciting the words, I hear the crunching of footsteps approaching the cave. Sami is back! I don't want to look silly, so I keep studying. I know Sami isn't like one of those men Zohra was talking about; he's happy that his wife can read. The footsteps multiply as he gets closer. I freeze. It's more than one pair of feet making the noise. I hear voices now too. The voices of men. I scramble, looking for my *chadari*. I finally spot it behind the box and quickly drape it over my head so it covers my body. I run to the farthest end of the cave, taking the box with me. I position myself where the bicycle is leaning against the wall.

Why would Sami bring people back with him? Is he okay? Was he spotted? Could it be Walid or someone else that Mullah Sarwar has sent? My heart races with fear. This isolated cave suddenly feels as exposed as our village homes. I rummage through the box, pull out the knife and clench the cold steel handle in my fist.

Through the small pinholes in the blue covering, I see the men approaching. I can't make out their faces as their shadowy figures now block the opening. I search for Sami in the group, but I can't see if he is with them. Instead, I see men carrying long weapons. And the fear I so easily let go of this morning comes flooding back, engulfing me.

Where is Sami?

Will I die here alone without him?

Twenty-seven

SAMIULLAH

I use my thumbnail to cut the last flower and add it to the pile I've stacked on the ground. The purple and white wildflowers strewn throughout the valley look like a drawing, but they are not as striking as Fatima. Knowing that she's my wife now, that I'll have her with me for the rest of my life, makes me happier than I have ever been. I hope these flowers are nice enough to make her smile.

It's the least I can do after ripping her away from her family. My grin fades when I think of how disappointed I am in my father for not siding with me on this. I had thought he was better than that. If he had accepted us together, he could have made Mohammad Aaka agree to it. Fatima's father is a good man—I know he would have come around if my father had.

I shake my head. That's our past life. It's not worth thinking about anymore.

I pick up the flowers from the ground, adding them to my latest bundle and breathe deeply. The scent is intoxicating. It smells like my childhood, like running around in the fields with Fatima. I hope she thinks so too. I mix in the dried weeds I found to burn if it gets too cold later. I haven't been able to find any wood in this rock-strewn terrain, so the weeds will have to do. I use my free hand to grab the bottle I filled with water from the spring and start walking back.

As I approach the valley where our cave is, I see a green pickup truck parked down the hill from our hiding area and start to panic. I sprint closer, but don't see anyone. The writing on the side says POLICE. I peer inside the dusty window and see empty leather seats. I take a look in the bed of the truck and see more seats. I swing my head in every direction, trying to get a better look at the hills and mountains to see where the police from this vehicle have gone. But the valley is as empty as it was when I left, except for the truck. I can hear my heart racing as I look up at the cave. Have they found her?

I begin to run, sliding on the gravel, kicking up dirt and pebbles. I catch myself from falling and use my hand to push up and forward into a fast sprint. *God, please let her be okay! Please don't let them have seen her.* Strange men finding a woman alone can only bring trouble here. It doesn't matter that it's the police. It's often worse when it's them! My mind races with stories of policemen who have raped women and children in various parts of the country, using their authority as impunity from law and morals. I read about them in the papers when I was in the *madrassa*. And I was told by our religious teachers to never trust the government. That's the one thing I learned there that I held on to. I feel sick to my stomach and run faster than I have ever run before.

I get to the entrance to the cave out of breath but full of force. It takes a moment for my eyes to adjust from the brightness outside to the shadows of the cave.

"*Asalaam aleykum.*" I hear a man's voice. My eyes focus, and I see two men sitting next to the wall. The same wall Fatima and I slept against last night. I dart my eyes to the other side and see Fatima wearing the blue *chadari*. I run to her.

"Are you okay?" I ask. Fatima nods, but I can tell, even through the blue fabric, she is shaking. "Everything will be all right." I reassure her, but I don't know if I'm lying.

"*Wah wa!* What beautiful flowers he has brought for you," the man says. I dart my head back at him and notice the officer to his right laugh, as he keeps his perverse eyes on Fatima. "You are a very lucky woman!"

"Who are you?" I ask with annoyance.

"Isn't it obvious?" the chubby officer on the left says as he puts a half-eaten date back into its box. He puts his hand to his green hat, tipping down and then back up. "We are the police. But the real question is, who are *you*?" He pops the date into his mustache-covered mouth and tosses the box to the side.

"My wife and I are just passing through," I quickly respond, glancing at Fatima. "And I don't appreciate strange men walking into our place of rest while I'm not here." I look back at him, eyeing him with contempt.

"Calm down, my dear brother. We are not here to bother you or our sister," he says, gesturing at Fatima. I adjust my body to block her from their unfamiliar eyes. "We've patiently been waiting here for you. Your wife hasn't said much to us, but she did let us know that you would be coming back. We didn't mean to offend you." The officer wipes his mouth and then nose with the back of his hand. "We're the police, not your enemy. There has been a murder in a nearby village, and we've been searching the area for the killer. I'm sure you had nothing to do with it, but we wouldn't be doing our jobs if we didn't ask you some questions, right?"

I nod my head at him but can't stop looking at the thinner one, who is staring at Fatima with snake eyes. They look bloodshot and dazed, like the men in town who smoke hashish from morning to night. And the only thing I see in them is deviance.

The officer who has been talking to me notices that I'm no longer looking at him and turns to his colleague. He slaps him on the back of the head. "*Boro berun, Fahim!*" he yells, telling the degenerate to leave. "Wait at the car until we are done!"

The stumbling officer can't be more than a few years older than me. His hat falls off during his tottering, revealing disheveled, greasy hair.

"*Ahmaq!*" His superior curses at him as he picks the cap up and exits the cave. "I'm sorry for his behavior."

"*Tashakur,*" I manage to say to the officer with the thick, bristly mustache.

"There is no need to thank me. I'm sorry," he says again, looking genuinely embarrassed. "They send me these useless recruits, and I try to train them, but it's hard to teach a man like that." He lets out a sigh. "My name is Commander Ahmadi."

"I am Samiullah," I respond. "Can you please ask your questions and leave us?" I have no choice but to be abrupt. These men obviously do not care that they have invaded my wife's privacy.

"Yes, yes," Commander Ahmadi says. "Where were you yesterday?"

"We were traveling from our village and stopped here for the night. We were going to leave soon," I say.

"So you didn't pass through the nearby villages?" he asks, raising a furry eyebrow that perfectly matches his mustache.

"Yes, we passed a few, but we couldn't tell one from another," I lie. "Who has been killed?"

"A mullah. His name was Mullah Sarwar," he says, making my heart rise up to my throat. The commander fixes his eyes on mine, and I try my best to stay composed.

"How did this mullah die?" I ask, averting my eyes from Commander Ahmadi's.

"He was shot and then hung." I feel my stomach clench

with nausea. "They put a paper in his pocket with the word *traitor* written on it." The commander shakes his head.

It had to be Latif and his men. Men who include my cousin Rashid now. They killed the mullah because of us . . . I fight down the bile threatening to rise in my throat.

"It's a shame. The mullah was a good man. I knew him. Looks like this was the work of criminals. We don't think it is the Taliban. Even the Taliban liked Mullah Sarwar—well . . . for the most part. We are still investigating."

I hear Fatima sniffle. A noise that doesn't go unnoticed by the commander.

"Did you know him?" He looks at Fatima and then at me.

"No. We're from a faraway village," I lie again and pray God will forgive me. We can't afford to be held up any longer. They found Mullah Sarwar and killed him for helping us. If those bastards can kill him, they will definitely kill us too. I can't let Fatima die. I won't let her die.

Fatima sniffles again.

"Are you sure you didn't know him?" the commander asks, looking back and forth at the two of us. Thank God the blue cover is hiding Fatima's sadness. For the first time, I wish I had a *chadari* so I didn't have to mask mine.

"We did not know him," I say, looking him in the eye. "I'm sorry, my wife is quite sick, and we need to leave soon to try and find her a decent hospital. Are you finished here?"

"Forgive me, I didn't know she was sick," he says. "She's barely spoken since we arrived. Where do you need to go?"

"We are heading to the big city to find a good hospital." I stand up in an attempt to get him to stand as well. And he does.

"We can take you to the provincial capital, if you'd like," he says, looking at Fatima and me. "We figure the killer has left the area or is hiding in villages we won't be able to enter because they are under control of the enemy." He puts his head down in shame.

If we did go with him, it would make our journey much faster. My plan was to get to Kabul, but any big city would be better than staying here. I don't think Walid will be coming back for us any time soon, and we can't risk being captured by the same criminals who killed Mullah Sarwar. I feel my heart aching again, thinking of his death. Shot and then hung. These are sick people. But then I remember that drugged-up officer with twisted eyes who is with Commander Ahmadi. His sinister stares are enough to make my decision for me. I don't want him anywhere near Fatima.

"We're fine, thank you," I finally say.

"Okay, if that is what you want. But be careful out there." Commander Ahmadi winks at me and then puts a hand over his heart. "Thank you for the delicious dates. *Khuda hafiz.*"

"Good-bye," I say, putting my hand over my heart as well.

I walk him to the end of the cave and watch him as he

starts down the hill. I make sure he is far enough away before running over to Fatima.

"Are you okay?" I ask as I lift up her *chadari*. I see her tearstained face. She's gripping tightly on to the knife from the plastic box Walid left us. "Fatima, it's okay now."

"I . . . I . . . didn't speak . . . My accent . . . They will know . . . I'm Hazara, you're Pashtun," she manages to say, through more tears. "Mullah . . . Sarwar . . . was killed." Her wet eyes look as big as I've ever seen them as she stares at me, still frightened. I loosen her grip on the knife, throwing it to the dirt floor. I pull her close for a hug, and her arms wrap around my back, pressing me in. I kiss the top of her head.

"I know. I'm sorry," I say feeling a tear fall from my eye and roll down the side of my face. I feel the guilt taking over. Even if I wasn't the one who pulled the trigger, I am Mullah Sarwar's murderer. It is because of me he died and because of me that his family will suffer.

"I love you," I whisper as I kiss Fatima's head again, trying to comfort her.

"I love you too," she says through her whimpers. And as much as my heart is breaking right now, her words seem to help.

Twenty-eight
RASHID

We are eating our kabobs in Latif's villa, but I can barely take a bite without thinking of the trail of blood and turmoil we left behind. I'm disgusted, but I can't show it. I'm afraid that if I do, I'll be next or my family will pay the price . . . again. The same family I have already betrayed and left behind to be here with these heathens. I don't know how God will ever forgive me. I pray he never forgives them.

"Here." Zaman passes me some bread. "You have to eat more, or they'll know that you're weak."

"I'm not weak," I say, grabbing the bread.

"To them," he says, looking up, "being different is weak. You must act as though none of this has bothered you."

"He killed a mullah last night, and now he's here laughing like nothing happened," I say, holding in my true fury. I look up and see Latif joking with one of the other men, who is basking in the attention. The sight adds fuel to my rage. I don't even know why I'm so angry. I just met Mullah Sarwar. I threatened him myself. But the old man had made me believe I could be absolved of my sins. That I could be forgiven by my living family, by my dead family and, most important, by God.

"No—he's there laughing like it did happen. He's proud," Zaman says, ripping into a piece of bread. "This has just made him mightier. He killed a mullah. A mullah he will say was teaching heresy."

Latif catches my eye and walks over to sit down in front of us. "How is your lunch?"

"It's delicious," I say, faking a smile.

"Juicy meat," Zaman adds as he continues to chew.

"Good," Latif says, looking around. "We should stay in the villa today and head back out tomorrow. I got a call saying they've sent police around in different parts of the province to look for that mullah's killer. They won't dare send anyone here—they're too scared." He grunts.

"Okay," I say, taking a bite in order to prevent any further conversation. I'm worried the words that will come out won't be to his liking. Latif starts picking at my kabob with his grimy hands until he finds a perfect, juicy square of lamb with traces of tender fat. He pops it into his mouth and starts chomping like a cow. He smiles at me, exposing his crooked, turmeric-colored teeth. I can see strings of meat stuck in between them.

"Killing a baby and an old man all in one day—I can't say it's my first time." His snicker makes my body tighten in anger.

"Snapping that little girl's neck was as easy as snapping a little chicken's." Sick son of a bitch.

"Latif! Latif!" One of the men runs to him. It's Fawad, a barrel-bellied mess whom I would consider amusing if the circumstances weren't so atrocious.

"What!" Latif rolls his eyes as he continues to gnaw on my kabob.

"I got a call from my brother." Fawad makes it to Latif's side. His scurry has left him out of breath. He rests his hand on the table, pushing it downward and lifting our end into the air. Both Zaman and I swiftly shove the plastic board down to keep it from flipping.

"You fat-assed fool!" Latif barks at him. "Be careful!"

"I'm so sorry, Commander!" Fawad straightens up, still taking deep breaths. "But I got a call from my brother. The officer. They have been on patrol all day, and he thinks he saw the boy and the girl." Fawad pauses to smile, obviously proud of the news he has just given Latif. "He was searching with his captain and found a young couple hiding in a cave not far from the village we were in yesterday."

Could this be true? Has he found Sami and Fatima? But why would they be so close? Why didn't the idiots keep traveling? They had so much time. Now they're bound to be caught by Latif! Sami, you fool!

"What?" Latif gets up from his chair. "What else did he say?"

"Fahim told me that it was a Pashtun boy, wearing a light-colored *payron tombon* and a *pakol,* and a girl covered in a *chadari* hiding in a cave. He couldn't figure out her accent because she didn't speak much. They had a bicycle and a little food," Fawad continues. "They managed to convince the captain that they were a married couple passing through, trying to find a hospital. And you won't believe it." Fawad smiles. "The boy was holding flowers when he walked into the cave."

Latif laughs. "Did you hear that, Rashid? Your cousin is a romantic!" He looks at me, and I force a smile. Sami used to pick flowers for Fatima and his mother when we were young. But how could he be so stupid, picking flowers now, when he should be running. Running from us.

"The police commander told them about the mullah's murder, but they said they didn't know him," Fawad says as his gluttonous eyes alight on our food.

"See!" Latif slaps his hand on the table and looks at me. "We were right. That old man did know where they were. Why else would they be hiding in a cave near *his* town?"

"Yes, you were right." It is all I can say to Latif as I try to figure out a way to stop us from finding them. As angry as I have been with my cousin, Mullah Sarwar's words have been running through my head since last night. And for the first time in a long time, everything makes sense to me:

Your rage is not because of Sami or that poor girl. The anger is a part of the darkness you are holding inside yourself. It's a darkness you must let go. No one can fix your heart but you. . . . If you don't fix it, your suffering will only increase as your sins grow in number.

I don't want my sins to grow any more than they have. My father told me as a child that my soul was as clean as a glistening white shirt, but even one small spot on that shirt could ruin the entire cloth. I had to work on being a righteous, moral and God-loving man to keep the outfit stainless. Right now, I feel as though I have soiled my soul with deep stains that may never come out. But I must try.

What my cousin did was wrong, but I don't think he should die for it. And as for Fatima, I can't expect forgiveness for what I have done to her. She must not even know that her little sister has been killed. I tried to make myself believe it was justified, but I can't pretend anymore. The guilt has been growing since last night and is festering in my soul. God must be so angry with me for using his name to rationalize murder—the way these thugs do. *God, please forgive me.*

I need absolution and will start by helping Sami and Fatima. Mullah Sarwar said it's possible, but I have to prove my sincerity. I'm ready to prove it now.

"I'll go and find them," I say to Latif.

He stares at me. "We'll *all* go."

"But isn't it risky?" I look at him and then Fawad. "You said yourself there are too many police in the province looking for criminals. Besides, I can trick them into coming back with me. They don't know I'm with you."

Latif stares at me with skepticism. "Why should I trust you?" he says. "You couldn't even get the old man to talk last night. You were too soft."

"I've learned from my mistakes. And you can trust me. I brought them to you," I say. "I can go ahead and give you a call if the routes are clear. I care about this more than anyone here!"

Latif contemplates my offer. "Fine," he agrees. "But you have to go with Fawad." The pudgy man droops at the mention of his name.

"He will slow me down." Fawad barely looks offended by my comment. In fact he seems pleased. "How about Zaman?" I offer before Latif can think of other options.

"Fine, but you must take only one motorbike," he says. "And keep calling with updates!"

"Whenever we can get service on our phones, we'll call," I say, feeling relieved as I look down at an annoyed Zaman.

"Give him your weapon," Latif says to Fawad, whose eyes bulge at the command. But he doesn't dare disobey; he takes the strap of his assault rifle off his shoulder and hands it to me. I strap it around my body so it hangs down my back.

"Let's go," I say to Zaman, who rolls his eyes before picking up his own rifle, still chewing on his last bite of kabob.

As Zaman and I load ourselves onto his motorbike, Latif yells out to us, "You better not kill them without me!" His menacing grin gives us another glimpse of his rotting teeth.

We enter a valley. This is the third that we have tried. Fat Fawad gave us a secondhand description of where his *charsy* brother found the pair hiding. He did warn us that his brother's description wasn't great because the drugs tended to cloud his memory, but this is ridiculous! What a useless bloodline. This valley is farther away from the main dirt road but still parallel in direction. As we enter, I can see the tracks of a truck—maybe the one that belonged to the police. I tap Zaman's shoulder and point up to a cave on our left.

Zaman stops the motorbike, and I jump off onto the gravel.

"You check, and I'll have a cigarette," Zaman says as he uses his foot to thrust the kickstand to the ground. "Shout if they're in there."

I climb the short hill up and make it to the cave. It's dark and empty inside. This is the fourth cave I've looked in. I'm about to turn around again when I see writing on the wall. I walk into the cave to look closer and step over a pile of wildflowers lying on the dirt floor. They have to be the flowers Sami gave to Fatima. They were here! I run out and look around the valley, but I don't see anyone except Zaman.

"Another empty one?" Zaman says, throwing his cigarette to the ground and pressing it into the earth with his boot.

I ignore his words as I run down the hill. My feet slide on

the gravel, but I don't fall. I look around for more clues and spot footprints in the dirt.

"What are you doing, *laywanay*?" Zaman says. I can't blame him for his words. I must actually look crazy right now.

"Get on fast," I say running back to him. "Go that way!" I point straight ahead. Zaman huffs and gets on the motorbike. I jump on behind him and hold on tight. "Hurry!"

He revs the engine, and we fly forward. At the edge of every mountain, I search through the passes for Sami or Fatima. But as we speed along, I don't see anything. Not even any birds. The place looks deserted.

But as we pass a towering mountain to the right, I notice a passage below. It's so narrow our motorbike wouldn't be able to squeeze through. If I were trying to hide, I would go that way.

I tap Zaman again and point back. He turns the motorbike sharply, leaning at such a steep angle I think we're both about to fall off before he straightens back up. We slow down as we make it to the opening. I jump off, peek inside and decide to climb through. There are bulky stones on the ground, making it difficult to walk in sandals. I slither and slide with each step. I notice an opening ahead. It looks like a patch of empty land entrapped by mountainous walls. I walk through, making my way into the clearing.

As soon as I step inside the opening, a creature pounces on me. It throws me to the ground, and I fear being gnawed to death. I start to fight, swinging my fists, when I realize it is not a wild beast. It's Sami.

"Sami! Sami!" I yell, but he keeps throwing punches. "It's me, Rashid!" He stops pounding his fist when he hears my name.

"Rashid?" he says as we lie there.

"Yes, it's me."

I notice him look up ahead. I follow his eyes and see her too, wearing a *chadari* to disguise herself. As I look back, Sami starts to strike at me again.

"Enough!" I say. "Stop! I'm not here to hurt you. I swear! So don't force me to!" Sami hesitantly stops his beating but is not letting down his guard. "I'm here to help you."

"Why should we believe you?" Sami says, getting off of me, but making sure he's standing between me and Fatima. I follow him up and wait for him to start slapping the dirt off his clothing, afraid if I look down, he will catch me defenseless again. We both start hitting our clothes but each keep our eyes on the other.

"I know I've given you no reason to believe me. But I'm telling the truth," I say. "I swear on the Holy Quran!" Sami is still eyeing me with suspicion. "Look, we don't have much time. You need my help. You'll die if you don't take it. And I can't let you both die because of me."

We hear noises coming from the narrow path. I put my finger to my lips to stop Sami from speaking. I peek through and see Zaman holding his rifle.

"Don't worry. Everything's fine," I say to Zaman, who keeps walking forward. I know the time has come when I have to tell him my true intentions and hope that he'll understand. I slowly start moving my rifle from my back to my side. I can feel Sami's eyes on me. I look at him and blink my eyes slowly in reassurance. "Really, everything is fine." I direct my words at Zaman.

"Then what were those noises?" he asks as he moves closer. When he finally makes it into the clearing, he sees Sami and lifts his rifle in that direction. Fatima screams at the sight, startling Zaman, who then turns his gun toward her.

"Put your weapon down," I say to Zaman. "They're unarmed."

"No! We've found them. Call it in," he says moving his gun side to side, aiming at both Fatima and Sami, who has already made his way to her and is trying to block her with his body.

"Please, don't kill my wife. She has done nothing wrong!" Sami screams. "Please! We've done nothing wrong. We're married now. We had a proper *nikah*. Please don't hurt her!" Sami's eyes fill with tears. I can't begin to make sense of all he just said as I try and focus on Zaman.

"Zaman, please."

He looks at me without moving his rifle. "But I thought you wanted them to be punished?" He eyes me. "Do you know what will happen to us if we don't phone Latif? I can't risk my family's safety because of this," Zaman says with fear in his voice.

"I know. I'm sorry I put you in this position. But we can figure something out," I plead as I move my hand as slowly and discreetly as possible to my firearm. "I wanted them to be punished," I say avoiding their eyes. "But not like this. They've been through enough. They don't need to die too."

Zaman pulls out his phone and starts dialing. I have to do it now. I quickly pick up my rifle and point it at him. But he continues to dial. I put my hand on the trigger and realize I've never used this rifle—or any weapon—before. But I must do it now, and I have to do it right.

"Stop!" I yell at Zaman, hoping he will put the phone down. If he does, I won't have to pull the trigger.

"Latif? *Salaam aleykum,*" he says, glaring at me. I twitch my finger, and I realize I don't have it in me. I can't take his life. I drop to my knees, put the rifle down and drown in my defeat. I look to the blue sky above and ask for God's forgiveness and for the forgiveness of the innocent souls I have infected with my poison. Tears rush down my face like rainfall from the sky.

I know I can't kill Zaman in cold blood, but now I am responsible for taking three more lives: Sami's, Fatima's and my own.

Twenty-nine
FATIMA

Through my *chadari*, I grab the back of Sami's *payron*, squeezing it. I don't know what else to do. Just knowing he's here brings me some comfort. And I know he loves me enough to protect me. I want to ask him to kill me before Latif's men can touch me. But that may be too much to ask. I could never kill him if he was the one asking. I'll have to kill myself.

I squeeze the steel handle of the knife in my hand and bring it closer to my body. I just need to know where to stab myself so I'll bleed out the fastest. Maybe my heart or stomach? I don't want to be alive for what comes next. Death is a better outcome than being taken by strange men who will rape me until my body is broken and mutilated. I've heard stories about Latif's men. They have no mercy. The blade is sharp enough to pierce through my flesh and rip apart my organs. I've decided I will dig it through my heart. It's a small organ but the most important.

"Stop!" Rashid yells at the man dialing the phone. I don't

understand why Rashid is helping us now, when he was the one who sent Latif's men after us in the first place.

"Latif? *Salaam aleykum*," the man says into the phone. Rashid drops to the ground.

I look at the black rifle lying next to him. That would be an even faster death. I wonder what would happen if I tried to grab it.

"Yes, yes," the man says to Latif. "No, the roads aren't clear. You shouldn't come yet. No, we haven't found them yet." The man's words surprise me. Sami seems bewildered too, as he moves even closer to me. "Yes, yes. We'll let you know if we notice anything. *Khuday pamon.*" He ends his conversation with eyes still on Rashid. Then he slides the phone back into his pocket and says, "You better come up with a plan fast!" Rashid looks at the man and then us. He seems to be in as much shock as we are.

"Thank you! Thank you, Zaman *worora*!" Rashid says with what sounds like relief. He then makes his way to us. "You have to trust me. We don't have time. Fatima, the provincial capital is only thirty minutes away. I can take you first. There is a place there I can drop you off that takes care of people. The mullah at the *madrassa* spoke badly about it because his wife went to them and they helped her divorce him and escape to Kabul." He turns his attention to Sami. "Then I'll come back and take you. They can then help you both get to Kabul. You can make a new life there." Rashid's eyes look possessed, but not in a sinister way. I still don't trust him. I can't. He's been spending time with Latif's animals, the same men who killed Mullah Sarwar. The same men who want to kill us. I push myself farther behind Sami.

"Just go back and say you never found us," Sami says, brushing him away. "We can find our own way."

"You don't understand," Rashid says desperately. "Latif has men everywhere! We found you because a police officer gave us your location. One of the ones who found you today." Could it be true? Why wouldn't they have just taken us? And I realize the young one on hashish must have been the spy. The captain probably had no idea. "But I can get you out now. And this office can help you get away from Latif and his men."

"Give us a minute," Sami says to Rashid, who nods and walks to Zaman. Sami turns around to look at me. Even through the blue cloth, I can see the concern in his eyes. He can't be thinking of following Rashid's plan.

All I can say to him is "No."

"But this could be our only chance," he says, his anxious eyes searching for mine through the fabric.

"What if this is a trap?" I say the words I know we're both thinking. His eyes are a deeper shade of green than I've ever seen before. And there's a tightness around them.

"I don't think it is," he says. "I believe my cousin regrets his actions."

"But I don't want to leave you," I say as my tears begin to fall and my throat becomes heavy.

"I know, but I need you to. And I swear I'll come for you," he says. "You trust me, don't you?" I nod my head, holding back my sobs. "Then go with Rashid."

"No." I start shaking. "No!"

"If you love me, with all of your heart—"

"I do!" I cut in before he can even finish.

"Then go," he says, forcing a shaky smile onto his face. His eyes are blinking rapidly; I know he's nervous.

I am flying through the streets on the back of Rashid's motorbike. As we ride, I keep seeing Sami's smile as he waved good-bye. I keep praying it's not the last time I will see his warm soft lips or his gentle green eyes. I can't stop crying, and I don't care what Rashid thinks of it. I hate holding on to another man, even if he is taking me to safety.

I don't notice we've arrived in the city until I hear car horns and motorbikes whizzing by. The city is even bigger than Mullah Sarwar's village. Every block we pass seems to hold hundreds more people. Our motorbike slows down, and I realize we've turned onto a side street. Rashid pulls up to a large building that is surrounded by tall cement walls and round wire at the top. A guard stops us at the gate.

"What business do you have here?" the guard asks.

"This is an emergency," Rashid says. "I'm here to drop off my sister-in-law. She's in danger. But I have to hurry and get my brother as well."

"Wait here," the guard says and goes back into his box. I can make little out through the holes of my *chadari*, but I can see him on a phone. He comes back and lifts the gate to allow us in. "Go over there for a security check." Rashid rides in and then helps me off the motorbike.

"That box seems to be the female check," he says. "I'll wait for you right here."

I feel vulnerable and alone as I become aware of my surroundings. The building ahead is bigger than anything I have ever seen before. There must be dozens of people inside, none of whom I'll know. But these strangers will help Sami and me? Why would they do that? I'm afraid of what is next and more than ever wish Sami were here. I lift the drape covering the entrance to the box Rashid pointed to, and I see a woman sitting inside. I hear noises from a radio. She puts down her glass of tea.

"*Salaam,* sister," she says. "Do you have a purse?" I shake my head. "Okay, then I'll just check your body. I'm sorry, but it's my job." I realize why she was apologetic after she slides her hand all over my body—from my head, down to my shoulders, around and under my breasts, on my butt, between my legs and down to my feet. The process is so violating, I'm even more frightened about this place. People don't do this in our villages. I don't know what kind of security check would allow a girl's body to be felt up by a strange woman. I realize I've started crying when the woman speaks again. "I'm sorry, *khwarak*, but I have to do this. It's my responsibility to protect the building from attackers. And lately people have been using *chadari*s to smuggle weapons and contraband into places. Especially places like this. You must be from a village, *neh*?" She pats me on the back and leads me out. "There, there. We're finished now. You're in good hands here."

When I walk out, Rashid is waiting. He must have had his check outside with the men sitting at the table in front of us. I'm thankful that mine at least was in private. We walk up some steps, and he stops right before we go into the door.

"Fatima?" he says. I turn and look at him. "I need to apologize to you." I continue to stare. I realize I haven't spoken to him at all today and feel a pang of guilt for being so cold toward him. "I wronged you and Sami. And I hurt your family." He begins to choke up. "You need to know something. And it's bad."

His words strike me like a knife hitting my gut. The look in his eyes tells me what I am about to hear will be terrible. Oh, God! Did he leave Sami to die out there?

"Sami?" I mutter.

"No. Sami will be fine. I promise," he says, and I let out a breath in relief. He hesitates for a moment before speaking again. "Latif... Latif... killed your little sister," Rashid blurts out. He continues to speak, but I don't hear anything after those words. Afifa? Afo? She's dead? She can't be dead. It's not possible.

"Liar!" I scream at him. "You're a liar!" I yell it louder and begin pounding my fist on his chest. "Liar! Liar! Liar!" I keep shouting and continue thrashing at his chest, hoping to hit his heart.

He doesn't stop my punches.

"I'm sorry. I'm so, so sorry," his voice cracks.

And that is when I know he's not lying. I drop to my knees on the concrete floor. "Afo..."

"Please forgive me," Rashid says through his own tears. "I didn't mean for that to happen. I didn't mean for it to go this far. I'm so sorry..."

"Afo..." I fall into a trance of memories. Helping my mother as she gave birth. My baby sister's smiling face. Her wobbly run. The way she jumped into my arms when I returned from Zohra's. The bangles around her little wrist. Her fiery-red hair on my fingers, the soft strands that I loved to stroke as she fell asleep looking like an angel. She's dead.

My *baba*! The pain he must be going through right now. Now he's lost Ali and Afifa. And me... His worst nightmare has come true.

Afifa's death also kills any of the dreams I had to ever go back. To ever seek their forgiveness and have them accept my choice. It was my choice that led to this. My choice has led to my sister's death.

"What can I do?" Rashid says through tears. "Please tell me, what I can do?"

I can't bring myself to look at him. I want him to leave. I want to see Sami.

"Bring Sami." These are the only words I can get out before my body is wracked with sobs.

Thirty

RASHID

As I whiz back through the mountains, I see the sun dropping. The orange orb is a ticking clock. I have to get to Sami, and I have to get there fast. My speed makes the motorbike jump every time I hit a rock, but I no longer fear falling. I've worked out the system and am feeling more confident in my riding. Maybe I can get Sami into the city in less time than it took me to drive Fatima.

But I have to get to him first.

I'm scared Zaman will change his mind and call Latif or that Latif will send someone to check on us. I can't take the chance of him catching us. I won't feel comfortable until I know Sami is in the city.

I turn the bike, ripping into the valley. And I can see them. Sami and Zaman are no longer hiding in the crevice. I'm almost there! I grip the throttle as tight as I can. The engine roars. As I get closer, I release the accelerator and hit the brake. I skid on the dusty pebble road, feeling the weight of the bike tipping. I come to a full stop, and the bike tumbles to the ground.

"Are you crazy?" I can hear Zaman yell as he runs over.

"I'm fine," I say.

"I don't care about you! I'm thinking of my motorcycle!" He inspects the vehicle as I pick myself up, feeling some soreness on my left thigh.

"Sorry," I say to Zaman before looking at Sami. "Are you ready?"

"Is she okay?" he asks with sunken eyes.

"Yes, she's fine. But we have to go now." I turn to get back on the motorcycle, but Sami isn't moving. "What's going on? We need to go!" I yell.

"Latif called," Zaman says. I turn to look at him again. "They're going to be here any minute now. You won't be able to outride them."

"What? Yes we can!" I turn to Sami. "Come on! *Rasa!*"

"I don't want them to know you took her there," Sami says. "If they catch us, they'll know to check the city, and they'll find her. I have to protect her."

"How can you protect her if you're dead?" I'm infuriated that my cousin can give up so quickly. "They don't have men in every building of the city. I took her somewhere he can't get to."

"Rashid, they called twenty minutes ago. They should have been here by now," Zaman says. "We can say we caught him and didn't see the girl." We both look at Sami, whose eyes are closed, as if he is praying.

"No!" I yell at both of them. "No! No! No!"

"I'm not getting killed for this!" Zaman yells back. But this time I ignore him.

"Sami, quick, take off your clothes," I say to my cousin. "Take them off!" I scream at him as I pull off my black top and bottom. He finally listens and starts taking off his beige outfit. I throw my clothes at him. "Throw me yours and give me the hat." Sami does as he is told.

"What are you doing?" Zaman asks, sounding agitated and annoyed.

"I have another favor to ask," I say to him.

"I can't help you any more," Zaman says, waving his hands as he starts walking back and away from me.

"I need your bike," I say. "I'll pay you back, you have my word." I can tell Zaman isn't convinced. "Listen! Saving an innocent life after all the blood we've spilled is our only way to receive forgiveness from God! Don't you want some good deeds on your list when we face judgment?" My words seem to be working, because Zaman looks worried. I keep staring at him and notice his eyes shift to Sami.

"Fine! Take it!" Zaman yells. "But what are we going to say, that we got robbed by this guy?" He gestures to Sami, who looks defeated and pathetic. For the first time, I notice he has lost some weight and looks weaker since leaving our village.

And then I hear a distant buzzing. Zaman and Sami hear it too. I run and jump on the bike. "Get on!" I scream, and Sami jumps on behind me. I can tell Zaman is already regretting his decision, but he doesn't stop us. "Tell them we found him but he climbed away through different crevices in the mountains. We separated to find him." The buzzing gets louder. The sound of many motorbikes making their way to us. "When you came back out," I say as I start the engine, "you couldn't find me and the bike was gone." I don't even wait for Zaman's response before speeding off.

"Can you hear me?" I yell to Sami, trying to talk over the roar of the engine.

"Yes!" he screams back.

"When I stop this motorbike, I'm going to jump off. I need you to make it to the city by yourself. Can you do that?"

"Why? Aren't you coming? They'll kill you," Sami says.

"Don't worry about me. Think of Fatima." I can't even believe the words I'm saying right now. "She's at the human rights offices near the blue *masjid*. When you get deeper into the city, ask anyone for directions, and they'll tell you how to get there."

"But what about you? What will you do?" he asks.

"Don't worry about me. I have a plan," I say. "But can you get there?"

"Yes," Sami says.

We both fall silent.

The truth is, I don't have a plan. I just know I have to distract them and give Sami a head start.

Latif has men coming to the valley, but he'll have others

making their way to the main road. *Inshallah,* they'll see me before they see Sami, giving him more time. And capturing at least one of us may satisfy their thirst for blood. I pray it will.

We've made it far enough, and I stop the motorcycle. I jump off, and Sami slides forward. "You need to go now! Keep driving, and don't look back!"

"Are you sure? Will you be okay?" he says. He's always been the worrier. Something I thought made him weak, but I realize now it made him stronger than me.

"I'm fine. Just go! Fatima is waiting for you." I pat him on the shoulder, but he pulls me in for an embrace. I give him a squeeze before letting go. "Now drive!"

I watch as the dust cloud trailing him gets smaller and smaller. My breathing steadies as he disappears. I start walking in the same direction. Anyone coming from the valleys will have to pass me first.

Minutes go by before I hear the buzzing of other bikes. I straighten out Samiullah's *pakol* and speed up. I recite prayers to calm my nerves, the same prayers Mullah Sarwar recited before Latif killed him. The buzzing eventually becomes a roar as the men get closer. Some start shooting in the air, trying to get me to turn around and face them. But I don't. I just keep walking. When they pull ahead of me, I drop to the ground face-down, tasting the salty dirt. The motorcycles all pull around me, and I can hear the men jumping off.

"You!" one voice howls at me.

"It's him. It has to be the lover boy," another says. "But where's the whore?"

"Get up!" the howler demands. But I don't move. The longer I stay down, the more time Sami has. "I said get up!" I feel a striking blow to my side. Followed by another and then another. It continues until he has managed to kick me hard enough to roll me over.

"Rashid?" I open my eyes and see that it is Azizullah. "What are you doing? Have you gone mad?" My lips begin to form a smile, and I laugh. A cackle that I can't stop. Maybe I have gone crazy. But I don't care anymore. "Have you found your cousin and that girl?"

I answer him with more laughter.

"He must have let those *kafirs* go!" I hear another voice yell. "He's not wearing the same clothes. Look!"

"Is that true?" Azizullah asks me, but I just keep laughing. "You stupid bastard!" He continues to kick me in between his orders to the other men. "You three, get on your bikes and ride toward the city—see if you can find them. I'll take care of this dog!"

Azizullah stops his kicking long enough to grab his weapon. The pause gives me a moment to feel the intense pain he has inflicted. And before I know it, he pounds the butt of his rifle over my lungs. The pressure knocks the air out of them and has me spitting out blood. Then he takes the head of the rifle and places it on the middle of my forehead. But I don't feel fear.

"Where are they going?" Azizullah asks me as he digs the metal deeper into my skull.

"Come here," I whisper.

"What?" he yells.

"Come down here," I gurgle through the blood in my mouth.

Azizullah looks around at his men and then back at me before kneeling down. "Now tell me, you *khar quss*," he swears. "Where are they?"

"Closer," I mumble. I allow him to get as close as possible before I use all the energy I can muster to shoot out a mixture of blood and spit onto his ugly face.

"You son of a—" He jumps up and fires his weapon.

I feel the pressure of the bullet hitting my chest, but I don't feel any pain. My vision becomes hazy, but it doesn't matter, because I no longer have the strength to keep my eyelids open.

My parents' voices fill my head, soft and pleasant.

I hear my mother teaching me my prayers. I can feel her gently stroking my hair. I hear my father telling me how to be a man. How to protect my mother, my sister, my family. And then I hear my baby sister's laughter. Sparkling, beautiful. I hear it all . . . and I know it's safe to take my last breath.

Thirty-one

FATIMA

I haven't taken my *chadari* off since I arrived, but even the covering is not protecting me from gawking eyes. There are only three other people waiting in this room, but it still feels too crowded. Two are women, neither of whom are wearing a *chadari*, just head scarves that cover their hair and are wrapped around their chests. The third is an old man with a white beard and turban. He is staring at the three of us, but mostly he's looking at them. The truth is I can't stop staring at them either. Their faces are chalky white, with spots of crimson added to their cheeks and lips. I've tried not to stare because when I do, bad thoughts go through my head about what kind of women they might be. And I know it is wrong to judge them—I don't even know them. It isn't fair. That's the exact mentality that I've been running from.

But I crave the distraction.

The problem is that when I bring my eyes down and look at the ground, my brain begins to fill with tormenting thoughts. A chill runs down my spine as I think of my sister's death.

My baby. My Afifa. My Afo. She did nothing to deserve this. I should have been killed, not her. Not the little girl who cried at the sight of my burns. The baby who brought joy into all of our lives when we thought the happiness had been sucked away by Ali's death.

And if I'm not thinking of Afifa, I'm thinking of Sami. No one told me to love him—they told me not to. But I couldn't help it. It happened. I've loved him all my life. And I know I will love him for the rest of it. No matter how short or long it is. But I can't help thinking the worst, the longer I sit heavy-hearted on this broken wooden chair.

A woman with a red head scarf finally comes out of a room and calls for the ladies across from me. They follow her, closing the door behind them, leaving only me for the old man's eyes. He doesn't look threatening, but I feel uncomfortable nonetheless.

A young man in a suit comes out and offers us both some tea. I look away and don't answer him. I'm afraid if I talk to him, they'll both judge me. The old man declines the offer of tea by sucking his tongue on his teeth.

"Okay, then," the man says, leaving.

After more time passes, the door opens again and the two ladies leave, whispering to each other.

"Excuse me, ma'am," the woman with the red head scarf says to me. "Please come into the office." But I find myself afraid to follow her into the room. I don't want to be alone. Where is Sami? "Sister, please come in."

I slowly get up, keeping my head down. She closes the door behind me, gesturing for me to sit. "Please take off the *chadari* if it will make you more comfortable." It won't. So I shake my head. "My name is Mahnaz. What is your name?" I stay silent in front of this new stranger. Until recently, I had always been surrounded by people I knew and who knew me. Now everyone I meet is someone new.

"You don't have to be nervous with me." She says those simple words with such ease.

But it's not that easy. I've been tossed away by my old world, and now I'm just supposed to trust this new one?

"We'll try to help you, no matter your problem," she continues, in spite of my silence. "I can tell that it was difficult for you to come here. You're very brave."

Suddenly I can't hold back my tears. Mahnaz gets up from her chair and starts rubbing my back.

"It's okay. Cry all you want. Get it out." She pulls some tissues from a box and hands them to me.

I bring my trembling hand out from the *chadari* for a moment to grab them but quickly bring it back in.

"Are you ready to talk now?" she asks as I wipe my nose and eyes. "I can't help you if you don't talk. Keep your *chadari* on. I won't know who you are until you're ready to share that with me, but just tell me why you're here."

Her voice is soft and soothing, and through my veil I can see the concern in her eyes. I know I have to talk because

I can't go back out to those crowded, frightening streets. I need this stranger's help. So I tell Mahnaz everything. As I talk, it becomes easier. Dozens of tissues later, I've finished my story.

I can't believe I told her every detail. I worry that I just gave her many reasons to kick me out: betraying my family, causing the death of my sister, being a slut who left her home for a boy. I look for shock and disgust in Mahnaz's eyes. But they are not there. She doesn't seem fazed by anything I've just said. She just looks . . . sympathetic.

"I'm sorry you went through all of this," Mahnaz says tenderly. "I'm so very sorry. And like I said before, we're here to help you. Whether you want to find a way to reconcile with your family or live with your husband. We'll do our best to support you."

"I can never go back to my family," I say. "Not after Afo's . . ." I can't say the words again. "I can never go back."

"I understand," she says, and I believe her.

She starts to speak again, but her small black phone rings. We never had a mobile phone in my family. My *baba* said there was no need for one, because everyone we knew was only a short walk away. I now wish they had one just so I could call and hear his voice, even if I never let him know it was me.

"I'm sorry," Mahnaz says as she presses one of the phone's buttons.

"Okay. Uh-huh. Yes, please. Thank you." She ends her conversation and looks at me. "There's someone here to see you."

For a moment, her words send chills up my spine, but her smile calms my nerves. I hear the door open and turn to look. Through the blue fabric, I see him. He looks exhausted and dirty. But his emerald eyes still shimmer. My face falls into my hands, and I can't stop my tears. But for the first time in days, they're not tears of sadness—they're tears of joy.

"Fatima?" he says. "Fatima, don't cry. We'll be okay. I promise." He walks toward me and brings me in for an embrace. I pull my arms from under the fabric and squeeze as tight as I can. In this moment I want to fly with him toward a secret sky. I want to take a step without feet, with only our hearts to guide us.

And I know we will.

AUTHOR'S NOTE

In its modern history, Afghanistan has been a country at war since 1979. It started with the Soviet invasion and was followed by a barbaric civil war, then by the Taliban rule and finally, and most recently, the invasion led by the United States in 2001.

The country is a complicated mixture of different ethnicities, ideologies and cultures, and a lack of understanding and knowledge among the groups and outsiders continues to lead the country into further chaos. Unification is only possible with time and education.

It is hard to define an Afghan because of the complex differences between groups. It is also hard to govern the people using one set of laws, for the same reason. Each group has its own laws, which have been passed down from generation to generation. Tradition, culture and family are what reign in most of Afghanistan, not the government— and even in this pious society, culture often triumphs over religion. Many refer to the area outside of the capital, Kabul, as the "Wild West," because it is hard to govern and primarily run by political families or criminal groups. That is the area in which this book is set.

In most Afghan cultures, a person's destiny is scripted

by others. This is especially true for a woman. Her destiny is written before she is born, formulated by her family and community. She has very little say. This norm is questioned only by a very few. Those who do raise their voices are demonized, ostracized and even killed.

In my experience, the majority of Afghan people want normalcy and peace; they are sick of the war and infighting. They want to live quiet lives in the same way their forefathers did in the past. They don't want war—but they also don't want to be told to change their ways, and change is inevitable. I fear that continued globalization may lead to even more cultural clashes in this traditionally conservative society. As television, radio, magazines and Internet become more available, more and more people will be exposed to new ideas and different ways of life, and—like Samiullah and Fatima—may no longer be content with the rules their families and communities have followed for generations.

Even though Afghans long for peace and tranquillity, the future of Afghanistan is as uncertain now as it has ever been for the past three decades.

Love is from the infinite, and will remain until eternity.
The seeker of love escapes the chains of birth and death.
Tomorrow, when resurrection comes,
The heart that is not in love will fail the test.

—*Jalal ad-Din Rumi*

GLOSSARY

Aaka: Uncle (Pashto)

Abdur Rahman Khan: Known as the Iron Amir, he ruled the country from 1880 to 1901. The Pashtun leader was revered and hated. Some Afghans believe he strengthened Afghanistan following the second Anglo-Afghan war. Others believe he was ruthless and slaughtered many Afghans.

Aday: Mother (Pashto)

Afghanis: Afghanistan's monetary figure

Agha: Sir (Dari and Pashto)

Ahmaq: Stupid or Fool (Dari and Pashto)

Allah tobah: God forgive—a reproachful expression meaning that one should show penitence to God (Dari and Pashto)

Aush: Afghan noodles

Azizam: My love (Dari)

Baas: Enough (Dari and Pashto)

Baba: Dad (Dari)

Bachi: Boy (Pashto)

Bia: Come (Dari)

Bitay: Give me (Dari)

Boro berun: "Go outside" (Dari)

Chadari: All-covering garment worn by women, also known as a *burqa* in the western world (Dari and Pashto)

Chai sabz: Green tea (Dari)

Chai: Tea (Dari and Pashto)

Charsy: Smoker of hashish (Dari and Pashto)

Dewana: Crazy (Dari)

Dewanagak: Crazy, in a playful way (Dari)

Dilta rasa: Come here (Pashto)

Distarkhan: Eating mat—similar to a tablecloth but primarily laid out on the ground (Dari and Pashto)

Dokhtar: Girl (Dari)

Dostit darom: I love you (Dari)

Gak: term of endearment usually directed to younger individuals often meaning "little."

Ghagayga: Speak (Pashto)

Ghengiz Khan: A powerful Mongolian leader who established one of the largest empires in the history of the world in the thirteenth and fourteenth centuries. He is revered by some and known as a ruthless killer by others. His many descendants have spread throughout much of the world—the Hazaras are generally considered to have Mongolian lineage, though others dispute the claim.

Gul: Flower (Dari and Pashto)

Hazara: An ethnic group primarily in Afghanistan, but populations also inhabit neighboring Pakistan and Iran. Hazaras are the third largest ethnic group in Afghanistan.

Inshallah: God willing (Dari and Pashto)

Jaan/Jaana: Dear, a term of endearment (Dari/Pashto)

Janem: My dear (Dari)

Jinn: Spiritual creatures that, along with humans and angels, make up the three sapient creations of God

Kafir: a nonbeliever (Dari and Pashto)

Kaka: Uncle (Dari and Pashto)

Karachee: Cart (Dari and Pashto)

Kalon: Big (Dari)

Kena: Sit (Pashto)

Khajoor: A deep-fried Afghan cookie (Dari and Pashto)

Khak da saret: Literally, "dirt on your head," said to wish for someone's death

Khala: Aunt (Dari and Pashto)

Khan: A leader, in this case the leader of a tribe (Dari and Pashto)

Khar quss: Derogatory curse word (Dari and Pashto)

Khastgaree: When a male's family approaches a female's family to ask for her hand in marriage (Dari and Pashto)

Kho/kha: Okay (Dari/Pashto)

Khuda/Khudaya: God (Dari and Pashto)

Khuda hafiz: Good-bye (Dari)

Khuday pamon: Good-bye (Pashto)

Khwarak: Sister, spoken as an endearment (Dari)

King Amanullah: King of Afghanistan from 1919 to 1929, known for his attempts to modernize the country. He was forced to abdicate and flee the country.

Koonak: Little butt (Dari)

Kor mo wadan: "May your house always be safe"—a way of saying thank you (Pashto)

Kuchi: A Pashtun group, nomads who live and wander in Afghanistan and Pakistan

Lala: Older brother, spoken as an endearment (Pashto)

Larsa: Leave (Pashto)

Laywanay: Crazy (Pashto)

Lungee: Long piece of cloth used as a turban (Dari and Pashto)

Madar: Mother (Dari)

Madrassa: Islamic religious school (Dari and Pashto)

Mahr: A mandatory gift given by the groom to his bride, over which she has sole ownership (Dari and Pashto)

Manana: Thank you (Pashto)

Mayan wogora: "Look at the fish" (Pashto)

Masjid: An Islamic place of worship, or mosque (Dari and Pashto)

Maymon khana: Guesthouse (Dari and Pashto)

Mainday: Mothers (Pashto)

Naan: Food or Bread (Dari and Pashto)

Neh: No (Dari)

Nikah: An Islamic wedding (Dari and Pashto)

Nikah khat: Marriage document (Dari and Pashto)

Pakhto ghagaygay: "Do you speak Pashto?" (Pashto)

Pakol: Type of Afghan cap made of wool with a rolled rim

Pashto: A language spoken in Afghanistan primarily by the Pashtun people

Pashtun: An ethnic group primarily in Afghanistan and Pakistan. Pashtuns are the largest ethnic group in Afghanistan.

Payron: Shirt—in this case, a long baggy shirt worn in some central and south Asian countries, including Afghanistan and Pakistan. It is often accompanied by a matching *tumbon*. (Dari)

Peghlo: Girls (Pashto)

Qari: A reciter of the Quran, often one who has also memorized the holy book (Dari and Pashto)

Quran-e-sharif: Islamic holy book

Quroot: Dried and hardened yogurt

Qussy: Derogatory curse word

Quza wa chilemchi: Watering can and bowl used to wash hands before a meal (Pashto)

Rafeda: Small pillow used to place bread in the tandoor (Dari and Pashto)

Rasa: Come here (Pashto)

Rawra: Bring (Pashto)

Saib: Sir (Dari and Pashto)

Salaam/Salaamona: Hello (Dari and Pashto)

Shadi gak: Little monkey (Dari)

Shaw bakhair: Good night (Dari)

Shayton: Satan (Dari and Pashto)

Sheen: Green (Pashto)

Sheen Chai: Green tea (Pashto)

Singaye/singa yasti: How are you? (Pashto)

Sufis: Muslims who practice a mystical form of Islam

Taliban: Literally "students"—an Islamic extremist political movement in both Afghanistan and Pakistan. The group controlled most of Afghanistan from the mid-1990s until their overthrow in the invasion led by the United States in the fall of 2001.

Tandoor: Cylindrical-type oven usually built into the ground (Dari and Pashto)

Tashakur: Thank you (Dari and Pashto)

Toophan: Storm (Dari and Pashto)

Toot: Berry (Dari and Pashto)

Toshak: Mattress pad (Dari and Pashto)

Tumbon: Trousers—in this case, long baggy trousers worn in some central and south Asian countries, including Afghanistan and Pakistan. It is often accompanied by its matching *payron*. (Dari)

Woror: Brother (Pashto)

Za: Go! (Pashto)

Ziyarat: Shrine

Zoy/zoya: Son (Pashto)

ACKNOWLEDGMENTS

This book would not have been possible without the incredible support of the Philomel and Penguin family, who immediately made me feel like I had always been a part of their team. A special thank-you to Jill Santopolo; her guidance and expertise were invaluable—as was her friendship, honesty and kindness. I cannot express in words just how deeply grateful I am to you, Michael Green and the entire Philomel and Penguin team—there are so many who worked hard and with kind hearts and I am very thankful to all of you. And I cannot forget Nick Schifrin for sending the e-mail that set this all in motion, *besyar tashakur* and *dera manana,* dear friend.

I also want to thank my family for the love, support and patience they showed as I immersed myself in the adventure of writing a novel during my breaks from work—spending less time with them and more time with my computer and imagination. They never stopped believing in me. First, I want to express my gratitude to my husband, Conor Powell: you are my everything; thank you for taking this journey with me and for always motivating me in all that I and we do. My mother, Mahnaz Abawi, whose prayers and love have guided me all my life. My father, Wahid Abawi, who was my rock and taught through his strength and kindness what a true Afghan man is. My brother, Tawab Abawi, and his wife, Kelli, for their encouragement and love. And the Powells and Phelans for supporting us always. God has blessed me with so much, but the greatest blessing of all has been my loved ones.

I want to take this opportunity to thank my brothers and sisters in Afghanistan who took me in as family and showed me true Afghan hospitality during all the years I lived there. They are an inspiration. Every Afghan has millions of stories trapped in his or her heart, stories most will never be able to share. One day I hope the world can see past the war and destruction and glimpse the beauty and wonders that lie in this tragic history. Very special thanks to Qari Saib Fazal Ahad for his research, to the Shinwaris for their help, and to Mandy Clark for her input. And to everyone else who has touched my life and given me knowledge of a country that continues to survive with the patience and hard work of the good people inside it—both Afghans and internationals.

I also want to say *teşekkür ederim* to the Starbucks on Istanbul's Istiklal Street for allowing me to write for hours on end as I sipped my coffee and tapped away. And thank you to Chantilly's regional library for giving me the same experience—minus the coffee.